An excerpt from *Disciplining the Duchess*

Court wondered what had come over him.

Well, any polite guest owed it to the hostess to participate at least marginally in the entertainments. Or become one, if circumstances called for it. He wasn't about to let Barrett drag off his sister before the whole group. The unfortunate young miss gawked at him. An offer of her hand would have been the appropriate way to proceed, but her brother still had her by the arm. Court glared at him so fiercely he released her and took a step back.

"Your Grace, I am d—deeply honored to introduce my sister, Miss Harmony Barrett."

Court nearly lost his composure over her name. Harmony? "Chaos" would have been more fitting. "Miss Barrett," he said, taking her now-proffered hand and raising it to his lips. "The honor is mine. Would you care to dance the next set?" He looked back at the massing couples, all of whom were staring at them. "It begins shortly."

Her pale blue eyes widened as her fingertips fluttered in his grasp. "Dance it…with you?"

He looked around. "Who else?"

She closed and opened her mouth again. "I— I—"

If she refused him it would be hilarious. It would be talked about in drawing rooms and ballrooms for years. He held her gaze, willing her to do as she wished, to refuse him if she wanted to. Blue, so very blue. Her eyes were a pale, clear blue and her features so delicately pretty.

"If you wish, Your Grace," she finally managed, nodding her head and bobbing an awkward curtsy. He held her hand tighter and led her to the center of the room as her gaping brother looked on.

Disciplining

the

Duchess

By

Annabel Joseph

Other erotic romance by Annabel Joseph

Mercy
Cait and the Devil
Firebird
Deep in the Woods
Fortune
Owning Wednesday
Lily Mine
Comfort Object
Caressa's Knees
Odalisque
Command Performance
Cirque de Minuit
Burn For You
The Edge of the Earth (as Molly Joseph)

Erotica by Annabel Joseph

Club Mephisto
Molly's Lips: Club Mephisto Retold

Coming Soon:

Waking Kiss
Fever Dream
Cirque Vivide

*For R., who somehow looks
exactly like the duke*

Chapter One:
Gossip

Miss Harmony Barrett gazed longingly at the door.

She knew the precise location of Lord Darlington's library, for she'd already stolen there several times to explore his impressive collection of books. She was certain he would not be angry if he caught her at it, but she still snuck in and out like a thief. Perhaps it was because the Darlingtons' library felt so private. It felt like a hideaway, a shelter.

She wished she could hide away there right now.

Instead she was stuck with her silly set of young unmarried women, listening to an endless, cloying dissection of each and every gentleman guest at Danbury House. The Earl of So-and-So had the most handsome blond curls, and Lord Whomever was the most elegant dancer, didn't everyone believe so? And had everyone heard that Sir Horrid Rake and Lady Poor Choices had stolen off behind the carriage house yesterday to be alone? That was the girls' cue to dissolve *en masse* into giddy giggles. Oh, and didn't the Honorable Mr. Barrett have the most beautiful eyes in the world?

Harmony cringed. Mr. Barrett was her scoundrel brother and he was to marry Lady Meredith Airleigh at the holidays. This did not prevent him from spending his summer fraternizing with all the ladies at the house party.

"Mr. Barrett is a cad," Harmony said, "if you must know."

"Oh, hush." Lady Mirabel Godwin tapped Harmony's head with her white lace fan. "Of course you'd think so, but I would forgive him anything for those eyes."

"He is going to be married," Harmony said stubbornly. "His eyes are betrothed to another." She didn't understand the girls' obsession with her brother's appearance. His eyes were a very plain shade of blue like hers, and his hair the same white-blond, and she was certainly not fawned over by any of the gentlemen.

Lady Mirabel sniffed and turned away from Harmony, edging her out of the group. "Do you know what I heard? His Grace the Duke of Courtland has finally arrived to the party, along with his mother and her companion. Perhaps we'll see them at dinner, although I am not sure I shall be brave enough to speak to such a lofty person. If I am seated beside him I might faint into my soup."

The idea of this sent the group off into more titters and swoons. A few older women came to join them now that His Grace was the topic. Harmony half-listened to their gossip about his wealth, his opulent estates, his appealing features. Another fine specimen for her contemporaries to prattle on about.

"Why do you suppose he has not married?" asked Miss Juliette Pettyfur.

"There are reasons." Mrs. Castleton's voice held a note of distaste. "I wouldn't set your cap for that one."

"All dukes must marry at some point," Miss Viola Burress said, but then another woman said something about "uncomfortable habits," and the older ladies shushed her and urged the younger women outdoors into the sunshine to take their tea.

It was there, with their heads bowed together, that the younger set of ladies whispered about what his "uncomfortable habits" might be.

"Well, if he is thirty years old and not married, that means he is a rake," said Mirabel.

"It does not mean that at all," Juliette retorted.

Lady Sybil looked around at the other girls with an expression of gravity. "I probably should not say this, but Papa has warned me against him."

"There, you see," said Mirabel. "He is a rake."

"I believe he must be something worse than a rake." Viola flushed. "Did you see the older ladies' expressions when his name was brought up?"

Harmony wondered what could possibly be worse than a rake. From the silent, uneasy pall that fell over the group, she supposed she wasn't the only one.

"Mrs. Castleton said there are reasons he hasn't married. What could they possibly be?" Mirabel whispered.

"I do not know," said Sybil, "but my brother spoke something of him to papa when he was considering the duke for my hand. Whatever he said, papa refused to repeat it to mama."

This elicited horrified gasps from the entire company.

"Perhaps he has killed someone!" said one of the more fanciful girls. "A duke could get away with it."

"I bet he has the most cold and sinister eyes," another girl said.

"I'm frightened," whimpered another. "Why would they invite him here among civilized people?"

"If he killed someone, why would the Darlingtons invite him into their home?" Mirabel asked. "A duke cannot run about killing people on a whim. Dukes are powerful, but not that powerful."

"Yes," agreed Juliette. "How silly to leap from 'uncomfortable habits' to 'murderer.' As for his cold and sinister eyes, I thought he was considered handsome."

"I have seen him in town," said Sybil. "He is uncommonly tall, with dark hair and attractive features. He is handsome. Dangerously so." She raised a brow for emphasis.

Harmony was not sure how one could be dangerously handsome. Perhaps women fainted just from looking at him.

"He probably keeps dozens of mistresses," Viola said.

"Maybe he cannot keep even one, because he is so awful to them," said the fanciful girl. "Maybe he draws them in with his attractive features and then trods upon their hearts."

"Or beats them," suggested another. "Or *kills* them."

Harmony sighed as the young women joined hands, promising to protect one another from the terrifying menace of his wiles.

"Perhaps it is only that he drinks too much at dinner," Harmony drawled. "Or eats too much, and belches loudly and repeatedly. That would be an uncomfortable habit indeed."

As usual, all the girls looked at her as though she were mad. Which she nearly was, after days of listening to them natter on about the stupidest subjects. She stared back at them until they all looked down at their plates.

"Well," Sybil declared after a beat. "All I know is that I wouldn't take him for a husband even if papa would let me, which he won't. In fact, I am determined not to speak to him if we are introduced."

One of the younger girls gasped. "Will you give the Duke of Courtland the cut direct? I should like to see you try it."

The girls all began to giggle again, proclaiming they would also be bold enough to cut the duke, and wouldn't it leave him red in the face?

Harmony doubted he would notice. If the duke was a rake and a bounder with armfuls of mistresses, he was unlikely to crumble at the disdain of a few young ladies. Thank goodness Harmony was not concerned with such nonsense. She was only here at this house party because her brother Stephen had ingratiated his way into an invitation. "It's for you," he had said. "For you to make a match. *Any* match. You aren't getting any younger, and father and I shall not support you forever." His pressure didn't help matters. When this cursed party was at an end, perhaps they would resign themselves to her inevitable spinsterhood and allow her to study and bide alone to her heart's content.

"Harmony?" Sybil's strident voice interrupted her thoughts. "Would you?"

"Would I what?"

The ladies sighed and exchanged glances.

"Of course she would," Sybil said under her breath. "Someone like her would not think twice about it."

"I haven't the slightest idea what you're talking about," Harmony said with a pricked temper. "And I'm not sure I'll answer since you used that mocking tone."

"I am only teasing you." She tapped Harmony's arm with her fan. Harmony thought she would break the fan over top of Sybil's head next time she was tapped, and enjoy doing so.

"Harmony!" Sybil said, breaking into her thoughts again. "I'm speaking of His Grace. Would you dance with the Duke of Courtland if he asked?"

"Tonight?"

Sybil threw up her hands in irritation. "Whenever. Yes. Tonight."

"He won't ask, so it's rather a pointless question."

Sybil looked at the others. "I told you. Yes, she would."

"You are all unkind," Harmony said. "Perhaps he is a fine gentleman. You haven't even met him, only shared gossip which is probably untrue."

"How earnest you are," Mirabel sneered, looking around at the others. "She has shamed us, hasn't she? Well, then, we shall leave his prodigious charms to you." All the young ladies found that idea hilarious.

"I have had enough fresh air." Harmony took to her feet, to the insincere protests and apologies of her friends. Of course they would want her to stay; she made such a pleasant target for their barbs. "The sun is too strong today. Have a fine afternoon."

She ignored their whispers as she left the garden and made her way to the house. The gentlemen were out hunting and the older ladies still at tea. It was the perfect time for a stolen couple of hours in Lord Darlington's library. She shed her bonnet in her room, then hurried down the main hallway to a staircase with a great carved banister that led to the main floor. With no footmen in sight, Harmony let herself into the library and closed the doors behind her. The room was tucked away in a corner of the manor, an intimate space with an ornate ceiling and tall, laden shelves. There were several chairs and a deep, tufted sofa near the fireplace, with a massive desk between the two windows, facing out into the room.

How Harmony would love a desk like that. After she scanned the shelves and selected a couple of titles, she crossed to the mahogany monstrosity, running her fingers over the carved edges. Why, the desktop was large enough to be a bed. She imagined lying across the top under a blanket, with a pillow cradling her head. Whenever she finished a book and wanted another, she would be right there in the library to fetch one. Bliss!

She moved to the chair, which was nearly as tall as she. With some effort she drew it back and sat down on its weathered seat. So this was how it felt to be lord of the manor. She planted her elbows on the armrests and snuggled back into the chair. If only she were lord of her own estate. Then she might do as she pleased without her brother telling her no, or that it wasn't ladylike, or she must ask her father or some other nonsense.

Halfway through a vivid fantasy about telling her brother off, she heard a creak and the sound of the library doors swinging open. She slid from the chair into the recessed underside of the desk. Was it only a servant come to dust and organize the books? Was it Lord Darlington, home early from the hunt? Why had she hidden? Now she would have to spring out and shock the person, or risk being found crouched down in this hideyhole, skirts tangled around her legs. Perhaps she would just be very still and hope she wasn't found. The person would have to leave eventually.

She made her ample figure as small as she could and inched a little farther against the back of the desk's enclosure, gripping her books in her lap. Quiet. Quiet as a mouse.

* * * * *

Court prowled the library shelves, relieved to be sprung from the confines of the ducal carriage, luxurious though it might be. It had taken an entire week to travel north from London to Harrogate, a week during which his mother and her companion's chatter never ceased. Court had nearly recovered in the lazy baths of the spa town when he had to travel again with the elderly ladies to this house party in Sedgefield. Then there would be the lengthy journey back to London in a few weeks' time.

He couldn't think of that now. He would put it out of his mind and enjoy the comforts of the Darlingtons' home. "Only the quality," his mother had crowed on the journey. "Such elegant affairs, always. There will be grand dinners and fine conversation, and music and dancing every night for the young people. With such bright company, how could a hostess resist? Perhaps we shall even watch affection blossom between some lucky lady and gentleman."

Mrs. Lyndon had grinned. "Oh, yes, madam. A country match and a winter wedding back in town."

Both old women had then looked pointedly at Court.

God confound him. Until a few weeks ago the matter of his marriage had been settled, the proper alliance decided upon when he was a young boy. Ah, Gwen, with her sleek dark hair, her wide, serene eyes. They had grown up on neighboring estates in Hertfordshire, and from their earliest years had understood their intertwined destinies. While other boys teased and chased her skirts, Court treated her with the tender deference due a future wife. When he'd gone to London as a young man, he'd been discreet in his wilder adventures lest he shame her or cause her discomfort. Court, his parents, and everyone in society had assumed she would eventually become the mother of the Courtland heirs.

Until her father, Lord Tremayne, announced her betrothal to the Earl of Wembley, a man lesser to Court in every way. A love match, Tremayne explained in an attempt to preserve the long-standing bonds between the families.

But there was more to it than that. Gwen had looked at him differently once the gossip started to surface, sordid tales and half-truths exaggerating his use of spanking parlors and brothels. Oh, Court was bad, but he wasn't *that* bad. Her worshipful gazes had become something more like fear. Didn't she understand he never would have exposed her to that side of him? On pure rumor—so much of it untrue—his Gwendolyn, the future Duchess of Courtland, had passed on his great wealth and attributes to marry a silly country earl.

Court would never admit to nursing a broken heart, but perhaps he was.

His mother didn't care about his hurt pride, his bruised feelings. She wanted him to choose a different duchess, the sooner the better, and produce a child. This foray north was a matchmaking caper, the house party a convenient aggregation of acceptable female blood. His mother ranted and railed on the topic of Gwen and assured him he could do ten times better if he applied himself. The problem was, after so many years, Court found it difficult to imagine marrying anyone else.

He put these maudlin thoughts aside to enjoy the ambiance of Darlington's library. It smelled of leather and faintly of cigar smoke, and contained a quantity of interesting volumes. Occasionally he took down a book and leafed through it, looking for some history or novel with which to pass the afternoon, for he was not a man at ease in leisure and he was far from the places he felt at home. His clubs, his political offices, his house in St. James Square. His country estate was off limits, now that Gwen had set up house with her new husband just a few miles from what ought to have been her home at Courtland Manor.

Blast.

Tomorrow he could join the gentlemen at fishing and hunting, tromp through fields, get dirty and vulgar and shoot a grouse or two. He was good at such sport like any member of his set, though he was generally disinterested in killing things. Something about handing the carcasses over to the servants to be duly prepared and presented at dinner always smacked of wilting affluence to him. He would much rather shoot and prepare his own game over his own fire and eat it standing out in the woods like a savage.

Perhaps that was his problem. There was a savage inside him, trussed up in a waistcoat, coat, and starched neckcloth, gasping for air. Add a couple of elderly companions, a society house party, giggling young ladies, and the savage was smothered completely.

Court gave up on the bookshelves and moved to one of the windows to survey his host's property. Lovely garden, lake, some outbuildings, and a glass house in the distance. It was very much like Wembley's estate. Grand but livable. Large, but not so large that one felt dwarfed. In other words, nothing at all like his houses. He crossed to Darlington's desk, a handsome wooden structure set between the two windows, and sprawled back in the chair. He slung one booted foot over the other and laced his hands behind his head. Ah, but it felt damn good to stretch his legs after so many hours in the coach's cramped interior—

But then his foot contacted some soft, resistant surface that emitted a feminine squeak.

He leaned down to find a pair of wide blue eyes staring back at him, framed by mussed blonde curls. At first he thought a child had escaped the nursery, but a glance at her bodice dispelled that notion. She was a woman—a beautiful woman—inexplicably crouching at his feet. "What are you doing under there?" His voice sounded sharp. Since the shock of Gwen's jilting, he'd come to abhor surprises.

"I'm hoping you will leave," she said in an earnest whisper.

"I would rather not leave until I know why you're hiding under Lord Darlington's desk. Are you in some sort of danger?"

"I—I might be." From the shadows beneath the desk he could see her shapely bosom rise and fall. She peered out at him, one long curl falling over an eye. "Are you, by any chance, going to leave directly?"

"No."

"Oh. I wish you would."

He could see a couple of books clutched in her hand. "What have you there? A pair of romantic novels?"

"No, sir. Not romantic novels exactly. Might I ask who you are?"

"I will tell you who I am if you will show me your books." He didn't know why he pestered her. Because it amused him. Because it had discomfited him so to find her hiding there, and he wanted to discomfit her also. She pursed her lips, then looked down to read from the spines.

"*A History of English Political Thought in the Sixteenth Century.*" She handed it up to him. "And *Genghis Khan and the Great Mongol Empire.*"

Not romantic novels. Not even close. Court placed the books on Lord Darlington's desk, feeling unwelcome curiosity about the creature. "Will you come out so I may introduce myself properly?"

"I would rather not."

"Because you prefer to read under there, or because you're embarrassed?"

"I am deeply humiliated and wish you would forget this encounter completely."

He frowned. "I doubt I shall manage that. However, since I am a gentleman and you have asked me twice to leave, I will comply with your wishes."

As he stood to go, he heard a soft sound from beneath the desk. "Please…"

"Yes?"

"Will you give back the books?"

"Of course." He passed them down, pressing them into the small hand that emerged. "I wish you good day."

Court walked out, thinking the house party was not off to the most auspicious start, when one was obliged to converse with a strange woman huddled under the host's desk. He walked the halls for a half hour or so, until he felt less rattled and more relaxed again. Back in his private parlor, he found his mother and Mrs. Lyndon returned from tea, trading captious gossip on the sofa.

"Did you find Lady Emberley's bonnet quite out of fashion?" his mother appealed to Mrs. Lyndon. "I was shocked at how dilapidated it was. That rose silk—I daresay it was from two seasons ago."

Mrs. Lyndon tut-tutted and agreed that she found it quite out of style for the wife of an earl, particularly the rose silk.

His mother looked up at him and indicated the chair to her right. "Come and sit with us, dear. Have you toured the house? Did you find it pleasing? And did you happen to glimpse Lady Emberley's bonnet?"

"The house is exemplary. And no, I did not see this bonnet." He strained to sound pleasant as he seated himself near the pair. "I'm sure, despite her bonnet's dilapidation, that the lady herself is all that is proper and *kind.*"

His mother's eyes widened at his subtle reprimand. "She would have been kinder had she worn a nicer bonnet. It hurt my eyes."

"What of Mrs. Dawson's hair?" Mrs. Lyndon asked. Both ladies tittered.

"Perhaps it is the style in Yorkshire," said his mother. "But I found it so very…ugly. Yes, I cannot think of a milder word."

"Hideous," Mrs. Lyndon offered.

"Hideous is less mild," the duchess chided her friend. "But called for in this case."

Court sighed, almost wishing himself back in conversation with the chit beneath the desk. At least then he had been repeatedly asked to leave, whereas now, since he'd seated himself, he was stuck by courtesy for at least ten minutes.

"Honestly, Courtland, I wish you would not look so sour." His mother leaned forward to tap at his knee. "You will have your hunting on the morrow, and many esteemed gentlemen to smoke and play cards with. And there are so many lovely ladies in attendance, all of them eager to meet a dashing and distinguished duke."

"Are there?" he asked in a bored tone. "Too bad they are stuck with me."

Her sharp hazel eyes snapped. "For Lady Darlington's sake, you must make an effort to engage with her guests. Particularly the ladies. It is high time you settled on a bride." His mother puffed up like a hen ruffling its feathers. "Perhaps gossip of your unfortunate proclivities will not have reached these remote moors."

Court grimaced and considered, just for a moment, flinging himself from the nearby window. "Do not be offensive, mother."

"Oh," the duchess exclaimed. "Speaking of offensive, you will never guess who is here. Lord Morrow's children! Do you remember the viscount? He was one of your father's odder friends."

"I never made his acquaintance." He knew of him, although Viscount Morrow had retired from society in recent years. He remembered him as a studious, serious fellow, forthright in manners, which Court respected. His son, Mr. Barrett, was a few years younger than Court and not a member of his set.

His mother pounced on this lack of knowledge, eager to share what she'd learned. "Apparently Stephen Barrett is not the best sort. He is given to vice and leisure as are so many young men these days, and his sister is five seasons out now, poor dear. The ladies say she is woefully

16

strange in manners. She must be tiresome to all the gentlemen," she said in an aside to Mrs. Lyndon, who sighed appropriately.

Court arched a brow. "I thought Lady Darlington's parties only had the quality."

"Oh, you are very rude today." His mother scowled and fluttered her fan. "Now, you see, Viscount Morrow was a particular friend of Lord Darlington in their younger days, and so they must be civil to his son and daughter. The son, at least, is engaged to the Earl of Needham's daughter. Mr. Barrett must be dashing to win an earl's daughter, or perhaps it's the Morrow fortune."

"What is left of it," Mrs. Lyndon intoned.

"But you shall have to avoid the sister," his mother said. "I heard at the Bettlemans' ball in London last season, Lord Bettleman took pity on Miss Barrett and offered her a dance, and she spoke to him nearly the entire set on the topic of *Mongol hordes*." His mother whispered the latter words as if they were not fit to utter aloud. "Can you imagine his chagrin?"

Mongol hordes? It could not be coincidence. Nothing in Court's blasé expression revealed that he had already met this young woman—or that he had spent the last half hour trying to forget the image of her peering up from between his legs.

"And there was some debacle at Almack's," his mother continued, "so traumatizing to those in attendance that the ladies will not speak of it."

The old women clucked at one another behind their fans. Miss Barrett seemed to have created significant mayhem across her five unsuccessful seasons, which wasn't surprising considering what he knew of her thus far.

His mother's lips went tight. "Suffice it to say, no one would associate with her after that. What a sorry situation for Lord Morrow," she said to Mrs. Lyndon, who nodded in mournful agreement. "An odd daughter and a son who does not understand responsibility and couth. It is heartbreaking when sons disappoint, is it not, Mrs. Lyndon? Although, at least, Mr. Barrett has managed a fine match for himself."

His mother gave him a speaking glance. Court ignored her and studied the floral pattern on the arm of his chair. "Perhaps Miss Barrett and I would make a good match. Perhaps I shall court her here in the north and bring home a bride. What do you think, mother? Might we suit?"

The duchess gasped and feigned a fit of vapors while Mrs. Lyndon shook her head, her loose chin skin wiggling like a turkey's wattle.

"You will do no such thing, Benedict Thomas William Hawthorne," his mother cried. "Imagine, the Duke of Courtland paying his addresses to the daughter of a viscount. A peculiar daughter at that!"

Court glanced out the window at the late-summer moors. "I might like a wife with whom I can discuss Mongol hordes."

His mother gave a beleaguered sigh and whispered viciously to Mrs. Lyndon. In truth, she had nothing to fear. He hadn't the heart to court any woman at Sedgefield, peculiar or not. He was for cards and a little hunting. Otherwise, he would make himself scarce.

He would survive this house party just as he survived all the others he was compelled to attend.

Chapter Two:
Magic

Every night after dinner, the entire company retired to Lady Darlington's largest drawing room to socialize and make merry, and every night Harmony lagged behind, dreading the proceedings. There were refreshments and punch, and pleasant music provided by the more talented guests. The gentlemen asked all the ladies to dance, except for Harmony, who had not yet been invited to dance by anyone. She hid within the protective circle of her acquaintances, perfectly happy not to reveal her two left feet.

At least Stephen was having fun mucking about with Lady Smythe-Dorsey and Mrs. Waring every chance he got. When Harmony had confronted him about being unfaithful to his fiancée, he'd laughed at her. "You don't understand the ways of society. These flirtations are perfectly acceptable. In fact, they're expected at parties like these. It is better to be a jovial, sociable guest than a prim stuck-up like you."

A *prim stuck-up*. Apparently this was the gentlemen's assessment of her, along with the other usual descriptors, "strange" and "odd." At least there was no gossip of her hiding under desks in libraries, even though three days had passed since her encounter with the Duke of Courtland. Something so horrifically embarrassing could only happen to her. She wondered why he did not tell tales about their meeting when he could so easily amuse his friends.

As for her friends' staunch intentions to snub His Grace—every topic of conversation now revolved around him.

The duke did not appear anything like the villain they'd expected. His teeth were white and straight and his eyes intelligent, set off by dark eyebrows. His face was neither broad nor narrow, but just right, with a masculine nose and fine, well-shaped lips. His chin was strong without seeming pointy or prominent. Taken together, the duke was indeed dangerously handsome, though not in a classical sense. It was more that when one looked at the Duke of Courtland, one wished to keep looking.

But Harmony dared not. The duke had noticed her at dinner the very first night, his eyes glinting in wary recognition. His arch expression left no doubt he remembered how they'd met. Since then, she had kept her gaze on her lap or the carpet, leaving her friends to comment upon his every expression and movement from the corner where they spied on him.

"He is so tall," Viola said breathlessly. "Each time I see him I am shocked by his height."

Mirabel fingered her fan. "Look how he stares about at everyone without smiling. He is too severe."

"His hair is disordered," said another girl.

"I thought he would look older," said Juliette. "He is old, is he not?"

"He does not dance with anyone," sniffed Sybil. "How rude. He probably doesn't know how."

They fell silent, peeking at him from behind their fans. Harmony allowed herself a long look too, now that he was occupied talking to his friends. The duke was in evening black with a neatly tied cravat and elegant jewelry glittering at his neck and hands. Nothing too ostentatious. No, the ostentatious thing was the air of power and hauteur he wore as easily as his fine clothes. His expression was carefully neutral, yes, almost severe. His handsome features were framed by dark hair worn slightly longer than was the fashion. He did not smile, not even once, in the course of his conversations.

"I believe he can dance very well." Mirabel's voice sounded slow, almost predatory. She looked over her shoulder at Harmony. "You are the one who was willing to dance with him. Go stand near him and see if he'll ask you."

The girls tittered. Harmony set her chin. "I never said I was willing. I dislike dancing."

Sybil's lips curled. "I can't imagine why. Come, ladies, let us rejoin the company of our young gentlemen. As for the Duke of Courtland, he may stand and glower all he likes but he shall not impress me."

Harmony stayed behind, as they doubtless intended her to. The girls massed in the center of the drawing room, arranging themselves with their favored beaux for the next set as an old matron plinked doggedly at the piano. Harmony shouldn't be jealous that her friends had such fun, that they enjoyed flirtation and the attentions of their suitors. She wished she wasn't jealous, but in quiet, weak moments, she desperately wanted to be like them. She wanted gentlemen to shoulder each other out of the way for her attention, to hang on her every word, however vapid those words would have to be. She wished a gentleman, just one gentleman, would notice her.

But then she remembered that she didn't like to be vapid, and she didn't wish her entire life to revolve around the attention of men.

There was only one man among the guests who interested her anyway, and that was the mysterious, worse-than-a-rake duke. What were his uncomfortable habits? How many mistresses did he have and what awful things did he do to them, that Lady Sybil's papa must strike the duke from his list of acceptable candidates for her hand? The duke did not seem at all perverse in his manners. In fact, he had been quite civil to her when she'd surprised him under Lord Darlington's desk.

Harmony watched as the wealthy peer drifted into the card room and out again, then went to the punch bowl for a drink. His hair was slightly unconventional, perhaps due to a mild case of curls. One dubious aspect of an otherwise very sedate person. Harmony dropped her gaze from his hair and stared at his gloved hands. Even across the room she could tell the duke's gloves were impeccably fitted, of utmost quality. Everything about him screamed quality and propriety, and nothing uncomfortable at all. She rubbed her eyebrows and forced herself to stop staring. She was no better than her friends, speculating endlessly about him.

"Miss Barrett. Must you hide your beauty back here in this corner? It is not fair." The booming voice of elderly Lord Monmouth startled her, along with the noisy creaking of his stays. Behind him, her brother gave her an urgent look. "Might I have the next dance, madam?" the old earl asked.

Harmony schooled her face to careful blankness even though she was quailing inside. Lord Monmouth was a kind man but his teeth were decaying and his figure was very…round. She forgot all about the sleek dark duke as she stared in horror at the earl's extended arm.

"Lord Monmouth, forgive me, but I'm not feeling my best at the moment. I'm really too…"

Her brother caught her eye and glared a threat at her.

"I'm really too…bloated from dinner to…dance yet…" she finished weakly, eyeing Lord Monmouth's rotund belly straining above his breeches.

"I am sorry to hear it," Lord Monmouth grunted, his expression hardening. "I pray you feel better soon. Good evening to you." Without further ado, he stalked past her brother and disappeared into the adjoining salon to join the other gentlemen at cards.

"Harmony!" Her brother vibrated with frustration. "Lord Monmouth is a widower. A *rich* widower, you twit. What of finding a match?"

"You cannot think I'd wish to marry that ancient gentleman?"

"What do your wishes have to do with anything?" Stephen pulled her up, wrenching her arm in the process. "I had to play nice with the man for nearly an hour, regaling him with tales of how sweet and misunderstood you are only to get him to come over here. And you—" He pinched her elbow painfully. "You tell him you are too bloated to dance with him? I am sure he's even now sharing that entertaining tidbit with his card partners, and they are all having a great laugh at your expense."

"Let go of me." If they pulled at each other any harder, they would draw attention to themselves. "Release me," she hissed. "You are hurting me."

"It's what you deserve. And if you are feeling so *bloated*, you can very well retire to your room for the evening. It embarrasses me, the way you skulk about. You won't be happy until we're both utter laughingstocks."

He grasped her arm and forced her forward so she had no choice but to trip across the room under his simmering control. They were nearly to the door when a sudden hush descended on the company. The Duke of Courtland stepped right in front of them, his face a polite but rigid mask. He nodded to her brother and then waited for Harmony to acknowledge him—which she did with a shocked stare. He bowed slightly.

"Madam, I am sorry to have not made your acquaintance before now."

* * * * *

Court wondered what had come over him.

Well, any polite guest owed it to the hostess to participate at least marginally in the entertainments. Or become one, if circumstances called for it. He wasn't about to let Barrett drag off his sister before the whole group. The unfortunate young miss gawked at him. An offer of her hand would have been the appropriate way to proceed, but her brother still had her by the arm. Court glared at him so fiercely he released her and took a step back.

"Your Grace, I am d—deeply honored to introduce my sister, Miss Harmony Barrett."

Court nearly lost his composure over her name. Harmony? "Chaos" would have been more fitting. "Miss Barrett," he said, taking her now-proffered hand and raising it to his lips. "The honor is mine. Would you care to dance the next set?" He looked back at the massing couples, all of whom were staring at them. "It begins shortly."

Her pale blue eyes widened as her fingertips fluttered in his grasp. "Dance it…with you?"

He looked around. "Who else?"

She closed and opened her mouth again. "I— I—"

If she refused him it would be hilarious. It would be talked about in drawing rooms and ballrooms for years. He held her gaze, willing her to do as she wished, to refuse him if she wanted to. Blue, so very blue. Her eyes were a pale, clear blue and her features so delicately pretty.

"If you wish, Your Grace," she finally managed, nodding her head and bobbing an awkward curtsy. He held her hand tighter and led her to the center of the room as her gaping brother looked on.

The set began just as they arrived, as if the other dancers had been waiting for them. Miss Barrett grimaced, flubbing very badly the first pair of turns. "I'm afraid I don't dance well," she said.

"You dance wonderfully." He gave her a nudge through the next step so she didn't turn the wrong way. She shot him a harried look that rather amused him. He caught a glimpse of his mother seated on the periphery with Mrs. Lyndon, all color drained from her face.

23

He grinned at Miss Barrett simply to goad his mother as they moved through the formations of the country dance. Over, under, turn left, turn right. He found dancing extremely boring, but partnering Miss Barrett livened up the proceedings. There were always stray arms to grab and adjustments in balance to keep him alert. His partner was grim-faced and silent, not once engaging him in a conversation about Mongol hordes, or Viking or Pictish hordes, or any other type of horde. For his part, he murmured encouragements when he wasn't managing her unruly arms and dodging the trods of her feet.

In addition to her lack of natural coordination, they were confounded by a marked difference in size. Until now he'd only seen her under a desk, or across the room where perspective was harder to judge. He was tall like his father and used to peering down at women, but Miss Barrett was shorter than most. Her chin barely reached the height of his chest and her hands were like little hummingbirds in his oversized grasp. She must find his hands monstrous; she eyed them frequently while they danced. At one point she turned the wrong way and collided with him. He righted her and she stopped short in the middle of a promenade.

"I am the very worst dancer," she said.

"Nonsense. You move with rare eloquence." She rejected this lie with a thunderous frown. "Perhaps we should take some refreshments instead," he suggested.

Miss Barrett agreed emphatically with that idea. He had the feeling she would have fled the drawing room if he hadn't tucked her hand in the crook of his arm. He led her to the punch bowl, nodding in response to Lady Darlington's smile, and got Miss Barrett a glass of punch she appeared too overwrought to consume. People pretended not to watch them but they watched nonetheless, and Miss Barrett clearly yearned for escape. He might have let her go at that point with a bow and a polite "good evening." He wondered why on earth he did not.

Instead he asked, "How are you enjoying your books?"

A flush bloomed on her cheeks. "I— Well—about that, Your Grace…thank you for not gossiping."

"I abhor gossip."

"I do, too." Her pleased look warmed him. "To answer your question, as a student of history I found the books fascinating."

"A student of history? I am glad to hear it. You've finished them already?"

"Yesterday," she admitted.

"And still they gazed, and still the wonder grew, that one small head could carry all she knew," he quoted in a fit of whimsy.

Miss Barrett looked alarmed. "I am not that intelligent."

It was a lie every bit as false as his lie about her dancing. She clamped her mouth shut, as if some monologue on the origins and habits of Mongol hordes might otherwise escape her. She was, as his mother had warned, woefully strange in manners, which disquieted and fascinated him at the same time. He took her cup and placed it on a nearby table.

"Miss Barrett, did you know our hosts own several paintings of historical interest? May I escort you to see them?"

She stared up at him. He felt a twitch at his lips, a smile not called up from some sense of politeness or propriety, but a true smile. She smiled back, then her face clouded.

"Is it entirely proper?"

"To view your hosts' paintings? Of course. They are just down the hall outside this room."

"Then yes, please. I would love to see them."

He offered his arm and she took it, holding herself stiffly beside him. She was worried about propriety, was she? His days of seducing young women in secluded galleries were long over, although he did imagine for a moment what it might be like to pull Miss Barrett into a dark corner and surprise her with a kiss. Would she react with a slap? A swoon? Not Miss Barrett of the Mongol hordes. She would more likely glower at him until he stopped.

He looked down and patted her gloved hand, trying to communicate her safety in his care. They left the brightly lit drawing room and entered the wide hallway. It was darker there, but adequately illuminated with lamps. The flickering light reflected off her disarranged hair. His fingers ached to set a couple of errant curls to rights, but it was not something a gentleman would do with any lady other than his wife or mistress.

"Here, Miss Barrett," he said, stopping at the first one. "A portrait depicting St. Joan of Arc."

She regarded the painting critically. "It is not how I would imagine her."

"Oh?" He had viewed this rendition of *Jeanne d'Arc* before and found her stark, severe expression moving. "She was not like an English lady," he explained. "She would not have a silk gown and her hair done up in curls. She lived long ago in France."

"It's not that I think she should look like the ladies back in the drawing room," sniffed Miss Barrett. "I am not an idiot."

Court felt laughter bubble up in his throat. He grunted to disguise it, rocking back on his heels. "I did not mean to insinuate—"

"I think the artist made her too pretty." She stepped closer, her arms at her sides, still staring at the painting. "Joan of Arc was a fierce warrior. I often wonder how she did it."

"Did what?"

"Convinced all those men to follow her, to fight and give their lives under her command. She commanded *armies* of men," she said, turning to him. "I wonder how."

A thought lodged in his brain at that moment: it was most certainly a blessing Miss Barrett did not know how.

As it turned out, her knowledge of Joan of Arc put his to shame. She told him all she knew of the woman's birth, childhood, political machinations, and eventual burning at the stake, while he occasionally contributed a polite "Imagine that," or "Fascinating." At last Miss Barrett lost interest and he led her to the next painting.

The work depicted a Persian prince surrounded by a harem of voluptuous slaves. *Nude* voluptuous slaves. The women sprawled on cushions and caressed one another while the prince surveyed them all, master of his domain. Court enjoyed the painting's sensual overtones, but in the company of Miss Barrett it created an awkward situation, not least because his lewd mind found her robust figure not unlike those of the prince's lush concubines, and Court momentarily pictured her there among them.

"What do you think of this work, Miss Barrett?" He cleared his throat as she studied it, adding, "It is composed in an appealing baroque style."

She considered it for a long moment. "Yes." Tentatively. Then, "Yes, it is very moving," with an ardent nod of her head. "I should very much like to lie around all day on pillows like those women. Although it might grow tedious after a week or two."

Court stifled a smile. "Tedious indeed," he said. "You prefer to stay busy?"

"I do prefer it. Although idleness can be pleasant enough in the right circumstances. And with the right company," she added, pointing out two embracing women. "They appear to be particular friends."

Court's lips twitched. "Shall we move on?"

They lingered next over a series of expertly crafted landscapes, which did not seem to interest Miss Barrett very much. Then they came to the large canvas at the end of the hall, a rendering of Camelot, King Arthur, Lancelot and his knights. She made an ecstatic sound.

"Do you enjoy the Arthurian legends?" he asked.

"I love them. I've read all the books I could find about King Arthur and Guinevere and the druids and priestesses and all those myths and legends." Her excitement delighted him, although no gently-reared lady would ever admit to being so well read. She studied the detailed painting while he stood silent, reluctant to interrupt her thoughts. Finally she turned back to him. "Do you think they really happened? The things that are written in those legends?"

She sounded wistful, as if she hoped they had. "I suppose some of the events really happened," he said, "while other parts were embellished or contrived. The magic parts, for instance."

"You don't believe in magic, Your Grace?"

"No," he told her truthfully. "Do you?"

She turned back to the painting. "I suppose not, although I wish I did. It is so pleasant a fantasy, that there is magic and mysticism all around us. But I haven't found it to be so. I suppose I lean more toward belief in fate, and chance."

"Fate and chance?" Court raised a brow. "Are they not in opposition to one another?"

She pondered this, a small wrinkle forming between her brows. "I think we all have fates to which we must submit ourselves," she said. "But we can also grasp at chances when they come to us."

"And perhaps change our fates?"

"We must try, mustn't we?" She regarded him as if he held the answers, but in truth, he'd never given much thought to any of this. He had been born to a fate of course, that of the Duke of Courtland. She had been born the daughter of a lesser—and peculiar—viscount. Her fate, his fate.

"You are very profound, Miss Barrett," said Court. "I have never conversed with any lady quite the same as you."

He meant it as praise, but frustration flitted across her face. "People always say that. That I'm strange."

"I did not say you were strange," he corrected her. "I said you were profound. Whenever I ponder magic, fate, and chance hereafter, I shall recall this fascinating conversation."

She tilted her head as if questioning whether he mocked her. He did not mock. In fact, he did not feel ready to return her to the greater company as he should. "Come, there is a striking painting in the ballroom. I believe you would appreciate it very much."

He drew her hand over his arm and she followed a little hesitantly. If odd Miss Barrett hesitated, Court should certainly know better. Why was he doing this? Perhaps because he'd had so little excitement in his life of late. As they walked at a leisurely pace around the corner and down another wide hallway, she did not prattle on as a typical young lady would, and he did not feel compelled to fill the silence. He enjoyed the novelty of strolling beside her lost in his thoughts…too many of which centered on her voluptuous attributes and that damned harem painting.

When they arrived at the Darlington ballroom, there was little light with which to see the painting. He walked in anyway, turning in the expansive, tastefully decorated chamber. When it was lit for a grand ball, as it would be at the conclusion of the house party, a thousand candles would illuminate the space, but at the moment only a single lamp cast shadows for any guest or servant passing through.

He turned to Miss Barrett, who waited by the door. "Are you afraid of the dark?"

She shook her head. "No, Your Grace. I am afraid of ballrooms."

He laughed at her jest—or perhaps it wasn't a jest—and beckoned her to join him. They would be here only a short time. Not that he believed Miss Barrett would try to entrap him in marriage, but her brother would in a heartbeat. He pushed that thought from his mind and crossed to pick up the lamp.

"Come." He led Miss Barrett to a large painting in the center of the far wall and held up the light so she might see it.

She recognized the subject at once. "It is Caesar in the Roman Senate."

"Yes."

"It's one of the few paintings I've seen of Caesar when he's not being stabbed to death," she said. "There is much more to his story than his assassination."

"I agree. I find Roman history interesting. What I know of it, anyway."

"Did you know there is an old Roman wall here?" She turned to him, eyes shining in the lamplight. "Well, not here, but north of here? It is very ancient. Thousands of years old."

"I did know. Have you been to see it?"

Her face fell. "No, not yet. My brother will not take me."

Court would have escorted her there if she'd asked him, taken an entire day to arrange the outing only to assuage her disappointment. Fortunately, she did not ask him. She was engrossed in the painting, her thoughts someplace far away. How novel, a young woman with such concentration, such intelligence to animate her.

He moved away from her because he had to. He prowled the shadowed perimeter of the ballroom, pretending to study the decorative wainscoting, the plentiful sconces affixed to the walls. When he was the length of the room away from her, he turned to discover the full force of her open gaze. It was enough to give a man thoughts, the way she stared at him across the darkness. In his peripheral vision he saw a footman enter and then back out again.

"Leave it," he said when the bewigged man moved to close the doors. With a bow, the servant fled.

Miss Barrett stared at the door, at the retreating servant. "We should probably return to the company."

Something guarded in her expression helped him regain his wits, or at least his sense of propriety. He carried the lamp back to its table near the wall.

"In truth, we've been gone too long." He straightened his waistcoat and coat before he turned back to her. "I shall escort you back to the drawing room."

"Thank you. And thank you for showing me the paintings."

"It was my pleasure."

He walked back with her down the hall, aware of her warmth, her closeness. Her fingertips tightened on his arm almost imperceptibly as they passed the harem painting, or perhaps he imagined it. She helped herself to another long glance. He enjoyed her freshness and curiosity. In fact, he had deeply enjoyed her company, but for appearance's sake, they needed to part ways—quickly. Publicly. When she told him at the door she would rather retire for the evening, he urged her back into the drawing room so everyone could see them, and delivered her back to her brother's side.

Court hoped it would be enough to hold the gossips at bay. They had been away from the group far longer than was appropriate. It was rare he behaved so clumsily, so foolishly, especially at a large party such as this. He decided from then on he would avoid her as much as possible. He really had to.

For her sake and his.

Chapter Three:
Wish

Harmony thought the Darlingtons' garden would be pleasant indeed if she could explore its charms in solitude, but instead she sat with the ladies, taking the sun and awaiting the gentlemen's return from the hunt. Nearby a lake glistened, surrounded by woods to the edge of the property. Flowers bloomed in a landscaped border and paper lanterns twisted in the breeze. It was very picturesque, all of it, but Harmony's peace was shattered by the constant badgering of her friends.

"You cannot tell us anything else?" Juliette pouted. "He did not act the rake in the slightest? No rude comments? No lurid glances?"

"No," Harmony said. "He was not lurid at all."

"Are you sure you're not leaving anything out?" Viola leaned closer. "We won't tell."

"I have told you all I can remember, many times over."

The Duke of Courtland this, the Duke of Courtland that. For a group of ladies so repulsed by the Duke of Courtland, they were obsessed with every aspect of the man.

"Are his eyes really green *and* blue?" Mirabel asked. "I wish I could see them close up."

"He has beautiful eyes," Harmony said quietly. "Very kind eyes."

"Kind?" Sybil huffed. "If he was kind he would be civil to the other guests."

"You mean civil to *you*," said Juliette. "He is civil to his gentleman friends, and the Darlingtons."

"He was civil to Harmony," Mirabel laughed.

"He should be civil to everyone." Sybil flushed a hot pink and fanned herself. "I don't believe he is kind *or* polite. In fact, I know he is not," she added, raising an eyebrow.

Juliette snickered. "You are only jealous he did not ask you to dance."

"I most certainly am not. If he had asked me to dance, I would have said no."

"Jealous, jealous, jealous," Juliette taunted under her breath.

This tedious banter had gone on unchecked for a week, ever since His Grace had introduced himself and asked her to dance. She had gone from the least respected member of her social group to the most admired, although in her opinion she was being admired for a very silly thing.

And since that day nearly a week ago, he had not so much as spoken to her, nor looked at her, nor smiled in her direction. He went out with the men to hunt and fish in the day time, and kept to cards and the smoking room at night. From time to time he'd make an appearance in Lady Darlington's drawing room to watch the dancing, but he did not ask her or any other lady to dance, even the older women who openly flirted with him. After a time, too short a time, he'd disappear back into the side rooms and the young ladies would wink at one another and whisper behind their fans about his showy clothes and his too-long hair, and his big hands.

Harmony did not agree that his clothing was showy. He actually dressed in a rather conservative style. His clothing only appeared showy for being so expertly fitted to His Grace's compelling physique. The ladies talked about that too, until Harmony's head would burst from it. His Grace's broad shoulders, His Grace's stern features, His Grace's fine legs revealed in alluring detail by his tight-fitting trousers. And yes, his shoulders were broad, his features were stern, his legs were fine, and his hands were…obscenely large.

"I believe he wanted to kiss you." Viola made a gleeful sound. "Do you think he meant to kiss you when he took you off to walk alone?"

"We only went down the hall to see some paintings. There were footmen everywhere."

Sybil tsked. "As if a footman would intervene with a duke. Fortunately His Grace did not choose to take advantage of you." It was an insult, sweetly spoken. Sybil had been the one most anxious to cut him, and now had become the one most jealous of Harmony's connection to him.

"The duke only invited me to dance to save me from a scolding," Harmony explained for the twentieth time. "It was very embarrassing, as I told you. Nothing romantic happened, not the entire time we stepped away."

She had not told them everything. She had not told them about the pleasant, relaxed way he conversed, or the way he listened when she talked. She let them believe he was what they thought: a highborn, stuffy gentleman, guilty of great perversions. The rest of it she kept in her heart, her special secret she refused to reveal. If they knew how much she thought about him they would never stop teasing her. If they knew the silly fantasies she harbored when her eyes lingered on him...

"Why do you blush every time you speak of him?" asked Mirabel. "If nothing romantic happened?"

"I know what happened," said Juliette, eyes dancing. "He dragged her into a corner and subjected her to his *uncomfortable habits*!"

"Oh, yes," Mirabel giggled. "He took unforgivable liberties, didn't he? Perhaps he wishes Harmony would be his mistress."

"What a terrible thing to say," Viola gasped.

"Goodness, how sensitive you are." Mirabel dressed Viola down with a sneer and excluded Harmony from the rest of the conversation.

She didn't care. She wasn't here in the garden to simper and chat, but to see the duke return from the hunt. He seemed particularly strong and manly coming in from the fields, in a way that very much affected her, even if he never had a word or glance for her.

It wasn't long before the hunting party appeared with their attendants and bags full of game. There was much silly flirting and mucking about as the men showed off for the ladies, but it was not the duke's habit to partake. His Grace ignored her friends when they crossed to his group and contrived to crowd nearby. It gave Harmony a certain sour pleasure that their fluttering and preening was for nothing, especially since they pretended to despise him.

Harmony drifted away from the milling guests to a quieter corner of the garden. She had enjoyed her glimpse of the duke, but she would not crowd about him with the other girls. Instead, she sat on a bench near a clump of flowers, inhaling their sweet scent. She wished she could turn her head and stare at him without inviting mockery. She wished to stare at him all the time, but she couldn't, which annoyed her. He had looked so earthy and capable in his hunting coat and trousers as he sauntered about the clearing, his shotgun slung over his arm.

Oh, he really had looked *so dashing*. She decided she would allow herself one more peek. Only one, and a short one at that. She turned to find him in the center of a crowd, talking to his friends as the footmen bore off the gentlemen's guns for cleaning and storage. Her short peek turned into an extended stare. She could see the ladies giggle behind their hands as his regard passed over them. Silly hens. She was glad now she had left them. She would rather hide here and—

"Ah, if it isn't the lovely Miss Barrett, fellows." A strident voice interrupted her solitude as a group of young fops descended on her. She recognized the one who addressed her as Lord Sheffield. She hadn't made the acquaintance of the others. They smiled at her but they didn't look like real smiles. She drew herself up, instantly on guard.

"Good afternoon, gentlemen. How was your hunting?"

"It was fine hunting. The Duke of Courtland snared a rare grouse, or so I heard."

"Eh, Sheffield, was it a Red Grouse?" one of the young men called.

"No, sir. It was a Blonde Grouse."

Harmony lifted her chin, turning her face away. "If you are making a joke, it is not particularly funny."

"Aww, Miss Barrett, we won't tell him you were hiding over here staring til your eyes popped out. Don't pout now. It's a lovely day."

"Not as lovely as you," one of them cried in a mocking voice. Lord Sheffield elbowed him and turned back to her.

"Don't be cross, miss. Me and my friends were just saying how majestic you looked sitting over here among the flowers. Like some pretty picture in a museum. I bet the duke likes you a lot. He asked you to dance, after all."

Harmony picked at a tiny snag in the fabric of her gown. "I do not care if he likes me or not."

"Don't you?" Lord Sheffield shifted and looked back at his friends. "You'd be a perfect match, you and that one." A couple of the young men burst into laughter and reeled away. Harmony stood and began to walk farther from the garden, leaving them to their stupidity, but Lord Sheffield and a few stragglers dogged her heels.

"Do you think he'll ask you to dance again?" Lord Sheffield's mouth curved in a grin she very much wished to slap off his face.

"I should think not," Harmony replied shortly.

"You ought to ask him. He seems so lonely without you."

Harmony seethed with irritation. Why could he not leave her in peace? No matter where she walked, he followed, and when she paused to face him he stared openly at her bodice, the nasty rat. She tugged up at it a little, and then he laughed, and she decided she had tolerated quite enough. She drew back her hand to give him a sound box across the ear—but then her fist was trapped in a firm grasp. She turned and locked eyes with the Duke of Courtland.

His gaze left her to settle on Lord Sheffield. "It is not at all the thing to pester a lady."

A low chuckle issued from one of Sheffield's friends. The duke silenced it with a cool stare.

That accomplished, he turned back to her. She'd forgotten how large he was up close. Intimidating. She took in his stern, chiseled face, his dark hair and the eyes of a color she still couldn't place. Green or blue? Dark greenish-blue. She did not know how to describe them, only knew that when he turned them on her she rather lost her ability to think.

"Miss Barrett," he said, placing her hand over his arm. "Will you walk with me around the lake before tea?"

He couched it as a question but it was a command. She knew she ought to reply with some fluttery thing—*Certainly, Your Grace. I would be honored, Your Grace*—but she could not summon a word in her disarrayed mood. He sent a withering glance over his shoulder at her tormentors as he turned her toward the path. "If you will excuse us, gentlemen."

His acerbic tone implied they were anything but. The men shrank away like beaten dogs, slinking toward the house. Why couldn't she command that type of respect? She hoped His Grace had not heard too much of their mockery, especially the part about her mooning after him. Of course, he probably heard worse things about her, wherever the men gathered and talked about the ladies. Her brother, who ought to stick up for her, probably spoke of her worst of all. Only this man, this near-stranger, had seen fit to come to her rescue—for the second time.

It was both wonderful and infuriating. And embarrassing beyond belief.

She looked away, at tree tops and blue sky, as a whirlwind of emotions assailed her. She didn't realize until now how much she'd craved his notice, but why did it have to come at a time like this, when she felt so irritable and bleak? She scratched her cheek and fussed with her bonnet's brim. "You needn't stay and walk with me," she said. "But thank you for sending those gentlemen away."

"I felt obliged to interfere." He helped her cross from the lawn to a narrow walking path beside the lake. "You might have knocked out Lord Sheffield if I hadn't." His deep, sonorous voice held a note of reproach.

"I did not— I would never—"

"Plant a facer aside Sheffield's crooked nose?" He patted her hand where it rested on his arm. "That's a lie. I think you tell a lot of lies, Miss Barrett."

She gawked. "I most certainly do not."

"You do. Out of necessity, I'm sure, but you needn't lie to me."

She stopped still and faced him. Beneath his handsome exterior, behind his intent gaze, she saw some spark of mayhem that unsettled her. She wasn't sure anymore if he'd rescued her or only wished to toy with her in private. When she spoke, her voice trembled. "I am too stupid sometimes to tell lies from truth. To tell sincerity from cruelty."

"Are you too stupid to realize when a friend stands before you?"

She had used the word stupid first. He said it with a touch of frustration that made it sound nastier perhaps than he meant. She glared at the burnished gold buttons of his waistcoat. "I can be eminently stupid, Your Grace."

He made a low, impatient sound. "Come, let us walk." He guided her forward at the same desultory pace with which he did everything. "If you do not care to continue as an object of gossip and teasing, you must refrain from throwing punches at gentlemen. You are becoming the party's entertainment and I doubt you wish to be."

She flushed hot at his words and tugged her bonnet again. "Are you trying to be gallant or to humiliate me?"

"Humiliate you? What an outrageous thing to say." His eyes were fixed on some distant point, his lips drawn down in what might have been a frown, except that he didn't look angry. "Why did you not dismiss the gentlemen when they began to tease you?"

"Dismiss them how?"

"A glare, some sharp words. Ignore them if you must. Those young bucks are nobodies, annoying gnats. If you swat at them enough, they will go away."

On the heels of the gentlemen's mockery, she must now endure this dressing down? Her throat worked with the effort of mastering her emotions. "The scene you witnessed was not the first nor the last time I shall be mocked," she said. "I do not suppose you know the feeling of being made fun of, but it is not a very nice one. I cannot come up with the correct words to say in friendly company, much less when I feel attacked." She stared at some point just above the wrist of his coat, then lifted her face to meet his gaze.

She oughtn't have. Her humiliation was complete, for he was looking at her with *pity*. His deep, rich green-blue eyes held hers and softened as if they shared her pain. But she mustn't be fooled by his beauty, his seeming tenderness. He belonged to the part of the world that ruled and controlled, socially and in every other way. He belonged to the circle that shunned her every chance it got.

"Please go," she said, turning her face from him. "I wish to be alone."

He did not go, which she supposed was a duke's prerogative. She tried to pull away from him, but his hand tightened over hers. "I walked you this far. Let us walk the rest of the way."

"I had rather go and sit—sit over there," she said, gesturing toward a remote glade.

"Miss Barrett, are you cross with me?"

Yes, she was cross with him, with his wealth and prestige, his easy manners. He might always do as he wished and look casual and confident about it, as opposed to her with her awkwardness and muddling. She tried to be like him, ruffled by nothing, her chin set high against the world, but it was only a charade. It was the role she played of necessity, when inside she felt lonely and hopeless, and so desperate for just one person to accept her. But she *was* hopeless. Again, she moved to pull away.

"No," he said, drawing her back. "Continue to walk with me. For a few moments only, until you gather yourself."

"Gather myself? I am perfectly gathered, thank you," she said in a strained voice.

They grappled there beside the lake, Harmony trying to retrieve her hand while he trapped it ever more stubbornly.

"Miss Barrett," he said as they struggled, "forgive me if I offended you. I only meant to help."

"I do not require your help." Harmony laughed bitterly at herself, at this entire situation. "I assure you, I am beyond help. Everyone believes so."

"I don't."

She went still at his staunchly spoken words. "You don't?"

"I don't," he repeated. "Now please, calm yourself and paste a pleasant smile on your face. At the very least, something besides that frown. They watch, you know. Always."

They watched, yes, all of them believing her beyond help—except him. She wondered if his words were true or only a gentleman's polite response. She wondered why she cared, since she'd given herself up for lost a long time ago.

Harmony relaxed her arm—and her expression—and allowed him to draw her back onto the path.

* * * * *

Damn and blast, Court thought. What a confounded situation. This was what came of meddling in young women's affairs. What had come over him, to barge in again like a white knight on horseback to rescue her from the likes of Sheffield? Or more accurately, rescue Sheffield from her?

He watched his companion master her emotions, take in air and square her shoulders. Her misery-pinched face relaxed by slow degrees into a shuttered mask that disturbed him almost as much as her glares and frowns. "I am better now," she said. "I am sorry I cut up at you when I was annoyed by someone else."

Court was sorry too. Sorry to know how sad and tormented this creature was beneath her false, forced veneer. He didn't want the burden of her woes, not on top of his own responsibilities. "It is no matter," he said in a brisk tone. "Let us forget this episode ever occurred." He led her nearer to the lake, being careful to not to trod the hem of her sage-sprigged dress. "We will have some light conversation until you are feeling completely yourself again. What shall we talk about?"

She thought for a moment. "Did you kill anything today?"

A bloodthirsty topic, but she was not known for her girlish repartee. "Yes, I did," he said aloud. "A hare and several pheasants."

She shuddered. "I hope the hare did not have babies. They will be crying now, wondering where their mama is."

"It was a male hare," he lied.

This did not placate her. "I'm sure other mamas were killed today, and on every other day you and the gentlemen go out to hunt. Is it necessary to kill helpless creatures?"

He gazed down at her, thinking how desperately the contrary young woman needed to be spanked. "Are you one of those crusaders who oppose blood sport, Miss Barrett?"

"I find it distasteful to kill things. To *want* to kill things," she added, giving him an affronted look, as if it was her own mama hare he'd shot.

"You feel strongly about things, don't you? Yes." He answered his own question. "But in this case you need more information."

"What do you mean?"

"Do you know about the benefits of culling? Reducing the herd? Hares are pests to the farmers and villagers, and with the rate at which they reproduce, they might soon overrun all the crops in England. What would be done then?"

They walked a few steps in silence as she bit her lip. "Oh."

"Counting out the inconvenience of not having enough bread or produce on your table, what would become of the hares—and the hares' *babies*—when their own sources of food became scarce through overpopulation?"

It was not a conversation he would have had with a typical lady, but he rather enjoyed watching Miss Barrett work through it in her agile mind.

"I had never thought of it like that. It would be quite disastrous, wouldn't it? Still…it seems cruel. Killing."

"It is cruel in a way, but kinder to shoot a hare or stag or fox than have them overrunning the countryside, forming packs and slowly starving for lack of food."

She would not meet his eyes. He was not forgiven yet for his gentlemanly crime of hunting. Perhaps he never would be. Young ladies' hearts were so capricious, which was why he avoided having anything to do with them. Usually. Until now.

They walked in silence for a few moments until they rounded the other side of the lake and headed back toward the manor. Her gaze fixed on the distant house guests. He detected a subtle stiffening of her spine. "Aren't you glad now you did not attack him in front of everyone?" he asked.

"He deserved a drubbing."

Do not laugh. Do not encourage her. "You must behave in a mannerly fashion, Miss Barrett. Without manners, we are…savages."

"I should like to leave," she burst out. "This instant, I should very much like to leave this house party and return to London."

"Shall I escort you to Sedgefield so you might hire a carriage and be on your way?"

She bristled at his mocking tone. "I wish you would. I'm sure my brother and our hostess would both find themselves well rid of an inconvenient guest."

"You are not inconvenient. Merely unconventional. And undisciplined," he added for his own private titillation.

She gasped, her eyes going wide. "I don't think it is very polite to call ladies 'undisciplined.'"

"I don't normally do so. But in this case…"

Her blue eyes snapped in irritation, for he was not being a gentleman. He did not feel, at present, very much like a gentleman. He felt the strongest urge to tumble her back on the grass and kiss her outrage away—after he disciplined her, of course. He settled for a much-more-appropriate shrug of his shoulders. "It is not that difficult a thing to use manners. For instance, in turning down a dance with creaky old Monmouth, you might more delicately plead the headache than profess yourself bloated."

Miss Barrett sputtered. "Did you— Who said—?"

"I fear nearly everything you say is repeated. If I were you I would use it to my advantage. Say some horrid things about that bounder Lord Sheffield, for example. They needn't be true."

"Your Grace." She tried hard to look shocked as she ought, but a smile played around the corners of her lips. "I was *not* bloated, by the way."

"Of course not."

"I simply didn't want to dance with him. I do not enjoy dancing."

"I don't either. Not these country dances anyway. In London, they waltz." He gave her a look he feared contained some longing. "Have you danced the waltz, Miss Barrett? In the ballrooms of London?"

She looked stricken. "I am not permitted to waltz."

"Not permitted? By whom?"

"By the patronesses at Almack's." She paused. "Rather, they revoked my permission. I am mortified to say why."

Ah, the Almack's debacle. Beautiful Miss Barrett, strewing chaos wherever she went. He could not laugh at the poor thing, not to her face, but his mind swam with comical images of what a young lady might do to have her dancing permissions revoked. He disguised his laughter in a ponderous frown. "I do not know the circumstances," he said, "but you ought not to have lost your waltzing privileges. It's criminal. A miscarriage of justice, I'm sure."

"Perhaps you can introduce a bill on my behalf into the House of Lords, Your Grace."

He nodded, enjoying her cleverness. "All young ladies should be free to waltz. Particularly you, Miss Barrett. Yes, it would make a fine bill, and take some of the wind out of those stuffy patronesses."

She sobered and gave a sad little shrug. "I do not care, anyway."

Court wished he might slip an arm around her waist and draw her close. He wished he might secure her little hummingbird hand fluttering at her throat and trap it in his own and waltz her around the lake until her sullen mood brightened. His hands flexed into fists, fighting the folly of his will. She stirred him. Her ample breasts, her delicate hands. Her full, pouting lips.

My God, he was developing a *tendre* for Miss Chaos. He took a deep breath to clear his head and let it out again. "You should not care," he said. "Almack's is a crashing bore."

"But those balls are only a few hours of torture. This house party drags on and on. All anyone does here is gossip, eat, dance, and kill things."

Court nodded at her accurate assessment. "So what are we to do with you? You dislike three of those four activities, and you cannot eat every hour of the day."

"Your Grace!" She halted him, eyes wide. "Be absolutely still."

She stepped forward, practically against him, and darted one gloved hand at his face. Before he could step away, her fingertip slid beneath his left eye, a fleeting touch. She drew her finger back and held it up to him. "You had an eyelash. Now you can make a wish."

He looked down at her finger, his dark lash perched at its tip. Everyone in the garden was surely watching this young woman plastered against his front. "Quickly," she said, "or it will blow away on the wind." She was so close to him now he might have kissed her.

"Quickly what?" he asked, befuddled.

41

Her blue eyes sparkled at him. "You must blow your eyelash away, Your Grace, and make a wish as you do."

There was no way he was going to blow his eyelash from her fingertip. Dukes of the realm did not do those sorts of things. He saw the moment she realized he would not do it, for her mood dimmed again.

"Why don't you take my wish?" he suggested, easing her away from him. "Wish for something marvelous."

She shook her head. "It doesn't work that way."

"Doesn't it? Why not?"

"It just doesn't." She rubbed her thumb over the finger and his eyelash flittered away, perhaps into the lake, the wishful opportunity squandered. She backed away from him, straightening her skirt and tugging at her bonnet. "I wonder if it's time yet for tea? I am feeling so much better now." She gave a decisive nod. "Completely better. I'm sorry to have drawn you away from your friends for so long."

"It is no matter. Let us return to the group or the gossip will be tedious."

Too late, Courtland. Far too late for that.

"I don't care about gossip," she said, staring out at the lake again. "But I regret for your sake that your name has become linked with mine."

"It is not a matter of our names being linked. Gossip can have dangerous results to a lady's reputation."

She gave him a weary look. "I am nearly twenty-three. I will not have another season and I will not marry. My reputation is no longer of any consequence."

He felt unaccountable anger that this young creature, however brazen, should feel her life over at such a tender age. Although, perhaps, her resignation was for the best. "Miss Barrett, I am sorry to hear you feel this way, but I hope you discover more enjoyment at Danbury House than you have had thus far. Why, have you been to see the artwork in the Darlingtons' East Salon? There is a gallery of notable family portraits there, if you should find yourself bored and restless." As he said it, he had inappropriate thoughts of another activity one might do while bored and restless. A considerably more carnal activity. Dukes could do almost anything, but there were a few things they couldn't do...

For instance, Court could not put his hand at Miss Barrett's back and guide her up the grand staircase of Danbury House to his guest bedchamber above the Great Hall. He could not, once there, remove her clothing and admire her voluptuous, feminine figure, run his hands over every curve and valley of her person as he clasped her against his front. He could not suck on the curve of her shoulder or fill his hands with the bounty of her tempting breasts. He could not push her back on his bed and tease and pleasure her until every hint of anxiety was erased from her pretty face. He could not drive inside her until his own sordid, restless cravings were expended again…and again…and again…

No. He could not do that. He should not even imagine it, not now, with sad, conflicted Miss Barrett leaning on his arm. Curse civilization and blasted manners.

They began to walk more slowly as they neared their company. The crowd in the garden had not dissipated in the slightest. If anything, the audience had grown. Court knew with some pain that the universal topic of discussion was them. He delivered her to the younger group of women, greeting the fluttering circle with a tight smile before bowing over his companion's hand.

"I wish you a pleasant evening, Miss Barrett."

I wish you were beneath me all this pleasant evening. But that is only because, deep down inside, I am even more uncouth and mannerless than you.

She inclined her head to him and muttered something he couldn't make out. Perhaps she said, "I wish it for you too." He heard, *I wish for you too.*

He thought of his eyelash, and her body sliding against his. *Make a wish. Quickly, or it will blow away on the wind.*

Chapter Four:
Escape

For three more days, Court managed to avoid contact with Miss Barrett. He turned his attention to cards and male conversation, and hunting, and more cards. And more male conversation, sprinkled with the squawking of his mother and Mrs. Lyndon, who'd heard the whispers about he and Miss Barrett. She ripped up at him the day after their lakeside stroll, berating him in their private parlor as the ladies took tea.

"She is so much worse than I expected," said his mother. "She lacks the most basic of manners. Why, she is practically a savage. It is unkind but it must be said."

"Her mother died too young," Mrs. Lyndon agreed. "She has no social graces."

"And now she has abandoned her set completely and taken to keeping company with Lord Darlington's books."

"I believe he granted her permission to do so." Court knew it, in fact, since he was the one who had quietly arranged it.

"She spends hours in there, reading!"

"Horrifying," he murmured. "If she does not take care, she may learn something."

In unison, his mother and Mrs. Lyndon puffed out their cheeks.

"You must avoid her, Courtland." Her eyes widened in horror, as if the savage Miss Barrett might rip out his throat. "I can't understand how Lady Darlington tolerates that girl and her brother under her roof. And to have her name linked to yours! You cannot imagine how humiliated I was when Lady Myra whispered you'd stolen off to the ballroom with her. Can it be true, my son?"

His lips drew into a tight line. "I was showing her a painting. Not that I must give an accounting to you, or to any of the gossips in this house."

His mother rapped her fan on the table at her side. "Ah, you will turn into that Barrett girl now, disregarding basic manners and acting like an impulsive child."

He believed he might. He felt the most impulsive urge to upend his mother's tea cup over her head, an urge he subdued with an iron will. He was glad "that Barrett girl" was likely engrossed in some book, blissfully unaware of the talk about the two of them. He was pleased for her to have that respite.

But for him, the house party lost much of its glow. Above and beyond his mother's fretting, the daily repetition of activities began to chafe. One could only shoot so much game before one grew bloody tired of the sport. One could only hash over so many political arguments and play so many hands of cards before one nearly lost one's mind. So when the other gentlemen amassed for their daily foray the fourth day after Miss Barrett's retirement to the library, Court begged off and donned his town clothes and walking boots instead.

He wasn't sure where he planned to go. Away. Away from the temptation of visiting her in the library. Away from salons and crowded halls and servants who spied. He wanted to go where he might be a solitary, anonymous man taking the fresh northern air. He strolled down the road from Danbury House into the outskirts of Sedgefield proper, realizing he should have dressed down if he'd sought anonymity. No one bothered him, but some of the children stopped to stare at the well-turned-out gentleman in their midst.

Court decided he would amble about Sedgefield until tea time, perhaps even longer. Perhaps he wouldn't return to Danbury House until dinner, until he had two great lungs full of fresh air to sustain him through another evening cooped up with irritating ladies and obsequious men. At least he would not have to contend with his mother; she'd set off that morning with Mrs. Lyndon to a nearby manor to visit a friend. With any luck, she would remain there a week or more. Not that he didn't love his mother—he just preferred her in small doses.

He walked past an inn and down the main thoroughfare of town. Though narrow, it was lined with thriving shops. He glanced in the window of a bookseller's and thought instantly of Miss Barrett, of her lopsided hats and bookish ways and large blue eyes. He thought of her curled up in one of Darlington's deep library chairs, her slippered feet drawn up beneath her as she devoured some volume of the Royal Historical Society. He thought of her too much.

Make a wish...

He had made no wish, though. He didn't believe in them. But he could still picture her dainty gloved fingertip in his mind, his curved lash at the end of it like some treasure she'd found. *Make a wish. A wish...*

He turned at the end of the street, surprised to see the figure of a well-born lady in the setting of an outdoor marketplace. Pretty dress, lopsided bonnet, fingers twisting in her skirts.

Bloody hell. "Miss Barrett?"

She turned and took a step back, looking as surprised as he. She stood by a rickety wagon, engaged in conversation with some village man. A farmer or tradesman perhaps, none too genteel or clean.

"What on earth are you about?" he asked. "I was only jesting about hiring passage back to London. Where is your brother? Your lady's maid?"

"My brother is out with the gentlemen, and the lady's maid from Danbury House would not come into this part of town."

"Wisely so." He cast a withering look at the man by the wagon. "It is not the thing for a woman of quality to tarry here. Particularly alone."

She released a stream of garbled explanation. Perhaps it only sounded garbled to him because he'd never had the experience of being talked back to by anyone, much less this slip of a woman who barely approached the height of his shoulder. He held up a hand and finally succeeded in silencing her.

"Miss Barrett, I must insist for propriety's sake that I escort you back to Danbury House at once."

She shook her head. "I am sick unto death of Danbury House. And this could be my one and only chance to go to the old Roman wall."

"Go to the old Roman wall? Now? With whom?"

She'd already turned from him, sweeping toward the wagon and its sagging horse. He moved to grab her arm.

"Miss Barrett—"

She tugged away, freezing his words with her glare. "The driver will leave without me if you do not let me go. I had to bargain for some time to gain passage on his wagon."

Court gaped. "Don't tell me you have hired a ride north with that man? Miss Barrett—surely—you cannot mean to—"

"I've always wanted to see the old Roman wall," she said slowly, as if she were explaining to a child. "My whole life, ever since I learned of it in geography and history books. When you joked about hiring a carriage in Sedgefield, I realized I actually might if I wished."

Good God, so this was his fault. The tradesman shifted from foot to foot, clearly growing uncomfortable with the situation. It would suit Court fine if he would just run off. Otherwise he might need to resort to force to dissuade Miss Barrett from setting off on this journey. There would be struggling and drama, a full scene right here in the heart of town. The idea appalled him, but to step away and let her go was not an option. He would not have her ruination on his hands.

He made one last attempt at reason. "Surely, madam, you are not considering taking an hours-long journey north, unchaperoned, with a perfect stranger. A man," he added with emphasis. "He is not a gentleman, and you've no lady to accompany you at any rate."

"Your Grace, you must understand—"

"I understand one thing only. You are about to do a dangerous thing."

She threw up her hands, then clasped them at her waist. "I have no choice, you see. I've asked Stephen to take me nearly every day since we arrived, but he is preoccupied with hunting and women. He has no care for history, for exploring the world."

"Exploring the world? Dear girl, your place is back in the drawing room, beside the fire. Leave exploring to those who are suited to it."

"I am suited to it," she cried.

He drew himself up, fixing her with his most intimidating stare. "I will not allow this caper to proceed. I cannot."

"You have no right to stop me. You have no power over me, Your Grace," she added for good measure. That was twice in five minutes she had mouthed back to him. Preposterous.

"It's unfortunate I don't have any power over you," he said when he recovered himself. "If I did, I could give you the sound spanking you so richly need and deserve."

47

The words were out before he could stop them. She looked appropriately scandalized and turned away, toward the shifty man and his rickety cart. He had to grasp her hand to stop her. Grabbing at someone else's person—him, the Duke of Courtland. He hadn't done such a thing since his childhood, and he'd done it twice with Miss Barrett now.

"The wall you speak of is at least six hours' journey from here," he said. "Perhaps more."

"But it's days from London, and Stephen says we are going home this weekend. Which is why I must leave now. I can be there tonight and take the mail coach back tomorrow, and my brother will never know. When he is at cards and women, he stays out all night and never wakes before two the next afternoon."

She was leaving. In three days. The thought upset him almost as much as her reckless plans. She yanked at his hand until he released her. "Why is it so important to see it?" he asked. "Will you risk your good name, your reputation?"

"I told you before, those things are meaningless to me now. I do not care."

"You ought to. You ought to have a care for the safety of your person at least." He shot a look at the driver, or tradesman or farmer, or whatever he was. "That man could take you somewhere and ra—" He bit off the word before he uttered it. "Bedevil you. How do you know he's an honest person? Not only that, but his wagon and horse are both dilapidated." He looked around at the curious townspeople beginning to gather. She was turning him from a refined peer to a public scold, damn her. "Miss Barrett, if you must continue on this ill-advised course, permit me to engage a more fitting conveyance for your trip, and hire a proper chaperone to ride along with you."

She seemed, finally, ready to listen to reason. "Will you? How long will that take?" she asked, watching him carefully.

Long enough for you to regain your senses. Or at least long enough for me to force you into a carriage and get you home. "It will not take long," he assured her.

Court offered her his arm, which she refused, but she followed. "I would lend you my coach but my mother is using it to call on acquaintances," he said. "I'll hire one at the inn."

"What if you can't?" came her small voice.

"There are very few things I can't do."

His tone of authoritative control worked to silence her. He walked quickly along Sedgefield's narrow streets in the mid-afternoon sun. He was angry, yet he felt some sympathy for her, some grudging admiration. Miss Chaos was willing to risk her life to visit Hadrian's ancient pile of rocks—it was not merely some passing fancy to her. Any other woman of her set would see the wall as nothing more than a background to pose against and look pretty, but Miss Barrett was not of that ilk. She refused to languish in the drawing room, even though, as a woman, that was her fate.

Ah, but he could not entertain sympathetic feelings for her. His pace quickened along with his temper, and he left it to her to keep up. After all, this was her fault. If he had not come across her by chance, what might have become of her? What would her brother do when he found out about her attempted flight north? Court remembered with some distaste Barrett's rough handling when she'd refused to dance with Lord Monmouth, and this was a considerably worse offense.

Well, it wasn't his concern to put down sibling squabbles, but to get her safely home. As soon as they arrived at the inn, he'd put her into the first carriage he saw, along with a maid, and send her back to Danbury House. What a load of trouble to take up his afternoon.

"The innkeeper surely has a lady's maid to spare," he lied over his shoulder. "It should be no great thing to hire a girl to take a couple days away. This is not, after all, a busy town like Harrogate. But Miss Barrett, it would be better to abandon this adventure entirely if you can bring yourself to do it. There are Roman antiquities to see in London." He paused and thought a moment. "I will take you to visit them someday, perhaps, with your brother's permission. And a chaperone, of course."

He turned to receive her response, only to find a village girl stepping along behind him with a covered basket. With great anger, he realized Miss Barrett had not been following at all, but stolen away at some point, probably while he was still going on about the carriage. The girl passed by him, dropping a curtsy. She must have thought him daft, prattling on to himself. Cold fury washed over him, and something else. Shock. No one, no mortal being of his acquaintance had ever made him feel hapless and furious and *powerless* like this. He stood for long moments, fists clenched, face flushed with anger, and considered his choices.

He could wash his hands of the whole affair, let Miss Barrett journey to the Roman wall alone, unprotected, across the moors. No, that was out of the question.

He could go in search of her brother. He might catch the gentlemen on their hunt, but he might not. He could wait at Danbury House for her brother to return and then notify him of his sister's situation, but by that time, Miss Barrett could be in some peril. The thought of that peril, the dangers a lady like Miss Barrett faced alone in the world, was what finally made him turn and continue to walk with great frustration toward the inn.

He would have to go after her himself. It was as reckless and dangerous a choice as Miss Barrett's, but what alternative did he have? By the time he found her and fetched her home, they would have been out and about together for some hours without a chaperone. Disaster.

Perhaps he could still catch her in time to return with her to Danbury House unnoticed. They could part at the gate. She could lie and say she'd been out walking and gotten lost, while he slipped in some back door unnoticed. Dissemblance never sat well with him, but the alternative…

He could not consider that now, or he would become too paralyzed to act.

It seemed an eternity before he reached the inn. He hired the most comfortable coach they had and waited impatiently for it to be prepared. By the time they were on the road to Newcastle, he'd lost almost two hours in his pursuit. He sat forward on the cushions, his gaze fixed on the way before them. The smartly-turned-out driver assured him this was the most traveled route to the wall, and Court had no choice but to believe him. He watched expectantly for an hour and a half or so, and then he began to worry.

If he found Miss Barrett, she was going to endure the full wrath of his temper. Here he was riding north, no valet, no clothes to change into should he become dusty or dampened. He hadn't eaten in hours, bringing a headache to go with the great storm of worry roiling around in his brain. They ought to have caught the wagon by now. What if she hadn't gone back to the driver she'd hired? What if she'd returned to Danbury House? Or hired a different driver? What if the driver had pulled off the road and was even now doing unspeakable things to Miss Barrett with rough, grasping hands?

For another half hour Court stared out of the carriage, stomach clenching with anxiety. Miss Barrett could be in great distress at this moment due to his ineptitude at controlling her. But people behaved around him, deuce take it. From the age of fourteen, since he'd inherited his dukedom, people had deferred to him, respected him. They had not argued or shouted, or pulled away or disappeared without permission from his side. Even before then he'd been a marquess, first son of a powerful man, and people had treated him with proper deference. He had lived an ordered life, observing conventions and doing those duties his title required, earning, in effect, the respect that *most* people showed him.

Most people, but not her.

He scrubbed a hand over his face and growled. Why was the esteemed Duke of Courtland crossing the moors of northern England to fetch an ill-behaved woman who was not his kin or even his social equal? Again his mind turned to thoughts of retribution. When he got his hands on Miss Barrett, he'd give her a tongue lashing she'd remember for the rest of her life. He'd give her that spanking he'd told her she deserved. She *did* deserve it. He'd punish her until she begged forgiveness for her behavior, her manners, her strangeness which had no place in polite society. And then— And then—

And then, out the window, he saw her pale gray frock, her bonnet perched atop her blonde curls as she stomped down the side of the road, and all he could think was, *thank you. Dear God, thank you.*

"Stop!" he called to the driver. Court was out of the door before the vehicle completely slowed. Once he assured himself it really was her, it penetrated his brain that she was crying. Not just crying—she was choking with sobs. "What happened?" he asked. "What has befallen you?" He took her shoulders and searched her person in a panic, fearing the worst. But it was not terror in those tears. She was whole and well. It was anger.

"He left me," she cried. "He promised to take me the whole way, but when we reached the crossroads a while back he said he must be off to some other place. He shrugged and said I must get down. I reminded him that I paid him for his services, but he claimed he only promised to take me this far!"

She appeared so injured, so distraught, that Court couldn't find the words to scold her. To say, *you should have known better. This is what you deserve.* He thought wildly of finding that man, of combing the countryside all around and bringing him before the law, but it would only delay him in fetching her back. "Miss Barrett," he sputtered instead. "Hell and the bloody devil. You frightened me."

She gave him a sideways glance as he fished in a pocket for his handkerchief. Once he handed it over, she ripped off her bonnet and swabbed at her tears. For a moment she seemed to him some unworldly thing, some mythological goddess who might shoot lightning from her fingertips or turn men to stone with her gaze. "Do not look at me that way!" she shrilled in a breaking voice.

Court blinked and spread his hands. "What way?"

"With that reproach and...and pity. I know you think I'm awful, that my behavior is impetuous and foolish, but I truly wished to see the wall, to see where the Romans walked so many centuries ago. If you do not enjoy history, you cannot understand! You cannot understand the way I feel right now." She wept still, even through her fervent speech. Not the pretty, polite tears of a well-reared young lady, but torrents of sorrow.

Court stepped closer as she mopped at her face. "Nor do you seem capable of understanding how I feel," he said. "If I had not found you— For God's sake—"

"That driver promised to take me. He lied." More heartrending, bitter tears. "He is probably somewhere now laughing at me. This is my life's work, I suppose—amusing others. I am sick of it. You cannot understand."

Court studied her, his anger tempered by alarm. He'd thought her manners at Danbury House outlandish, but they were nothing compared to this fit of passion. It could be called nothing else but a *fit*. "Miss Barrett," he said. "Was it his lie that has distressed you so, or your disappointment in not getting to see the Roman wall?"

"I am going to see it," she bawled. "I am going to walk."

Court rubbed his upper lip, finding his own emotions in surprising upheaval. Before he could think what to say she was off again, trudging down the road in her dusty gown, her bonnet dangling from one hand.

"You must return home and give this up," he pleaded. "It grows late."

"I do not care."

"You cannot walk all that way," he said to her back. "It is not possible for a lady of your constitution. Even I could not do it."

She half-turned, her quavery voice propped up with an underlying note of conviction. "That is because you are not as determined as me."

For a long, dreadful moment he watched her stride away from him, her back squared and stiff. He stared, he struggled, his future unfolding before his eyes. What might have been with Gwen...and what increasingly seemed likely as Miss Barrett soldiered down the road.

He counted very slowly and deliberately to ten. Then a stream of profound vulgarities sounded in his head, accompanying the realization that he was going to take her. Take her to the wall, take her on a journey, unchaperoned, that would require a stay overnight at an inn. Perhaps she did not realize the repercussions of such, with her single-minded unconventionality, but he did. He would be saddled with her then, this hopeless, passionate creature.

Damn him. Damn him a hundred thousand times.

"Miss Barrett." He sighed momentously. "I must insist you get into the carriage." She spun to face him. Before she could refuse, he held up a quelling hand. "I will take you to view your pile of Roman rocks, although I believe we will both come to regret it."

She stared at him as the coachman inched up the road, following them. The entire tableau was comical, as ridiculous as the woman standing in her bedraggled dress before him. All of it, farcical. He swung an arm in the direction of the coach. "Get in."

"Do you promise, Your Grace? You will not have your man start back to Danbury House the moment I embark?"

The prospect was tempting. He took a deep breath and let it out, praying for sanity.

"I swear on the graves of every Courtland duke before me." He turned to the coachman, who was doing an excellent job of keeping a straight face. "Will you kindly convey us to the Roman wall at Newcastle and back to Sedgefield on the morrow? You will be well paid for your time and trouble."

The man touched his cap and nodded. Court turned back to Miss Barrett with a scowl. "I will give you exactly one minute's time to board the carriage before I lose my temper and do something we shall both regret."

For a moment, she looked like she might reply, but then she wisely bit her tongue and let Court assist her up the steps and into the traveling coach.

Chapter Five:
Cage

Court settled heavily into the seat opposite her, then the coach started forward with a lurch and a squeak. Harmony waited for it to turn and change direction, but the duke kept his word and they continued toward the wall.

She knew he was angry. Furious. Perhaps he thought she would make marital demands on him as a result of this mad dash. She could, easily, but she wanted nothing less on earth. All she wanted was to get to the wall. She would not even broach the subject of compromising situations and propriety, because she didn't care about that at all. If only her original plan had worked, if only that cursed farmer hadn't stranded her in the middle of nowhere. If only the duke hadn't come across her in Sedgefield...

How awful that he was involved. *I will give you exactly one minute's time to board the carriage before I lose my temper and do something we shall both regret.* She supposed he was speaking of the spanking he'd alluded to earlier, the sound spanking she "so richly needed and deserved." It was impossible to imagine the duke turning her over his knee to punish her, but what if he did? It would hurt, she knew that. She stared at his large hands resting on his thighs and, to her horror, felt some small pang of excitement.

54

For shame, Harmony. What is wrong with you? She couldn't think about such things now, not with him sitting across from her glowering in such a grim way.

She had been prepared to walk to the wall, only to prove that for once she could do as she wished. For once, her desires and dreams would not be denied her. That line of thought only brought more tears and the beginnings of a headache. She pressed His Grace's handkerchief to her eyes, taking deep breaths of its folds. The linen held his rich, heady scent of musk or cologne and now she smelled of it too. When she finally calmed, she offered it back to him.

"Put it in your reticule, madam," he said tautly. "I do not doubt you will need it again."

Yes, he was furious. Perhaps she ought to just tell him she'd harbor no expectations of him, but she had no idea how to say it without embarrassing herself. She shrank as small as she could to give his legs more room. It was not a large coach but it was much more comfortable than the wagon she'd engaged. His scowling regard heightened her feelings of shame, but no matter. Thanks to him, she would get to see the ancient wall. She chanced a look up at his eyes, at his rigidly composed features.

"Have you seen it, Your Grace? Hadrian's Wall?"

"I have. I'm not sure from my recollection it is worth all this trouble but perhaps you will feel otherwise."

"I love history," she offered, as if that might somehow disperse his ire.

"So I gather."

His short, curt answers unsettled her. The times they had conversed at Danbury House, he had been formal with her, but not unfriendly. Now he was a dark cloud of disapproval hovering over her, promising a storm. She had earned a storm, she supposed. They rode an hour or more in heavy silence before Harmony delivered her carefully rehearsed apology.

"I am so very sorry to have inconvenienced you this day, Your Grace."

He answered her sincere effort with an inelegant snort of a laugh. "Inconvenienced me? *This day*, my dear girl? You are a genius of understatement."

"The wall is not so far from here. We can return to Sedgefield on the morrow."

He gazed at her and then down at his hands, stretching his fingers before clasping them in his lap. "You understand we will have to stop at an inn when we reach Newcastle."

"I am sorry for the expense." She was, truly, although she knew that wasn't the point he meant to get across. "I will ask Stephen to repay you for the night's lodging if you wish, as well as the cost of the coach."

He gave a great sigh and looked to the heavens. "It is not the expense of the inn or coach that angers me. You realize I will have to send word to your brother explaining our whereabouts? It is the dinner hour and you are nowhere to be found. They will be organizing search parties, fearing the worst."

"Oh." Harmony had only fretted about her brother finding her out, but the ladies would worry when she turned up missing. "I have behaved very impulsively. I did not think things through."

"As I tried to explain to you earlier. When they realize I am also missing..."

She could see she was making him angrier by pretending not to understand the gravity of their situation. "If you are worried about proprieties, Your Grace, I wish you would not. I'm sorry I've involved you in this disaster but I'll not... I won't..."

His eyes widened and bored into her, silencing her reassurances. She would explain her position later. She had the feeling she'd annoyed His Grace enough for one evening. She squinted into the waning summer sun, ashamed to think how much she'd irritated him during their limited acquaintance. Now he would have to bide at some country inn on her account, believing he was stuck with her for life.

"I'm sorry," she blurted once more. She was afraid she'd begin to cry again, just from the exhaustion of the day and the duke's scorn. She closed her eyes and tried to find a comfortable position on the carriage bench, but the vibration of the road prevented any relaxation.

"Are you tired, Miss Barrett?" the duke asked.

She tried to rouse herself. "I can stay awake until Newcastle."

"I imagine we are an hour from there. Perhaps more. You must be hungry as well."

This too was her fault—starving the poor man. "I am so sorry, Your Grace."

He looked at her a long time but made no response aside from a slight tightening of his lips. The other women at Danbury House talked about the Duke of Courtland as if he was a dangerous sort of gentleman, but he wasn't. He was fiercely angry at her now and hadn't laid a finger on her.

"All the ladies tell tales about you," she said. "That you are cold and not at all nice. But I never believed it. I told them..." Harmony paused. Why would he care about the women's silly gossip, or her defense of him? "I told them they ought not to spread gossip about you," she said anyway. "I think you are only...misunderstood."

His eyes narrowed slightly. "I hope you will remember those words, should occasion come that you and I are not on good terms."

Harmony thought that over, wondering what he meant. Then she didn't know what happened, only that she woke up some time later on the opposite bench with her head bobbing against his shoulder. His coat was soft against her cheek, his bulk so solid. In the dim light she could see his fine gloved hands resting in his lap, the long outline of his legs beside her skirt. This was a dream, surely. She'd never been so close to a man before. She was leaning right against his person and it gave her an odd, secure feeling she couldn't remember from anytime before. *This is not proper*, she thought to herself, but she was too tired to sit up and behave as she ought to. Next she knew he was rousing her gently. The carriage slowed, moving over bumpy cobblestones into the courtyard of an inn.

"Miss Barrett, we have arrived at Newcastle. Will you collect yourself?"

She mumbled something, trying to awaken, to get her limbs to cooperate. She searched for her reticule in the darkness, finding it on the seat beside her. The coach door opened and candlelight shone in her eyes. She heard the duke confer with the driver, then heard the distant, obsequious tones of what must have been the innkeeper. Yes, he would be honored to make two rooms available for His Grace. Yes, he could provide a valet and lady's maid at once. Yes, he would supply a dinner in the private dining room.

"I am too tired to eat," Harmony said, wishing to free His Grace from keeping her.

"You will dine with me," he replied in a quiet but inexorable tone.

* * * * *

Miss Barrett stifled a yawn as an endless parade of servants brought refreshments to lie before them. "It is so late to make them wait upon us," she said.

He shrugged. "They are servants. They serve."

The coachman had delivered them to the inn of greatest prestige in Newcastle, and while Court found the establishment not so impressive as the lodgings nearer to London, it was nonetheless clean and well-managed. He would wager the beds were free of fleas. There was really only one thing wrong with this inn—he should not be here.

He had sent a messenger with a terse note to her brother as soon as they arrived.

Miss Barrett is safe and under my protection. We return tomorrow.

Courtland

There was nothing more to say. He had progressed from fury to chagrin, then to a calm state of resignation. He had considered hiring a lady to accompany them back to Sedgefield in some attempt to lend respectability to their wild adventure, but such measures would be for naught. Barrett would question his sister. The truth would come out, and Court would rather not look like a coward or shirker. He would not attempt to back out of his responsibilities even if this whole thrice-damned mess was not his fault.

As for Miss Barrett, she appeared to be in great confusion as to the consequences of their actions. *I am sorry I've involved you in this disaster but I'll not... I won't...* Wouldn't what? Force him into marriage? Her father and brother would have a fair piece to say about that, once they'd alerted their seconds. In point of fact, there was no chance of escape now. Court was leg-shackled. To her.

But if she'd rather be obtuse and cling to denial, he would allow it for the time being. He didn't wish to take away from her excitement over the old wall, or perhaps he didn't wish to deal with the anxiety which would result when she realized she'd trapped them both in an unholy marriage of inconvenience.

He studied Miss Barrett silently, trying to imagine her as his wife. It was difficult. Disturbing. The Duchess of Chaos, forever at his side. She picked at cold meats and stewed carrots, eating little. Let her choke on her guilt. She deserved it.

"Might I be excused, Your Grace?" she asked, although she had barely touched a morsel of the feast laid before them.

"No. Not yet." If he could give up any hope of a reasonable marriage for her sake, she could sit in her chair a few more minutes and attend his pleasure until he finished eating and could escort her upstairs.

"I am tired," she said a moment later.

"As am I," he snapped. "Due to your intransigence, I am very tired and very cross. You will not leave this room unless it is in my company. You are under my protection and shall be for the foreseeable future. By your choice," he added sharply at the end.

She blinked once, twice, then turned her face a little. "I suppose I deserved a good scolding."

"You deserve much more than that."

He was astonished he would say such a thing, and more astonished still when she lifted her chin and asked, "Are you going to spank me?"

Court lowered his eyes to his plate, stabbing through a chunk of roast beef. "Young ladies should not be shocking."

"You are the one who said it. You said that it was unfortunate you had no power over me because if you did—"

"I remember what I said." Good God, his reckless leg-shackle. He let out a long breath and sat straighter in his chair. "If you must be so discourteous as to remind me of my comment, then I will be discourteous enough to repeat that yes, you are in dire need of correction."

"I cannot imagine anything so fantastical as you spanking me."

"Can you not, Miss Barrett?" he asked coolly.

She found the idea fantastical, did she? It would take very little effort to make it seem less so. Perhaps he should beckon the helpful innkeeper and request a stout birch rod be delivered to Miss Barrett's room abovestairs. That would surely cause it to seem much less fantastical and rather more possible. Court could guide her upstairs, one hand on her elbow. He would make her lie on her narrow inn bed with her head buried in the pillow, and then he'd remove his coat and waistcoat, roll up his shirtsleeves and take the birch in hand and—

His mind stopped there, incapable of going further without being too tempted to act. He gave Miss Barrett a warning look. "Your need for discipline notwithstanding, this is not an appropriate topic of discussion between us."

"You were only blustering then, when you said you would give me the sound spanking I so richly—"

"If you were mine to correct, Miss Barrett," he interrupted, "your bottom would have been striped with a sound switch long before now."

She swallowed hard, her expression miserable. "Oh, my. I'm sure I deserve it."

Court leaped to his feet, his chair scraping back with a grating sound in the quiet room. Miss Barrett leapt up too, taking up a place behind her seat. "Your Grace, I am just so sorry about today. About dragging you here. I cannot explain— If I could go back and do things differently—" She pressed her hand to her mouth, her eyes shining with tears.

In two steps he was at her chair. He placed one booted foot upon it and reached for her. Her eyes went wide but she did not resist him. *Right*, he thought to himself. *She's earned it.* He tossed her face down over his knee, arranging her bottom to be spanked. A birch switch would have been preferable, but his hand worked just as well. He delivered four well-placed smacks before she reacted. A small kick and a gasp of surprise, a whispered *oh, no*.

It was a bit late for *oh, no*'s. He wouldn't have done this if he didn't believe they both needed it, he for his irritation and she for her emotional distress. He held her at the waist and delivered a series of sturdy wallops to the accompaniment of her shocked cries. Ladies' fashions these days provided little in the way of padding, which suited his purposes nicely. Her small kicks became bigger ones, her muted whines louder pleas. It did not deter him from meting out the discipline she required.

"This is for scolding me" *whap!* "and evading me" *whap!* "and leading me on a merry chase across the county with my heart in my throat." *Whap, whap, whap.* She clutched his leg but didn't try to get away. She was crying, but then, she'd been crying before he even started. "It's also for being generally thoughtless and headstrong." *Whap, whap, whap.*

"I'm sorry. I'm so sorry," she wailed.

He paused after a particularly throaty sob and tightened his hold at her waist. "Do you know, Miss Barrett, I am actually feeling less cross now." Another volley of hard spanks across both globes of her posterior, and then he let her up, setting her on the floor. She backed away from him, her eyes wide and wet with tears.

"Where is your reticule?" he asked.

"Wh— What?"

He located her small gray bag and extracted his handkerchief from within. He pulled her toward him, using the linen to dab at her cheeks. "I told you you would need it again."

She made a little choking sound as he gathered her into his arms, but she did not resist him. He stroked her face, soothing and calming her. "There now," he said. "Your penance has been paid. You needn't continue carrying on."

"I can't help it," she said on another sob. "I did not think you really would—"

"I really would," he said. "You practically begged to be spanked, I assume because you felt such guilt. Do you feel less guilty now that you've been punished?"

She mopped at her eyes and took a hard breath. "I will feel guilty as long as you are angry with me."

"I will be less angry if you assure me you have taken a lesson." He held her so she was forced to look at him. "Tell me what you've learned."

"Not to go off on my own," she sniffled. "Not to scold and inconvenience Your Grace."

"Not to scare me," he said, his arms tightening around her. He should not be holding her so close, but he couldn't let go. "I have come to care for your safety. My anger was born of worry more than anything else."

"I am sorry," she whispered. "I truly am."

"Then you are forgiven," he said, forcing himself to release her. "Let us make a fresh start from this moment."

She nodded, wiping away the last of her tears. "I would like that."

"As would I. And perhaps you will find your appetite returned with the loss of your guilty burden."

She took the hint and sat gingerly on the edge of her chair. Court sat too, to finish eating along with her. His perverse fantasy of spanking Miss Barrett's bottom had become, abruptly, a reality, stirring his loins to a quick and uncomfortable stiffness. It wasn't only the act that aroused him, it was her penitence, her tears, the comfort she found in expiation. He had given her that feeling, restored her peace of mind—and her appetite too.

But he felt like a man starved.

He had never spanked any woman but a courtesan. Spanking Miss Barrett had not felt the same, nor had she reacted in the same way the courtesans did. He understood why, but he'd never imagined how satisfied it would make him feel, to spank not just for pleasure, but for emotional reasons.

Miss Barrett peeked across the table at him every so often. He did not frown, nor smile either—although he wished to grin in jubilation. He wished to fall on her and press himself inside her fiercely, and whisper to her that she'd taken her spanking well and he was so, so proud of her.

He wanted to wed Miss Barrett after all.

She would torment and aggravate him hourly, he was sure of it, but at least if she was with him he would know she was safe. He had the power and influence to shelter her from the consequences of the numerous scrapes she would likely get into over the course of her unconventional life. Even better, such numerous scrapes would call for many spankings on her alluring posterior. He felt a softening, a rueful acceptance of her, and in some part of his mind, at that moment, the iron bars of his protection wrapped around her like a cage.

"Your Grace?"

"Yes, Miss Barrett?"

She caught his eyes a moment, then looked down at her lap. "Can you not... Will you tell my brother about..."

He raised a brow. "About what just transpired between us?"

She blushed. "No, about...about my rash actions which have caused us to be here." She wrung her hands, turning her fingers as pink as her cheeks. "Well, I suppose either way he will find out."

"Yes," Court agreed. "I fear we have passed the point of secrecy and discretion, even if we left here and returned at once."

"Please, let us not. At least let me see the wall first, if I must endure the consequences of his anger."

"I promised to take you to your wall and I never go back on my word. I also promise your brother shall not lay a finger on you when we return."

She looked skeptical. "How will you prevent him? He'll be livid."

"As I said earlier, there are very few things I can't do."

She still looked afraid. There was no way at present to soothe her. If he told her she was now safe in his figurative cage, it would only frighten her. She might mistake safety for captivity, even with her sharp intellect. But in time she would see.

"Might I ask your name, Miss Barrett?"

"My name?" she asked, confused.

"Your full name."

She looked suddenly, charmingly shy. "It's Miss Harmony Louise Barrett."

Harmony Louise. A beautiful name for a beautiful, if quite impossible, woman. She looked at him expectantly.

"I have four names," he sighed. "Five, including my title."

"It's good that I have an excellent memory."

He shot her an arch look before he recited them all. "Benedict Thomas William Hawthorne, His Grace the Duke of Courtland. A mouthful, isn't it?"

"What do your friends call you?" she asked, as if his string of fine British names and impressive title was of no consequence.

"My acquaintances call me Courtland or Court." He waited.

"May I—"

"No. You will continue to address me as 'Your Grace' or 'sir,' as is proper."

She regarded him with a thoughtful tap of her lip. "Acquaintances, you said. Haven't you any friends?"

"A duke does not require friends."

"Only underlings?" Her eyes were wide with innocence, but he saw the sparkle beneath.

"Miss Barrett, you are exceedingly brave to tease me."

"I only think it's sad you haven't any friends."

"I have friends." He waved a hand. "Gentlemen I know, men of my acquaintance. Really, it is not at all like you and your giggling group."

"They are not my group. I am forced to socialize with them because we are alike in social standing."

"It is very much the same with me and my friends."

She played with the silverware. He squelched the urge to correct her like a nagging nurse. "Well," she said at last. "I will be your friend, Your Grace. Perhaps you will be mine."

He sighed and leaned back in his chair. "I am not at all sure you're giving me a choice."

She lowered her face and he had the sneaking suspicion she stifled a smile. How silly it was to speak of friendship when they were all but betrothed. They were both of them going daft at the late hour, or perhaps it was her sweet expression making him feel not at all himself. For a wild moment he thought about seduction, about taking her to his room and kissing her pretty face, caressing her figure, examining her reddened

63

bottom, which was far more voluptuous than any virginal English miss had a right to. She was to become his wife, after all. Why not?

Because he was a confounded gentleman and must act as one.

"I'll be right next door," he said when he left her upstairs, "should you need me. Otherwise, stay to your room." He emphasized the "stay" with a steady glare. "In the morning we shall see this adventure out, shall we not?"

"Yes, Your Grace, thank you," she said with a bob of her head and an off-balance curtsy. His wife. Blast and dash it.

She was going to be his *wife*.

Chapter Six:
Wonder

Harmony awakened the following morning to the sound of the maid's timid tapping.

"Good morning, ma'am," the girl said through the door. "His Grace asks that you rise now. I'm to help you dress."

For a moment Harmony panicked. Her gown was nowhere to be found in the small room, but then she saw it draped over the maid's arm as she entered, the worst of the dust and stains brushed out.

"Oh, thank you," Harmony breathed in relief.

The girl looked surprised at her gratitude but gave her a broad smile anyway. "No need to thank me, ma'am. We rarely have such fancy guests here. I'm to help you wash and dress your hair also if you wish it. You were sore tired last night."

At mention of the word *sore*, distressing memories assailed her. His Grace the Duke of Courtland had spanked her last night, and yes, she had goaded him to it. She'd seen with her own eyes the scarlet blush left behind on her bottom. It had hurt to be spanked by him, but afterward she had felt so much better, as if everything was in balance again. He had held her very gently and even stroked her forehead to soothe her. How confusing. How...extraordinary. How painful, but somehow it seemed worthwhile, even if her bottom still ached slightly as she sat up on the edge of the bed.

Aside from the problem of her smarting posterior, Harmony was bodily sore, and bodily tired. She was not accustomed to riding in a bumpy wagon and she'd done quite a bit of walking before His Grace caught up with her. She bit back groans as the maid assisted her at her ablutions and helped her don her newly-freshened gown. Even her slippers had been passably cleaned and mended. The talented girl tamed her curls into a dainty style, smoothing the rest of her locks neatly against her head. Harmony felt better, certainly, but her excitement to see the Roman wall was tempered by lingering embarrassment over her comportment in the duke's company. Not to mention her sojourn over his knee.

She would never forget it, not her entire life. It had been so smoothly and easily done, as if spanking a full-grown woman was of normal consequence to him. She wondered if this was the "uncomfortable habit" to which the older ladies alluded. If his habit was spanking errant women, he must have thanked the stars above the day he met her. When she added up all her faults and breakdowns and large and small trespasses since she'd made the duke's acquaintance, she couldn't blame him at all for punishing her the night before. Perhaps it would inspire her to curb her improper impulses and stay in the drawing rooms where she ought to.

She shuddered. No, that was no life in her eyes. She would rather be spanked and lectured for her faults than sit like a puppet on some divan making polite talk about gowns and which young man was the season's best catch. She had attempted that her first season, and her second, and failed miserably. She would simply have to face His Grace this morning and hope he could forgive her for the muddle she'd temporarily made of his life.

Once she was dressed, the maid led her downstairs to the dining room. The duke stood as she entered, looking as composed and severely handsome as ever, even in yesterday's clothes.

"Good morning, Miss Barrett."

"Good morning, Your Grace." She hesitated just inside the door. "I really must... I must begin with another apology. I know it changes nothing, but I am so sorry, so truly sorry for all of the inconvenience I've caused."

"As you know, your apology has already been accepted, and matters settled between us." He arched one dark brow ever so slightly.

Heat flooded her face. "Oh yes…that."

The brow arched higher. "Yes, that." She stared at him, mute with embarrassment and a strange delicious dread. "I trust you suffered no lasting damage?" he asked.

"No, sir." She flushed even hotter, if such a thing was possible. "In fact, I slept quite well."

"I'm glad to hear it. Join me and take some breakfast." He gestured to the empty chair opposite him.

The sideboard was laden with enough food to feed a dozen people. Either the duke had the appetite of a horse and had requested this largesse, or the innkeeper hadn't been sure what to serve, and so served a little of everything. The duke had already finished his plate. He watched her take some toast, marmalade, and a hard-cooked egg.

"And you, Your Grace?" she asked politely once they were seated opposite one another. "Did you sleep well?"

"No, I did not."

There went her appetite. She tried to eat a few bites of preserves slathered on toast anyway. He watched her, his eyes brooding, his mouth drawn down in a slight frown. There was a strange formality between them now, a new gravity. He was not precisely cross—he had forgiven her, he said. But he was not at ease either. Still worried about marriage, she supposed, but how to go about assuring a man like the duke that he did not have to marry her? It would seem awfully awkward and perhaps even presumptuous.

Unable to bear the tension, she pushed her plate away. "Can we go to the wall now?"

"When you have finished your breakfast."

She pulled it toward her again, forcing down toast and dry eggs and blobs of sweet jam because he expected her to. She couldn't help wondering, just a little, what it would be like to be married to him. He made her feel fluttery and excited, even times like now when he was in a prickly mood. Wicked thoughts plagued her all through breakfast, and continued to plague her as they took leave of the inn and climbed into the carriage. Thoughts of him touching her, holding her. Thoughts of his strength and virility. It was worse in the carriage because he was so close. She stared at his knees, his hands, his calves.

Even through the traumatizing experience of his spanking, she'd been aware of his body wherever it touched hers. He had been so firm, so powerful in the way he handled her. So capable and...large. Did his clothes not fit far too well, revealing too much beauty and grace in his physique? He should have pity on the ladies and wear shapeless garments instead of expertly tailored ones. She tried to imagine him in a loose dressing gown like her father wore, with a wool nightcap over his dark, unruly hair, but she couldn't envision it. Her mind got stuck instead on the thought of how His Grace might look without any clothes at all.

She shook her head violently and stared down at her lap, rearranging the folds of her dress.

"Miss Barrett? Are you quite well?" he asked with a concerned expression.

"I am very well," she said quickly. *Or I would be if you were not so terribly handsome. If you were not so lofty and commanding that I feel giddy a lot of the time.*

"We will arrive soon," he said. "I only hope you are not disappointed. It's a crumbling stone structure stretching across the countryside. You will not see Romans there, nor anything very exciting."

"Of course I know that. It's the historical significance of the place that excites me, not anything I may or may not see."

His Grace regarded her a moment, then leaned back in his seat. "I must confess, I am curious how you became so interested in the study of history."

"I suppose I love history because it provided...I don't know...some pleasant form of escape."

"Escape? From what?"

She shrugged, recalling so many hours hiding away behind doors, beneath covers, seeking solace and companionship from a book in her lap. "Well...from things that challenged me in my day to day life. You know, my father styles himself a gentleman historian and has collected many books on the subject. At home we have a library of three hundred or more books. Papa is very proud of it. He let me read every one."

"Every one? You've read three hundred history books?"

"More than that. I used to borrow from Papa's friends."

"You used to? You don't anymore?"

She met his gaze with a bit of temper. "My brother began to complain about the way I read and study. I beg him to take me to book shops in London but he says no. Papa would take me but he rarely leaves the country anymore. Now and again I use my own money to buy books but I have to hide them. If Stephen finds them he takes them away."

"Why would he do such a thing?"

"He wants me to be like other ladies, primping and flitting about town. He says I am too bookish and he gets into a temper and scolds me and…well." She looked out the window, then back at him. "It is very tedious, as you can imagine."

The duke steepled his fingers and brought them to his lips. "I dislike your brother intensely."

"I do, too, most days. He won't understand that I hate taking part in society functions. I would like nothing better than to retire to the country alone, with my books, and stay there for life." There, she'd practically come right out and said that she didn't expect him to marry her.

If he received her underlying message, he made no sign, only pulled at the hem of a sleeve, looking very serious and ducal. "I have a number of history books I no longer read. When we return to London, you may view my collection and choose whatever you like to further your studies."

Harmony could barely believe his generosity. "Your Grace, you are so kind."

"No," he said. "I am not kind enough."

The carriage halted and the driver appeared at the door to let the stairs down.

The duke leaned forward, offering his hand. "We are here, Miss Barrett. Prepare to bask in the glory of your old Roman wall."

* * * * *

Court was incorrect on two counts. Miss Barrett was not at all disappointed in the crumbling wall. And she saw Romans everywhere.

The awkward young woman he knew was replaced with an eager historian walking along the periphery of the wall as if in some dream. *"Just imagine,"* she'd murmur every so often. Or *"They walked right here."* Or *"I wonder…"* She wondered very many times about very many things. She wondered if the view was the same in Roman times. She wondered how many invaders had trod the ground upon which she trod. She wondered, perhaps gruesomely, how many had perished in the very place where she stood. She put her hands right on the crumbling stone, gently, as if she might damage it with her delicate fingers.

69

"I wonder who built this," she said. "I wonder who placed this very rock, and what his hopes and dreams were when he was alive so many years ago."

It seemed to him that she wondered more than any person he'd ever known. She looked achingly pretty flitting about the historic site, with the sun in her hair and excitement in her eyes. He enjoyed her intellect at times like these, when she was not irritating or challenging him.

In truth, he thought, she would make an interesting wife.

But it was difficult to imagine her as a duchess, particularly when she seemed set on some solitary country existence. She would have to come to terms with her place in society as the wife of a high-ranking gentleman. With effort and attention, the worst of her shortcomings could be corrected, but Court feared she'd never achieve the arrogant finesse of those who would make up her set.

As if to prove his point, Miss Barrett scrambled up a small rise adjacent to the length of wall they were exploring and flopped inelegantly on her back. She took no care to adjust her skirts—several inches of her ankles plainly showed. He was torn between insisting she compose her appearance and staring at the elegance of her shapely, stockinged leg. The part of it he could see, anyway. He had very little difficulty imagining the rest.

But he must not slaver over his soon-to-be betrothed. It was not the thing to do, when there was a world of courtesans, actresses, and dissolute women who made themselves available to men of his rank. He had always imagined he would continue to use such professional services after marriage, but he wasn't so certain now. He hadn't lain with Miss Barrett—Harmony—last night, but even the spanking had far surpassed any experience he'd enjoyed in the company of a professional. Now he stared at her rashly bared ankles and wondered how she might slake his other lusts.

"Your Grace, you must lie back with me and look at the sky!" Her delighted voice interrupted his lurid fantasies. He felt so guilty he actually complied, strolling over and sitting beside her, but not too close, and leaning back on one arm. He raised his eyes and noted there was indeed a lovely sky today. All blue, no clouds whatsoever. Late summer in the north of England could sometimes be...magical.

"No, you must lie completely down," she scolded with good nature. "I know you shall sully your beautiful coat just a bit, but believe me, the view is worth it."

He scoffed. "I have not sprawled back on the grass like that since I was a child."

"That's a shame. When you lie back and look up, it's like the sky is a large blue bowl above you. There is nothing but endless heavens. I wonder what it would be like to see the earth from up there." She reached to the sky as if she could capture it. "I wonder how high a person might go."

I wonder... I wonder... I wonder... With a sigh, he lowered himself back, and for the first time in many years stretched his full length along the ground. The earth was a hard bed, but not unpleasant.

"I wonder how many people have lain back here, just like us, to gaze at the sky," she continued softly. "Romans, or even those who came before. Perhaps a young herding boy or a girl daydreaming of a suitor. Perhaps some Romans had an assignation here beneath the blue sky and sun."

"Miss Barrett, you are scandalous."

She ignored his teasing, carrying on in her wistful voice. "It is entirely possible, you know. This wall has been here for nearly two thousand years."

"And before the wall?" he asked. "Even before the wall, people walked here. Creatures, perhaps, that we have never even known."

"Dragons," she breathed.

"Perhaps. The world is ancient, and everything in it."

Her eyes shone with new thoughts, new questions yet unspoken. How whimsical he was becoming, to encourage her so. Perhaps, rather than improving his wife's peculiarities, he might become over time as peculiar and ill-mannered as she. His mother had already accused him of such. Harmony was looking over at him now with the most sincere gaze of...adulation.

"Yes, Your Grace. Everything is ancient, as you say. How can we ever understand all of it?"

"We needn't," he said, a practical stick-in-the-mud. "We need only understand the questions and concerns that affect us directly."

She turned away to look back at the sky. She was thinking so hard he expected her to pass out at any moment from the pressure of all the "I wonder's" in her head. She closed her eyes and spread her arms outward.

"I can feel the earth moving under me," she said.

Nonsense, he thought.

"Can you feel it, Your Grace? The sway of the earth beneath you?"

71

"Yes," he lied, only to hear her sigh of pleasure.

"It's like a mother rocking a baby to sleep, don't you think?"

"I surmise we are the babies," he intoned lightly.

He waited for the next "I wonder" but none came. After several moments of silence he became aware that Miss Barrett had drifted to sleep there beside the Roman wall, rocked by the earth under her big blue bowl of sky. He leaned up quietly so he would not wake her, and regarded her for some time with his head propped on one hand. It seemed too intimate to watch her sleep, although they were both fully dressed and outdoors within view of the coachman, who waited patiently some distance away.

He noted that the little thinking lines on her brow eased as she fell into sleep. As time passed, as her slumber deepened, her lips parted a bit so her pretty mouth took on a sensual air. He very much wanted to kiss those lips, but he did not. He wanted to place his hands against the softness of her waist, run them over the silhouette of her breasts and hips, so erotic beneath the propriety of her gown. He wanted to clasp her to him and bury his nose in the curve of her neck, breathe her in and then lick the steady pulse that jumped just under her skin.

She was too vulnerable and sweet in sleep for him to think about the carnal things he'd like to do to her then. Instead he admired her delicate blonde lashes resting against pale skin, and thought how very many wishes they might bring him if only he believed. Then those lashes fluttered open. For a moment the big blue sky was reflected in her sleepy, unguarded gaze. He could not have looked away from her at that moment, not for any amount. Then the thinking lines were back. She looked past him, around them, remembering where she was.

"Oh, bother," she said. "I fell asleep?"

"For a short time."

"You ought to have woken me up."

"You looked tired." She still looked beautifully, drowsily tired, but they couldn't tarry much longer. Their small escape out of time and place was at an end. "We must return soon, Miss Barrett."

A frown chased away the last of her sleepiness. "I would rather not."

He watched her, but no, still no acknowledgement of their situation or the repercussions thereof. So be it. He would rather travel back with her in a state of comfortable companionship than hysteria over impulsive mistakes. There would be enough hysteria later, from all concerned parties. His mother would keel over dead.

"My brother will be so, so angry," she sighed as she sat up. "Really very angry."

Court rose to his feet and extended a gloved hand to help her rise. "He will get over it. Everything will be settled soon enough."

"And I shall have to travel all the way back to London with him tomorrow. A whole week's time to endure his endless scolds."

"I'm sure it will be nothing like that."

Her gaze met his with resigned sadness. "I shall miss you very much when we part, Your Grace. Perhaps I shouldn't say such a thing, but it is the way I feel in my soul."

How dramatic she could be. He turned away from her to brush at the sleeves of his coat. "You forget. I have made promises to you. To give you some of my books, at the very least. There is no need to speak of missing one another."

It was quite ridiculous to speak of missing one another, considering the scene that would play out when they returned. He could not decide yet if their situation was tragic or hilarious.

Somehow, he imagined it would end up being both.

Chapter Seven:
Discussion

They rode the few hours back to Danbury House in comfortable silence. Harmony was too caught up in her memories of the day to carry on polite conversation, and the duke seemed reluctant to talk. She enjoyed that about him, his reserved, taciturn nature. She liked his stares, his mysterious expressions, because they gave her more to wonder about.

She liked *him*.

She looked up at him furtively for what must have been the hundredth time. She liked him very much indeed, and would miss him when they parted. She would miss his thoughtful blue-green eyes and his large, capable hands that looked only slightly more civilized in gloves. His hands were too large to be gentlemanly, it must be said, but he was an eminently civil man. One got the feeling around him that he rarely became flustered or lost control, which was a rare trait in her experience. Her brother was the opposite. He was constantly fretting and whining, and doing things that showed an intolerable lack of restraint. Of course, she probably appeared the same to the Duke of Courtland.

Harmony stole so many glimpses she began to feel embarrassed about it. He occasionally, unknowingly, obliged her by turning to stare out the window. Then she might gaze openly at his robust posture, the masculine set of his jaw. She remembered the day by the lake when she'd strolled beside him, how very strong and firm his forearm had felt beneath his fine coat. Now she truly knew the strength of that arm.

She hadn't forgotten about that, her spanking. She would not tell the other ladies about it, for they would never understand. It hadn't felt mean or cruel, more a natural extension of his obvious need to control, to rule. To behave as a disciplined person and sometimes exert that discipline upon those around him. Those needs were just one more intriguing aspect about him, and not exactly repulsive to her mind. Strange? A little, perhaps. He was still a kind man. She was certain of that.

But he was a duke, at the end of it. He always would be, and she would always be odd Miss Harmony Barrett who had never found her place in the world. She would doubtless have many regrets about their journey when they returned to Danbury House, but she knew she could never be fully sorry because she had enjoyed her time in his company.

Oh, she would miss him so much.

"What is the matter?" he asked in a quiet voice.

"N—Nothing, Your Grace."

"You look troubled."

Harmony swallowed hard. "I was just thinking that I have enjoyed knowing you, but we are very different from one another."

"We are. But in some ways, I imagine we are the same."

"What ways?"

He gave her an unfathomable look. "A puzzle for you, Miss Barrett. To occupy your time. How are we the same?"

"I don't know." She studied him, wishing she knew him better. Wishing she had more time to discover who he truly was. "What is the story of your life, Your Grace? What has made you into the man you are today?"

He pondered a moment, rubbing his fingers over his lips and then brushing them down his chin. "I was born to the Duke and Duchess of Courtland thirty years ago. I was raised from the most tender age to succeed my father to the title, which occurred when I was fourteen years old."

She waited, but he said nothing more. "That's it?"

His cultivated features took on a severe air. "That is the story of my life. I left out the minor details."

"You left out *all* the details."

"I shared the details I wished to share. But you see the man I am before you. What brought me to this state is irrelevant. All that matters is the manner in which I conduct myself going forward."

"I see," she said. "How philosophical of you."

His lips tightened even further, before relaxing into what might almost be called a smile. "I would ask the story of your life, but I expect it might take a week or so for you to relate it and we are nearly to Danbury House."

"Your Grace is incorrect," she said. "It would take at least a month."

He laughed then, a short burst of mirth that transformed his shadowed face. His smiles were never grins, but more like secrets he shared. "I wonder, Miss Barrett, if you will not end up being the story of my life."

With those words, the carriage crossed through the gates. It was late, the dinner hour, but a crowd materialized as they clattered round the front of the manor house. There was her brother at the front, looking red-faced and furious. Stephen yanked open the door the moment the carriage stopped.

"I can hardly believe it, Courtland." He glared into the coach at the two of them. "And you'll drive up here to the front door with all the pomp of a bloody king. No, I can't fathom it at all."

"This will not be handled publicly," His Grace said. "If you will meet me in Darlington's library, we will discuss the situation."

"Discuss the situation?" Stephen snarled as the duke stepped down. "If you think you can talk your way out of this with your fancy, pompous—"

"Stephen!" Harmony pleaded. "Do not speak to him so. This was all my fault. Let me explain."

Stephen cursed and leaned into the coach. "Yes, you had better explain, sister. What were you thinking, to run off this way? The gossips have come up with the most vicious names for you, all of them deserved." She cringed as he raised his hand but it was halted before it could fall by the duke's rigid grip. Harmony stared as the two men locked eyes.

"I wouldn't do that," the duke said in an icy murmur.

Stephen's mouth fell open. "Oh, that is rich, coming from you."

The duke's grip tightened around her brother's wrist. "We will go talk—privately—before you humiliate Miss Barrett any further."

Her brother gave her one last aggrieved glare, and then he and the duke were gone, and Lady Darlington reached in to her.

"Oh, my dearest. My darling girl. Whatever has happened?"

Harmony regarded the white-faced matron. This was so uncomfortable, this fall from grace. "I am sorry," she whispered. "What must I do? If you wish me to leave tonight, I will go at once to pack my things."

"Leave? Oh, no." The lady squeezed her hands. "Darlington will clear everyone away and then you must come inside and let me help you. I am so, so sorry, my dear. Everything will be made right, I am sure of it. But what on earth have you done?"

* * * * *

The entire house reverberated with the thrill of a scandal. It sickened Court, but there was nothing for it.

Lady Darlington had wisely steered Miss Barrett upstairs. Court had enough on his hands dealing with her brother; he couldn't tolerate female histrionics, not now. Lord Darlington accompanied Court and Mr. Barrett to the library, although he kept a discreet distance from the two men. Tension thickened the air, but Court, for one, was not anxious. Fate had made a comic but inexorable circle. It was in this very room he'd first stumbled upon Miss Harmony Barrett, and in this room that their betrothal would be set.

"Before you cut up at me again," he said to the red-faced Mr. Barrett, "I will marry your sister. It shall be done before the holidays, in London, in a large, lavish ceremony so there will be no hint of scandal attached to our match."

"It's a little late for that." Her brother approached him, shoulders squared. "How dare you? How dare you abduct my sister?"

"There was no abduction. Are you mad?" He pushed past Barrett and threw himself into a chair by the fire. "As it happens, she wanted to go see the wall."

"What wall?"

Court glared at him. "The wall she asked you to take her to. Repeatedly."

"She didn't ask me to take—" The man stopped. "Well. She went on about some Roman wall but I didn't have the least idea what she was talking about."

Court sighed, leaning back and crossing one leg over the other. What he wouldn't give to have this nonsense over with, and go upstairs for a wash and a fresh change of clothes. Not to mention a bloody drink. "There is an old Roman wall a few hours north of here. Since you wouldn't take her, your sister decided to go alone and very nearly did."

"How would she do that?"

"She hired a wagon in town, if you can believe it, and he put her off not halfway there. If I hadn't come upon her walking the road to Newcastle, who knows where she'd be now."

The young man paled and started pacing the length of the library. "Stupid girl," he cried out. "Not a bit of sense. No brain, no anything. She's always been that way."

"You speak of my future wife," Court reminded him in a brittle tone. "The future Duchess of Courtland, who shall outrank you by a fair margin."

"Well, you ought to know, sir. She is blasted difficult to manage."

"Is she? I hadn't noticed."

The young buck ignored his dry wit, blustering on. "Now she is yours, like it or not. The both of you have been gone all night. You have to marry her."

"I've already said I would. But I would not lay this matter completely at her feet, nor mine."

His words seemed to shame her brother into some small amount of remorse. Barrett rubbed his ear and sank down in the chair across from him. Seeing enough amity to suit him, Lord Darlington stood and left.

"So...Your Grace..." Court was edified to see the young buck's manners had returned. "Your Grace, you will not...you will not be cruel to my sister?"

"As I imagine you frequently are? She was terrified to face you."

Barrett's gaze flew to his. "I don't mean to be gruff with her. It's only that she's so difficult to control. She's my responsibility, now that my father's put his feet up in Hampshire."

"She's a woman. They are easily controlled with the right methods."

"You say that now, but you'll see. She thinks too much. She's bookish and headstrong, always yammering away with questions and bumbling about with her head in the clouds, when she isn't smarting off."

"Do you want me to marry her or not?" Court interrupted wryly.

"I am only saying—" He seemed to screw up his courage. "I wouldn't think it right if you resented her for this match. If you treated her badly in your marriage and so on. My sister addles me no end, but I would not wish a life of misery on her."

Court leaned forward in the chair, working hard to rein in his ire. "A life of misery, Barrett? What an unflattering assumption you make."

The man did not back down. "It is not an assumption. It is common knowledge why Tremayne's daughter jilted you. I hear talk from those who know you. I know what you get up to and I don't like to think of my sister being exposed to that nonsense. She's crazy, perhaps, but she's been gently raised."

Barrett held his furious gaze for long moments, and Court felt an unwilling softening of his feelings toward the wretch.

"If you care for your sister, why did you let this happen?" he asked.

Barrett's lips tightened and he tugged at his cravat. "I suppose because I've always cared more about myself than whatever she wants."

"Well, you see," Court said, "I intend to care at least as much about her happiness as I care about my own. So it seems your sister will be better off under my protection than yours."

"I'm not perfect. I admit it, but you can understand why I have misgivings. I am only warning you—"

"Warning me about what?" Court knew the point Barrett was dancing around, but he enjoyed making the man squirm.

"Don't abuse my sister," he burst out. "I haven't the power and fortune you wield, but if you torment her I will not hesitate to call you out."

Out of respect for Mr. Barrett's brotherly bravado, which he believed was motivated by a sense of honor, Court did not smile nor laugh, although he found the idea of Barrett saving his sister from him a rather ironic one.

"I swear on my honor I will never hurt your sister. Will that do? In fact, I cannot imagine any man so weak and soulless that he would stoop to torment a gentle soul such as her." He saw the barb hit home. Barrett swallowed any further protests or excuses. Court regarded him, pressing his advantage.

"Why won't you take her to libraries and bookstores if she wishes to read?"

Barrett looked confused. "What?"

"Your sister is an avid student of history. Why do you not support her in her endeavors? Why do you strip her of her books?"

The younger man shrugged. "It's not natural, a young lady filling her head with such stuff. And we don't have money for it anyway. Not lately. My father has debts."

"They are your father's debts, or your own?"

Barrett bristled. "Well, that's a rather personal question."

"So it is." Court relented. It was poor form to confront a man about money—or lack of it—so instead he spoke generally and deliberately to some point just past Mr. Barrett's left shoulder. "I think it very wise in general to accrue little debt. At least, to not accrue debt one is not capable of eventually paying. And it would be wise of any man not to expect assistance from some other...source...to finance his own self-indulgent life choices. In fact, I believe it wise for men of your age and stature to settle down to a calm and respectable life. Wouldn't you say that's so? Fill the nursery and all that?"

"You're older than me," he said morosely. "And I don't see you with a nursery full."

That comment came with a mental picture. Miss Barrett...and children. His children in her arms, at her breast. Which led his mind to the begetting of children...

"I take your point, Your Grace," the gentleman muttered with a regrettable lack of deference to a person so much more distinguished than himself. But Court supposed it must do. He would soon be related by law to this repugnant young man, all because of his recently-developed taste for heroics.

"I will wait to speak with your sister in the morning if it's all the same to you. She is doubtless tired." Court frowned at him. "And unless you are of a mind to be exceptionally kind and supportive, I had rather you left her alone too. Lady Darlington has her in hand."

"But the gossip," her brother said. "How shall we show our faces?"

Court wasn't looking forward to mingling with the other guests this evening, but it had to be done. Hiding away would communicate guilt and shame and feed rumors. He rose and stared into the fire. "I cannot speak for you, Barrett, but I shall do as I have always done. Hold my head high like a gentleman and act the part."

"You make it sound so simple."

"It is simple." Court turned to look at him. "Men behave as men. That's the way of the world. My world anyway."

80

At that couched insult, Barrett stood and prepared to quit his company, but halfway to the door he paused and turned back.

"Man to man, Your Grace—I know I said all those things about not hurting my sister. But I wouldn't blink too hard should you see fit to give her a good leathering this once, for this stunt she pulled over on you."

Court's features hardened as he regarded the brash young man. "If you ever so much as touch your sister in anger again, I promise I shall destroy you, which I am quite capable of doing. Do you understand?" He glowered at him until a "Yes, Your Grace," mumbled forth, which he answered with a nod of acknowledgement.

"I am glad that's settled, Mr. Barrett. Now kindly get out of my sight."

* * * * *

Lady Darlington and two maids fussed over Harmony as if she were the survivor of some dire tragedy. "Are you certain you are all right?" Lady Darlington looked completely vexed. "He did nothing to…to insult you?"

"Oh, not in the least," said Harmony. She outlined the main points of their adventure for her hostess, leaving out the humiliating part about the wagon leaving her in the middle of nowhere, and His Grace rescuing her from the moors, although it had been quite dashing and gallant of him. She left out the part about the spanking too, for that was too mortifying to be mentioned. "He was entirely a gentleman," she finished on a weak note.

Lady Darlington became marginally less agitated, but she still frowned. "I am happy to learn His Grace did not take any liberties with your…your person, but there is still the unfortunate fact that the two of you were together, alone, all night!"

The maids' eyes widened. Lady Darlington turned and shooed them off, sending them for a dinner tray to be delivered to Miss Barrett's room.

"You poor thing," Lady Darlington said, turning back to her. "Your sweet mother couldn't explain to you. Your father ought to have, at least. Did you not learn from your friends? It is never acceptable for an unwed man and lady to be so long alone in one another's company."

"Oh, I know that." Harmony squeezed her hands together in her lap. "But I wanted to see the Roman wall and he offered to take me. It seemed preferable to walking."

The woman gaped at her. "Preferable to...*walking*?"

Harmony paused for a moment. "I understand what is to happen as a result. I know that everyone shall have to cut me now, including you."

"My dear—"

"But he is a duke and I cannot possibly make demands on such a distinguished person. I am a woman of no consequence compared to him."

"But he compromised you."

"He was trying to be kind, Lady Darlington. I can't reward his kindness by expecting him to marry me."

Lady Darlington blinked and shook her head. "I don't know that the choice is yours, my child. Whether he is your social equal or not, the Duke of Courtland compromised you. He is obligated to offer for your hand."

"We did not do anything inappropriate," Harmony said. "We did not even stay together at the inn."

"That doesn't matter. You traveled with him alone, in a closed carriage, to a town many hours distant. It was not proper. The duke understood that, at any rate. I cannot imagine what he was about."

"He was being kind," Harmony repeated. "He went out of his way to help me at great personal inconvenience." Why must Lady Darlington frown at her so? It was such an embarrassing situation. From what she could fathom, everyone believed they had run off on some secret, libidinous assignation. How crude really, and how ridiculous. She tried to imagine herself and the duke locked in a fervent embrace, doing the lurid things everyone believed they'd done. Not that such an image was unpleasant...it was just beyond belief.

"Do not fret," Lady Darlington said, patting her hand. "Your brother will insist the Duke of Courtland make things right. I believe His Grace would have anyway. He is not a man known for skirting duty. Even though... Oh, my dear." Lady Darlington patted her hand again. "He may not be the *ideal* husband, but he is a duke and he is quite wealthy."

"There is no need for marriage," Harmony said, yanking her hand away. "To be honest, I would rather retire from society and live quietly somewhere for the rest of my days."

"And what of the shame to your family? Your father and brother? And the duke?"

Harmony stiffened. She had not considered his reputation in this matter. "I have made matters very awkward for His Grace, haven't I?"

"Why do you think the gentlemen retired to the library in such haste? There now, I am certain you shall be redeemed."

"I don't *want* to be redeemed," said Harmony. "He was only trying to help me."

"You have no mama to act on your behalf, but I shall do so for you, and tell you that this marriage is a necessity." The woman nodded as if that settled things. "I know it seems frightening but he is a man of great prestige, and a formidable catch. You will realize all this in the morning when your mind is calmer. You just need a warm spot of tea and some rest."

All of Lady Darlington's words, all her assurances seemed completely bizarre. "I will explain to my brother that nothing of any romantic nature occurred between us," Harmony said stubbornly. "I will explain that I don't wish to saddle His Grace with any expectations. I told him so already, in as many words. Mr. Barrett and I will leave in the morning with many thanks for your kindness."

There was a tap at the door. Harmony was relieved to see it was only the chambermaid returning with her dinner tray. It would have been terrible for His Grace to arrive in the midst of such a mad conversation. Lady Darlington touched Harmony's cheek, gazing at her with a great deal of pity.

"It has been a trying day for all of us, my dear. I think..." She clasped her hands before her. "I think it would be best if you kept to your room unless you are called for, until this entire situation has been straightened out."

"I agree, ma'am. I'm tired anyway."

"Very good. I hope you will enjoy your dinner and take some rest afterward. Please call for a maid or footman if you need anything at all, or if you need me, dearest."

Lady Darlington, bless her heart, was about to "dear" and "dearest" her to death even in her disgrace. "I will, ma'am. Thank you."

With those words the lady swept from the room in a quiet swish of skirts, leaving Harmony alone. She began to laugh, soft chuckles that soon transformed to something more like sobs. Peculiar Harmony Barrett as bride to His Grace. It was too outrageous to imagine, but some small part of her still wished it might be.

But it could not be.

She hoped the duke stood up to her brother and Lord Darlington. She would hate for him to throw away all hope of future happiness only because she'd wished to visit a Roman wall. It was worth it for her, whatever happened, but him…

She had never meant for him to be punished too.

Chapter Eight:
Honor

The next morning, Lady Darlington led Court into a little-used drawing room removed from the main area of the house. Muted sun warmed the space, rays of light arcing across patterned chairs and sofas.

"You will have privacy here." She turned her head with a bit of annoyance. "You are both entitled to privacy, despite what the other houseguests think."

"I am sorry, madam, to have caused such disruption to your gathering."

"You have turned it into the social event of the year. But it is not my guests I worry about." Lady Darlington's children were grown up and launched, but the mother inside her was still in plain evidence. "Poor Miss Barrett," she said, shaking her head.

He tried not to take offense, and she quickly remembered herself, flushing pink in the cheeks. "Of course I do not mean— Your Grace—"

"Of course not."

"She is only so confused. I fear for her. Honestly, I do."

"You needn't fear for her any longer."

She pondered the intent of his words and smiled. "Yes, of course. She will no longer be a woman alone, dependent on an absent father and that gadabout brother of hers. Just know that Miss Barrett will not come to you prepared to accept a marriage proposal. She does not seem to understand the gravity of her situation."

"I will handle it," he said with strained patience, "if you will kindly deliver her here."

"Certainly, Your Grace."

His hostess left, leaving Court to await the appearance of his future bride. Miss Chaos, the rampant new force in his life. He moved across the prettily decorated room to gaze from an oversize window. Such a bright, clear morning. Really, the weather thus far had been beyond reproach.

He hoped Miss Barrett had not spent a restless night. He had slept the sleep of the dead, the sleep of a man with no avenues left but the one he'd embarked on and thus must follow without question or thought. He would propose to her, she would accept, they would marry and have children, and that would be his life. It was not so very bad.

"Your Grace?"

He turned to find her hovering at the door. She was in pale pink, her hands clutched in a ball before her.

He bowed in greeting. "Miss Barrett, please come in and sit down."

She hesitated for a moment but then obeyed, perching on the edge of an overstuffed divan. She did not look particularly well, but she wasn't sobbing either. He walked closer, clasping his hands behind his back.

"Miss Barrett—"

"Your Grace, please, I—"

"If you do not mind," he interrupted, "I would prefer to speak first."

She swallowed hard and clamped her lips shut, her hands squeezing and fidgeting in her lap. Even agitated as she was, she looked lovely and fresh, her blonde hair coiffed to doll-like perfection.

"Miss Barrett, I am not a particularly sentimental man," he began, "but I find you have touched me in some way that is rather…unexplainable. I have developed a great fondness for your unique and amiable nature."

"Your Grace—"

Again he held up a hand. "Kindly allow me to finish. I confess I have become so taken by your charms that I have asked your brother for the honor of your hand, that I might make you my wife."

He was rather proud of the way his speech had turned out. He believed he sounded quite sincere in his proposal, but she was on her feet, shaking her head until her curls trembled.

"No, please," she said. "This is absurd."

"I promise you, it is not absurd. I have come to feel a deep regard for you. You have brought a light to my life that is...quite...unmatched by any other light."

"No more of these preposterous endearments," she cried. "None of what you're saying is true. All of this, because we rode to Newcastle together? Has the entire world gone mad?"

He wished this was not so difficult for her. His own temper had cooled, his practical side demanding that he make peace with this match. Of course, she had no such practical side—or if she did, he had not yet seen it. Court stepped closer, reached out and touched, very softly, the downy curve of her cheek. "I have besmirched your reputation, and things must be put right."

She shied away from him. "I told you, I do not care for my reputation. You cannot mean to marry me."

"It would be most disrespectful to you if I did not."

"But—"

"There is nothing to discuss. I only await your acceptance of my suit. We will be wed in London, as soon as can be done, in a large and respectable ceremony." He reached for her, troubled by the way she backed away from him.

"But...if you will only wait and...and let me speak to my father..."

"I will not bend on this, I'm afraid. Nor would he. Perhaps you've no care for your reputation, but I am the Duke of Courtland and I do have a care for mine. I will not be seen as a less than honorable man."

At that, Miss Barrett burst into tears. Court reached into the pocket of his coat for yet another handkerchief and offered it to her, but she did not take it. She collapsed back into the divan, hiding her face against its padded arm and weeping with alarming vigor.

"Come now," he said, kneeling beside her. "Are you so distressed at the idea of marrying me? Here, look at me." He touched her chin, made her raise her head up.

She gazed at him through tears. "Please. This cannot be. It is so ridiculous."

"And what if it is?" He stroked her brow, her little thought lines. "You told me once you did not believe I was a cold man. Have you come to think otherwise? Why this hysterical display?"

"I did not think it would come to this. I did not. I made this terrible mistake, and now you are forced to pay for it for the rest of your life." She bawled some more, wetting the arm of Lady Darlington's divan until he finally managed to press the handkerchief upon her. "Your Grace, I am so mortified. I'm so sorry to have caused this disaster for you."

Two days ago, a week ago, he would have agreed they were barreling toward disaster, but somewhere along the way his feelings toward her had softened. He thought it odd, but in the end he was not one to question things he could not change. He tried to catch her gaze, to reassure her. "It is not a disaster. We will make the best of things."

She waved his handkerchief about in agitation. "How shall we do that? I never meant to entrap you. Somehow I never imagined..." She threw up her hands. "I never imagined anyone would force such an uneven match."

"You believed you would be allowed to creep off to the country in disgrace?"

"Yes!"

"While I went about my life without a thought to your lost virtue?" He frowned at her. "You must think me a scoundrel."

"Not a scoundrel, but a great personage above me. A duke!"

"The fact that I am a duke does not signify. All gentlemen and ladies must follow proprieties."

"That's what Lady Darlington said." Miss Barrett released another barrage of tears.

He eased onto the divan beside her with a sigh. "It is very provoking to have a proposal of marriage reacted to in such a way. My feelings are bruised."

"I'm sorry!" she wailed.

"Miss Barrett, let there be no more apologies between us. May I hold your hand?"

She sniffled and nodded after a moment, but kept her eyes fixed on her lap. He wished to calm her, to see her smile again as she had the day before at the Roman wall. He first removed her glove, then his. He took her delicate hand and trapped it in his own. "You see, what is done is done. We cannot go back now and change things," he said, leaning his head to hers. "Allow me to fix this muddle we've created. Please agree to become my wife."

"But you could not want me," she whispered back. "I will be a tedious wife to a man like you."

"Whatever do you mean by that?"

"What about your...mistresses?"

Bloody hell. "I have no mistresses. Not even one. You have been misinformed."

"But... But... The women, they said..."

"None of these are things with which you must concern yourself."

"Oh." She turned her face against his shoulder. He felt frustration, disgust at himself that he'd made such a muck of his reputation. Curse him for his courtesans and parlors and whores. The only reason he could deny he had a mistress was because a mistress would have displeased Gwendolyn, the one-time love of his life.

"Miss Barrett, I swear to you, I will be a kind and civilized husband. I would not wish you to enter this union in a state of distress."

She was quiet for some time, her fingers fidgeting against his. When she spoke, it was still in that small, fearful voice that troubled him. "It is only... I am afraid I will be an annoyance and a burden to you. That you will come to...to despise me or..." She hiccoughed violently. "Or feel ashamed of me whenever we are out in company. I am afraid I will make you ashamed, Your Grace. Each and every day. In fact, I'm certain I will. I wish you would not go through with this."

His fingers tightened on hers. He continued silent because he did not trust himself to speak. He was the one with the black reputation, with the cynical soul. He was the savage and sinner who ought to feel ashamed. Now, with her trembling against him in panic, he thought he could never be worthy of her.

"You will not make me ashamed," he said gruffly. "I do not want you to worry about such nonsense."

"It is not nonsense." She stood and pulled away from him, and crossed to the window. "Right now, they are laughing, you know."

"Who?"

"Everyone. All the guests here."

He stood with a frown but stayed where he was. "If they are, they are laughing at both of us. Not only you."

"I am accustomed to it, but you—"

89

"Miss Barrett, if you are trying to talk me out of marrying you, I beseech you to stop." He softened his voice, which had risen with his frustration. "If they are to laugh, I would rather they laugh at us together than apart."

She turned to him, her blue eyes red-rimmed, glistening with tears. "May I ask you one thing?"

"You may ask me anything."

"You must answer honestly!"

"I will."

"Do you think I shall bring you any happiness, Your Grace? Any at all?"

He crossed and stood before her. He put a hand on her arm, then cupped the side of her face. *His wife...*

"Because if I c-can," she stammered, "then I will not f-feel so very—"

It was not at all proper, but he kissed her. Hard. Their first kiss ought to have been a tender sort of thing, planned and executed with the greatest care, but instead he kissed her fiercely, holding her face and pressing his lips right against her trembling mouth. Her lips parted at the slightest pressure, allowing him to delve deeper. To possess her. To quiet her. He put an arm around her to steady her, then sighed and pulled her close. How he longed to trace her curves, to fill his palms with her breasts, but he contented himself with the feel of her solid warmth against his front. He didn't want to frighten her—he despised himself for this clumsy attack—but once he'd tasted her sweetness it was impossible to draw away.

Make a wish...

He forced himself to gentle his assault. He caressed her cheek, then slid his hand back to stroke the softness of her hair. Her innocent sigh brought his rising erection to instant, painful hardness. He held his body away from hers but still he kissed her, drunk on her loveliness.

"Your Grace," she whispered when she surfaced for air. He waited for what must follow. *Your Grace, release me. Your Grace, how dare you?* But no such remonstrance came, only a sigh and blush as she touched her lips. Court wondered why he hadn't done this earlier. Why he hadn't kissed and caressed her during every one of those endless hours in the carriage, since it was always going to come to this.

This. Him and her. A marriage.

"Now please, dearest Harmony." It was the first time he'd spoken her given name. He rather liked the feel of it. "Tell me you'll marry me so I can be at ease."

She turned her head a little and lifted her chin. "You still haven't answered my question."

"I can't remember the question," he said, eyeing the bee-stung fullness of her lips.

"Will I bring you happiness? Could a bufflehead like me truly bring you contentment in marriage?" Her fingers curled around his arms. "Tell me the truth."

He searched for the right words to reassure her, to put her fears to rest. "The responsibility is not all yours. We shall bring one another contentment in marriage. I would like us to try, anyway."

She blinked, then blinked again. He held her gaze, thinking to himself, *all those eyelashes.* He could not guarantee her a happy marriage, but he would try if she would only agree to try along with him.

"I will marry you then, Your Grace," she finally said. "I accept."

She sounded resigned rather than joyous, and she did not smile. It wasn't the way he'd imagined a lady's acceptance of his marriage proposal, but matters being what they were, he supposed it must do.

* * * * *

Humiliatingly, their connection was painted by the gossips as a love match, he the passion-struck fool who could not resist a young lady in such dire need of discipline. The worst of it was, they came awfully close to the point.

Miss Barrett returned to London with her brother, and Court followed a couple weeks later in the company of Mrs. Lyndon and his mother, who was not kindly inclined toward her future daughter-in-law. As the caricatures and *on-dits* hit the town papers, the duchess took to her bed in offended grief. She wailed about the sullying of the Hawthorne name, the destruction of the ducal line with "that willful hussy's blood." She refused to receive Miss Barrett or her brother to their house in St. James Square.

Court might have insisted on such niceties, except that Harmony was still struggling with the idea of becoming his wife. Rather than strengthen her objections by exposing her to his mother's animosity, he called instead twice a week at the Morrow home in Brook Street.

The first few visits were nothing but ducking, stammering, and choked out apologies. She still spoke as if they could extricate themselves from their engagement, even as he tried to orient her to the ongoing plans for the wedding. As he traveled to visit her today, he wondered what he might do to move her past her self-reproach.

What she needed was a lecture and a spanking, but that wasn't precisely courtship behavior. Too bad, since his spanking hand itched like the devil whenever she was near. Didn't she realize most of the *ton*'s social-climbing ninnies would give their pincurls to be in her position? Her position as his betrothed, that was, not her inevitable position over his knee.

Well, today he would be firm and insist she set her mind to their union. He braced for battle while one of his footmen delivered his calling card to the door. Moments later Court emerged from the warmth of his carriage to sail into the Morrow residence, following the butler to the small, rather shabby parlor where Miss Barrett and her chaperone received him. The shabbiness of the parlor was always forgotten as soon as Miss Barrett appeared at the door.

She looked sweet as ever, feminine and fresh and possessed of such picturesque curves. Court openly ogled her. This was allowed, surely, to a man regarding his future wife. She was wearing one of the new gowns he'd commissioned from Mrs. Oliver, one of the *ton*'s top modistes. The pale blue suited her nicely and the trimmings and styling were more appropriate to a duke's future wife.

"Your Grace," she said with a pretty curtsy.

"Miss Barrett." Court bowed. "I am delighted to find you so well."

"I am very well. I have been looking forward to your visit."

This cursed formality. She sat beside him on the sofa, leaving an appropriate amount of space between them. He would have loved to cross that polite space and draw her into his arms. How he ached to kiss her again, to feel her trembling response. Her innocent curiosity. *I wonder...*

He held her hand, the hand he knew as well as his own, for he had traced every vein, every downy hair, every contour of it during their limited times together. It was the only part of her he was allowed by social convention to touch. Once they wed, a few weeks hence, he would be free to know her entire body. *Every vein, every downy hair, every contour...* Court pushed those thoughts aside and drew a bracing breath. Across the room, her dragon of a chaperone scowled.

He leaned close to Harmony's ear. "What have you told her about me, that she glowers every time I call?"

"It's not you, Your Grace. She's peevish to sit with us when she has so many chores to do."

"Can't your lady's maid act as chaperone?"

"I don't have one."

"Ah." Amazing, that she didn't have a lady's maid. His mother kept four. "Before we wed, we must advertise and find you a lady's maid, unless there is someone in this household you're fond of?" He dared a glance over at the housekeeper and received a sour look for his trouble. "The sunny Mrs. Jenkins?"

"Goodness, no. But you needn't advertise. I'm not used to having a lady's maid."

"You will need a maid to help you manage your wardrobe and your day-to-day affairs, especially as you accustom yourself to your new life."

She got the sick, worried look on her face he was coming to know all too well. "My day-to-day affairs?"

"As the Duchess of Courtland," he reminded her gently. "There will be dinners, parties, social events and calls to make. Which reminds me, Mrs. Oliver will be returning this week."

"Why?"

"You will need more gowns for the upcoming season, and a bridal trousseau. I did not know if you had someone to manage it." He slid a look at the dragon. No, never her.

"I don't know a great deal about fashion," Harmony said. "I—I believe I have quite enough to wear already. Your Grace—"

He cut off her protests before they could be voiced. "Mrs. Oliver is a respected couturier. She knows exactly what a duchess needs to complete her wardrobe. You need only be available for the fittings."

Harmony seemed to shrink within herself, staring at the floor.

"Are her visits so tedious?" he asked. "Don't you wish for pretty things?"

"I— Well, I am grateful—ever so grateful for your generosity—"

"It is hardly generosity. Every husband clothes his wife."

"You ought to have had a better wife," she burst out, taking her hand from his. "Please, Your Grace, I don't wish for all these..." She gestured down at her new gown. "All these stylish and fanciful things. Really, a plain style will do better for me."

"So you might disappear at my side? Become invisible?" He seized her hand again, turning to face her on the patterned divan. "Look at me if you please." After a hesitant moment, she complied. "You cannot believe that this marriage shall be averted now, at this late date?"

Her eyes skimmed away, but he tightened his hand and she drew them back again.

"There are but weeks until our nuptials. Workers have been hired, orders have been placed. Whole blocks of rooms at St. James and Courtland Manor are being refurbished for your use. The engagement has been announced in the papers and spread in whispers through every salon in town. You must set your mind to the things you cannot change."

She held his gaze a long moment. He tried to impart a sense of authority and kindness in the face of her fears. He understood she didn't want this marriage, as insulting as that was. He didn't want it either in an abstract sense, but more practically, he enjoyed her and was prepared to make the best of things.

"You are speechless," he said when the silence spun out.

He saw a spark of rebellion in her eyes. "There is not much I am allowed to say, is there? Except that I will go along with what you and everyone else insists I must do?"

"I insist because you will be irreparably harmed otherwise."

"My reputation will be harmed. I will be fine and you will do much better without me."

"We shall be married," he countered. "And all will be well."

His fiancée gave a great shuddering sigh as if she were being forced to marry a mollusk. "My father has written. He will arrive in town soon to stay until the wedding. He will contribute what he can to the preparations."

"He needn't contribute anything." Court wished she would smile again, as she had when he first arrived. "Why are you so cross?"

"A porter has delivered forty gowns so far," she said grimly. "Actually, forty-two."

"You will need twice that or more for an entire season."

"But the expense—"

"It is nothing."

Her gaze fell to his lips, then up again. Torment. She fretted over gowns when all he wanted to do was kiss her.

"Lady Darlington said you knew." She looked at his lips again, the little tease, before her gaze meandered back to his. "She said the whole time we were at the wall, you knew you would have to marry me."

"Yes."

Her brows drew together, tiny thinking lines. "Why didn't you say anything? Why didn't you..."

"Warn you?" he asked. "You weren't of a mind to listen. You wanted to go to Newcastle and wouldn't be persuaded otherwise. Once I took you into the carriage, I accepted that I would have to marry you. You left me no other choice."

"You could have let me walk," she said stubbornly.

"No, I couldn't." Now he was the one to stare at her lips as he gathered his thoughts. "You spoke to me once of fate, and how we might grasp at chances. I wonder if I wasn't doing that, now that I look back."

"I think you were doing what you felt you ought to do."

"What I had to do. You were my fate. An inescapable consequence." She looked stricken at that idea. He ran the tip of one finger down her delicate cheekbone, ignoring the chaperone's faint tsk. "Either way, the outcome is the same. You are going to be my wife. Fate or chance, it makes no matter now. Things will seem strange between us for a while but it won't be so forever. I am fond of you and you seem to have no great aversion to me, as much as it galls you to become my wife."

"I doesn't gall me. It's only... I'm just worried that—"

"That you will make a poor sort of duchess?" he provided bluntly.

Her gaze shied away from his. "Will you spank me after we are wed?"

Ah, did this have something to do with her misgivings? Court glanced over at Mrs. Jenkins, feeling a blush rise beneath his cravat even though the servant was too far away to hear them. "I suppose that will depend on whether you are good or bad," he said in a low voice.

"I have never been a wife, or a duchess for that matter. What if I don't know what is good or bad?"

"That is one of the purposes of a spanking, to teach appropriate behavior." God blast it, just like that, his cock was about to burst. The little minx. She didn't mean to tease; she really wanted to know if he would spank her as he had at the Newcastle inn.

And yes, he would.

"I promise I will not be a beast and abuse you," he said, leaning close. "I won't cuff you and yank you about if you are not the perfect wife. I shall never be brutal and impatient with you."

"Well, that's a relief, because I won't be perfect. I just know it." She gave him a pained look. "I'm sure I'll deserve a spanking now and again. Perhaps...perhaps that pleases you."

How to explain what he himself barely understood? "It will please both of us to know the way of things," he said after a moment. "To know what is expected from either side."

"I have never really lived like that. I have lived in a very haphazard way."

"Have you enjoyed that sort of life?"

She was silent a while, mulling over his question. "Not always."

"I believe a clear system of expectations and consequences will suit us both in this marriage."

Her hand fluttered in his as she gazed into his eyes. "You mean, spankings when I am bad?"

"More or less."

He watched as she worked through this proposal in her mind. "I... I suppose I agree to that. I fear I shall make a terrible muck of your life, but with your guidance...perhaps..."

"With my guidance I believe you will be a much happier woman."

She gave him a look of such vulnerability that he ached to draw her into his arms. She probably did not understand yet that discipline would not always feel like something she wanted, or needed. That knowledge would develop in time, just like the closeness between them.

"I will try to be good," she said softly, "so you needn't spank me *too* often."

"I am sure you will try very hard, my darling." Either way he would be pleased with her. The darlings, the dears, they came so easily now. The Duke of Courtland, who was not romantic or sentimental in the least, feared very much he was falling in love with Miss Harmony Barrett. "You must not be afraid. You are not to worry about anything," he repeated, stroking her trembling fingers. "Anything at all."

Chapter Nine:
Discipline

Thanks to the talented Mrs. Oliver, Harmony felt assured she looked every inch the future duchess as His Grace squired her through throngs of promenading ladies and gentlemen at Hyde Park. Mrs. Jenkins had helped her dress in an elegant amethyst and ivory striped afternoon dress, along with a matching fur-lined cape and tasteful lavender beribboned cap. Her blonde hair had been tamed into a pretty upsweep by the hard-faced woman, framed by some artful curls at her temples. For once, the frowning housekeeper had almost seemed pleased.

Harmony hoped she pleased the duke. She would never be described as lithe or graceful but with Mrs. Oliver's gowns, she was at least in the latest fashion. Over the weeks of their courtship she had come to believe he cared for her, even if she'd never believe herself fit to be his wife. If he was going to be stubborn and insist they go through with this ill-conceived marriage, what was she to do?

He drew her close as they strolled through the crowded lanes, keeping her arm linked through his. What a fine figure he made in his tailored great coat and high hat. He never minced or pranced about like some of the gentlemen. When he walked, his leather boots sounded steady and measured upon the ground and his capable manner relaxed her. She felt safe with him. When any man dared stare or any woman sneer, he froze them with a glance.

Gossip continued, and perhaps always would, but in the last weeks it seemed people did less whispering and more smiling. He insisted on escorting her about town, to the theater, the opera, to book stores and art exhibits. She thought she would enjoy being married to such a man, who did not force her to stay at home and pretend to be brainless. But then she'd get a snide look from a passing lady or gentleman and long to be at home, away from the public eye. A duchess! The Duke of Courtland's wife! It was a ridiculous situation.

A situation she couldn't get out of. Not now.

But she wouldn't dwell on such thoughts, not walking out in public with him. He nodded to a pair of acquaintances and made a deeper bow to a friend's wife. How could he feel so at ease and behave with such cool politeness in every situation? She felt she might suffocate in the tumult of chattering, milling people. She tightened her hand on his arm and he looked down at her in sympathy.

"It's a crush, isn't it?"

She nodded as another couple brushed by them with murmured greetings.

"This is the place one goes to see and be seen," His Grace said. "It's not nearly as crowded now as in summertime."

"How do you remember them all, and recall their titles and connections?"

He shrugged. "It is necessary to remember. You will learn them too, in time. It is not hard if you apply yourself."

He made it sound so simple. He also made it sound obligatory. "I shall never get used to such a large social circle," she said. "Nor such great crowds."

"Did your brother never walk with you in the park? Or the young men who courted you during your seasons?"

"No one courted me."

"No one? Surely you exaggerate."

What worried her most about His Grace was that he seemed to have no grasp of what a social failure she was. "Did you court many ladies here?" she asked to change the subject.

"A few."

"I imagine you were a dashing suitor."

He pursed his lips. "My dear, I only courted one woman with any seriousness and she denied me in the end."

Denied him? The Duke of Courtland? "I can hardly believe it," Harmony said. "She must have been mad to do such a thing."

"This from the woman who has repeatedly tried to extricate herself from our betrothal."

A flush stole across her cheeks. "We are in a different situation. If you courted this lady honestly, how could she resist your attentions?"

"You are kind to flatter me, but she fell in love with another. We did...not suit."

She and His Grace did not suit either, at least by society's standards. Harmony felt somber, almost mournful. The duke was bold and wealthy enough to have lived a life full of adventures and romantic relationships—including one that made his voice sound oddly tight.

"Did you love her terribly?"

"Harmony," he murmured.

"If she was the only one you courted—"

"In the end, we did not suit," he said firmly, the edge in his voice warning against further questions. "I am utterly content in my choice of wife." He squeezed her hand where it rested on his great coat. She believed he was content, the foolish man. He was so certain all would be well, based mainly on his intention that it be so.

As for her, she was coming to adore him far more than she should. She wanted him in a selfish, breathless way, at least when she listened to the cravings of her heart. But when her mind considered day-to-day life with him...to include marital matters... Well. Husbands and wives shared intimacies she knew very little about, except that they were very *intimate*. She would be expected to do intimate things with him. She still remembered his commanding kiss in Lady Darlington's parlor. How shocked she'd been, and yet how intrigued...

She peeked up at him as he guided her through a particularly dense group of gentlemen and ladies. It was difficult to look at him now, so proper and controlled, and imagine he was the same man who'd taken her in his arms and pressed his lips to hers, and grasped her close and held her right against him as he'd kissed her...

A throng of young dandies stepped out of their way and they nearly collided with another couple as groups pressed in from both sides. She felt His Grace stiffen. A young woman with large, beautiful eyes and dark hair stared at the duke while the mild looking fellow beside her blushed behind his tawny beard.

"Your Grace," said the woman with a slight curtsy. "How wonderful to see you. You look well."

"As do you." His voice sounded as taut as his stance. "Lord Wembley," he said to acknowledge her husband. "Good to see you both in town."

"We hear felicitations are in order," said the man, his gaze settling on Harmony. Court drew her forward and made the introductions. Lord and Lady Wembley were apparently Hertfordshire neighbors, and the lady a childhood friend. Harmony felt a wave of jealousy. His Grace was affected by this woman. Around them, people stared in that delighted way they had when something awkward was going on. She realized with a shock that this must be the woman who'd rejected his attentions.

Harmony felt in a panic to get away, but the duke stood and made polite, inane conversation another minute or two, until the crowd made it necessary to bid the couple farewell.

"Come," he said, gathering Harmony close. His smile didn't quite reach his eyes. "Let us extricate ourselves from this press and find some fresh air."

He led her through milling groups and lines of curricles and carriages to a less populated area of the park. He found a bench on a slight rise and beckoned her to seat herself. She drew her pearl-trimmed slippers beneath her skirts and pulled her cloak closer around her in the chill air of the fall day.

"Now," he said with a sigh. "Perhaps we can collect our wits."

"Those of us with wits." She laughed far too loudly at her own joke. *Hush, Harmony. Be ladylike. Don't cackle out silly jests.*

But he was smiling, not frowning. The problem was, his smile looked wistful. She didn't want to ask but she had to know. "That was her, wasn't it? The lady you courted. With the dark hair and violet eyes."

"Yes, Lady Wembley. Growing up, I knew her as Gwen." He scratched twice at the side of his neck and his nostrils flared the slightest bit. "You will hear the tale sooner or later, so you might as well hear it from me."

"There is a tale?"

"Only that we were always meant for marriage, but in the end she chose not to accept me. Or rather, she accepted another before I could officially offer my hand. In any case, it was a very public and humiliating jilt."

"She is beautiful, but not at all above you. I cannot imagine why she rejected you."

He looked over at her, lounging back on one arm. "You are supposed to be jealous, dear. You are supposed to tell me how plain and feckless she is."

"I am the one who is plain and feckless. Well...what does feckless mean?"

He smiled again, but it looked more real this time. "It means unthinking and lacking in vitality. In other words, the exact opposite of you." His words sparked a pleased, proud joy inside her, even if young ladies weren't supposed to be too thoughtful and vital. His eyes were warm, laughing almost. How stern he could look, the maddening man, while his eyes laughed the whole while. She wished he would lean closer and kiss her. They were in a secluded area of the park, but she'd lay odds they were being watched by more than a few pairs of eyes. He fussed with the trim at his cuff and looked back at her. "At any rate, handsomeness and beauty is skin deep. A strong marriage isn't built on appearances. There must be a foundation of practical matters."

"Like similar circumstances and temperament?"

"Exactly." He cursed under his breath. "I mean, no. Now you've made me use inappropriate language."

"I'm sorry, Your Grace."

He tilted her chin up until their gazes met and locked. "You are not sorry in the least, and we both know it. Once we are wed, these impertinent challenges of yours will have consequences. Do you understand?"

She leaned into the heat of his palm, staring into those eyes that promised as much wickedness as propriety. Perhaps he whispered her name or perhaps she only imagined it, but then his lips pressed to hers in a sweet, chaste kiss. She sighed as he pulled away, and with a small groan he kissed her again, then again. She felt alarm—anyone might see them—but she didn't want him to stop. What was this terrifying pull between them? When he got too close, when he touched or kissed her, it was as if she lost all sense of reason. He drew away and muttered "Blast," then scowled at her. "See, you've done it again."

She touched her lips and grinned. "Is 'blast' a curse?"

"You are a curse. I always behaved impeccably in public until you came along. Let my mother hear that I was pawing you in the park. She will take me apart at the seams."

"Your mother seems an overbearing sort," said Harmony. "I cannot imagine your life as a boy."

His jaw tightened. "I understood what was expected of me at a very young age. My mother only bore one child, you see. I was the only chance at continuing the Courtland line."

"So they raised you strictly, without allowing any wildness or joy?"

"No, there was joy. Surely there was. But more of lessons, discipline and expectations. Even on Christmas mornings I did lessons." He shook his head with a soft laugh. "Funny that I remember that…and whippings in my father's study. I got my fair share. To this day I can't step into that room without suffering a chill."

"Ah," said Harmony.

He frowned with one raised brow. "Ah? What do you believe you've discovered about me?"

"That you like to mete out discipline because you were a strictly disciplined child."

He waved a hand. "One has nothing to do with the other, believe me. And I will not fault my parents for the way I was raised. If they'd allowed me to be weak or shirk duties, there was no younger son to take my place. There was no measure for failure. They only had one chance to mold me into the man I had to be."

"My brother was my parents' only chance and they didn't raise him so strictly."

"Your brother is an ill-mannered rake." He put a hand over hers, where she picked at the edge of a bench slat. "Stop that. You will damage your gloves."

She ceased her fidgeting and folded her hands in her lap. "We will have children, won't we?"

"Yes, of course."

"What if I only have one son? Will he be raised as you were? What if I do not bear any sons at all?"

"We shall see what transpires," he said stubbornly.

She knew she shouldn't rip up at him. It was not something a fiancée or a future duchess should do, but she needed him to know before they married that she would demand a say in the raising of their children—and that she would never allow lessons on Christmas morning, or frequent trips to a dreaded study. "Whether I have one son or ten," she said, "or only ten daughters, I will be a loving and kind mama. I will not be like your mother, and allow my children to be raised without joy."

"My mother loved me in her way."

"She doesn't even use your given name."

"Neither do you." His voice sounded heated, almost as heated as when he'd scolded her on the side of the road. He drew a deep breath, then let it out. "No one uses my given name. I prefer they don't."

"You don't like the name Benedict?"

"It doesn't represent me. Courtland is my name. Courtland represents my dutiful side. I have responsibilities to a lot of people. I provide a great many people a livelihood and property."

"What does Benedict represent?"

"A child. Someone that doesn't exist anymore. I was Lord Raymore from the day I was born. Our first son will be born to the title too."

"Lord Raymore," she echoed, feeling sad for him, for all the poor little first-born children who were never allowed to be children. "How terrible, to make a child give up his own self to the cause of a family line."

"Harmony. That is quite enough. I am a grown man and I would prefer not to spend my time with you hashing over my boyhood days, particularly since you disapprove of them. What do you wish me to say? That you may raise our children differently? I wish you would, but I warn you, they will not be permitted to run wild and undisciplined."

"Like me?"

He gritted his teeth. "Like you and your brother, yes. Our children will know duty and responsibility. Our sons will be gentlemen and our daughters will not run about the North Country in search of damned Roman walls, trapping themselves into marriages with beleaguered aristocrats."

She inclined her head to him a little, her lips curving in a smile. "You cursed again, Your Grace. But I understand your annoyance."

He took her hand in a rough, affectionate way, perhaps as an apology. "Somehow I imagine I shall curse my fair share before our days are over." With a great sigh he took to his feet and helped her rise. "I must see you home. I do not look forward to Mrs. Jenkins' countenance should I deliver you one minute past the appointed hour."

"Are you vexed with me?" she asked, straightening her bonnet.

"Only if you are vexed with me," he answered lightly. "It cannot be easy to be affianced to such a dull stick. All the way home, I shall berate you with observations about the weather."

He did no such thing, although they avoided fraught topics by silent agreement. In the name of peacemaking, she invited him to tea even though she knew he would decline. He'd developed quite an aversion to the hovering Mrs. Jenkins, and Harmony suspected the housekeeper made the tea intentionally weak to discommode him. At Brook Street, His Grace helped her down from the curricle with his hands at her waist as if she was light as a feather—and she was nowhere near light as a feather. As he led her to the front door, it opened to reveal a portly gentleman and a beloved, familiar face.

She pulled away and ran to her father's arms. "Papa! You have finally come." She turned back to the duke, her eyes shining. "Your Grace, now you must join us for tea!"

* * * * *

Court could refuse her nothing, even if it meant an exceedingly awkward hour in the Morrow's cramped day room with Mrs. Jenkins scowling over the tea tray.

Lord Morrow was the polite, pleasant fellow he remembered, although he was given to unusually prolonged silences. Court couldn't tell if it was social ineptitude or disapproval of his company. Court had, after all, run off to Newcastle with his daughter, whether it was his fault or not.

Despite the tension, he enjoyed watching father and daughter share pleasantries and catch up on news of their country estate in Hampshire. Lord Morrow flattered Harmony's new gown and listened patiently to talk of the wedding. Then, just as Court was about to make his excuses, Morrow stood and fixed him with a look.

"Shall we have a smoke in my study, Your Grace?"

Court didn't smoke, but since his fiancée's father was asking, the only appropriate answer was, "Yes, of course, sir." He bid Harmony a chaste farewell under Morrow's watchful eye and proceeded to the gentleman's study at the back of the house.

Once there, the contemplative viscount lit an old-fashioned tobacco pipe and offered Court the same. He refused, but settled with Lord Morrow into worn leather chairs before the fire. The study was pleasing, a comfortable space lined with books. The fire was warm but not hot, and the aroma of Morrow's pipe pleasant. The room reminded him not at all of his own father's study, thank God, although he did feel called on the carpet a bit.

"Yes, well..." Morrow began, clearing his throat. "I've spoken at length with my son Stephen about this engagement. I admit I had questions when I first heard the news."

Court regarded the man through a haze of smoke. He could glean nothing from his mild tone. "Have your questions been answered?"

"With Harmony, my questions are never answered, or, as soon as they are, more questions crop up in their place. She has a talent for getting into scrapes even though she is a docile woman."

Court's face nearly cracked, thinking of Harmony as a "docile" woman. With effort he schooled his voice to seriousness. "It is true our courtship and engagement did not proceed in the traditional manner, but we have become quite fond of one another."

"I sense she is reluctant to wed you."

Plain-spoken. Was this a quality he had appreciated in the man? He appreciated it significantly less when the directness was aimed at him. Court decided to offer it back, like for like.

"Her reluctance springs from a sense of unworthiness. Not that I have ever expressed to her that she was not worthy of being my wife."

Morrow fingered his pipe, blowing out a series of smoke rings. "'Tis true she has not been groomed to be a duchess. I thought to set her up in the country with a small allowance. You know, she is happiest with her history and her books."

"I do know." Morrow gave him a long steady look that had Court clearing his throat. "Of course your daughter shall be free to pursue her studies after we are wed. I am not one of those men who believes females should be blank and silent." *Even if life would be easier that way*, he added to himself.

Morrow nodded. "I'm glad to hear that. It eases me to see you together, to see that there is affection between you." His voice trailed off as he blew out another puff of odoriferous smoke. "The fact is, Your Grace—"

"We are to be family. Call me Courtland."

"As you wish. The fact is, Courtland, since the engagement I've heard tales that sound amiss."

"What sort of tales?" Court asked tiredly.

105

"It hardly seems gentlemanly to discuss it. I'm not one to heed gossip or believe the more outlandish things I hear—but I'll tell you this plain. I care for my daughter's welfare. I'll not stand by if I think she's being ill-used."

"Your son and I had this conversation already." As much as he wished to be on good terms with Harmony's father, he couldn't keep the haughty offense from his voice. "As for ill use, it was perhaps unwise to place her in the care of Mr. Barrett if you wished her to live a cosseted life."

Morrow took this criticism with the slightest twitch of his features. "Perhaps. I haven't been as involved as I should have in recent years. Harmony has always been a self-reliant soul. I encouraged this quality in her."

Court remembered her stalking, alone, down the side of a deserted road. *I am going to see it. I am going to walk.* Where might he be today if he had allowed her to walk? Relaxing in the country? At the club preparing to take dinner with friends? He would not be sitting in a smallish study being scolded by an impoverished viscount while swathed in smoke, that was a certainty.

"We must speak of her dowry," Morrow said abruptly.

"There is no need of a dowry."

"I'll not allow her to bring nothing to this marriage, and leave her dependent on your good will."

"Dependent on my—?" Court sat up straighter, very close now to losing his manners. "My dear Morrow, I assure you the honor of her hand is enough to secure my good will, but if you must—for pride— offer a dowry, it shall not be refused."

"I am a proud man," her father shot back in a coughing splutter of smoke. "I do not adhere to the niceties as my late wife would have wished, nor do I cut a stylish figure, but I have a thought or two about things and I would have my only daughter happy in wedlock. I would not have her come to you feeling less than she should be."

"That makes two of us." Court sat back in his chair again, gazing at the fire. "I have a lot of books, Morrow. Piles of them. More than will fit on my shelves. I have patience…more than most men, if not as much as I'd like. I try to be an honorable gentleman in all things." He looked back at the old man. Not many fathers of his rank would sound out a duke before giving his blessing to the match. Most would push their daughter toward any husband of his stature, even if he were abusive, moon-mad, and riddled with pox. "I admire you for loving and wishing your daughter to be happy," he said. "I promise to do the same."

Morrow held his eyes for a long moment, then gave a short nod. "Sure you won't have a pipe with me? I get my tobacco from a gem of a shop over on Broad Street."

Again, Court respectfully declined, then offered the man an open invitation to call at St. James any time. The viscount's manners would addle his mother no end, which Court would heartily enjoy. No matter her feelings, in a few weeks time they would all be family. His mother, blunt Lord Morrow, Mr. Barrett, Court and his lovely Harmony.

How odd that he would find her worth all these lowering trials. How odd that he'd been drawn to a rapscallion like Morrow's daughter—dutiful, sedate man that he was—nearly from the start.

Chapter Ten:
Her Grace

Harmony's wedding took place on a late morning in November at St. George's, the grand cathedral filled to capacity with guests of His Grace. She stood beside him at the altar in her gown of embroidered ivory satin and shook down to the soles of her slippers to be on such display. His steadfast presence was the only thing that saved her. How serious it all was, and how overwhelming. By the time the ceremony was over, she felt ready to collapse.

They rode to his home in St. James afterward to receive their wedding guests. She had not yet been to visit and the sight of the place was a shock. There was no comparison between the duke's house and her father's house on Brook Street. The edifice stretched an entire block and rose four stories high, with numerous wide windows trimmed with carved cornices. She knew her new husband was wealthy and powerful, but it hadn't crystallized in her mind just how wealthy until now. She stood before the grand curving staircase in the main hall, marveling at the luxurious white paneling and gawking at paintings and tapestries and chandeliers. This was not even like Danbury House. This was something quite a bit beyond.

She smiled and nodded through introductions and well wishes, her mind a boggle of faces, names, and titles. Her father, by tradition, was seated near the duke's mother and Harmony feared he caused her great displeasure from the harried look on her face. From time to time Harmony met the duke's gaze to reassure herself, and he'd look back at her with an expression that spoke of things she didn't understand. He was her *husband* now. She both dreaded and craved to be alone with him in the way of married couples. For days, she had thought of little else.

What would it be like? She couldn't put together a sensible possibility from any of the gossip she'd overheard, and there was no one to talk to save Mrs. Jenkins, who'd silenced her vague questions with a scowl. Of course, Harmony was an educated and well-read woman, and knew in general terms what was to go on, but the specifics... If only her mama were here to enlighten her. Harmony searched out the duke's mother across the ballroom. The formidable dowager had taken a dislike to her from the start. She would receive no motherly advice from that quarter. She ought to have asked Lady Darlington some of the finer details while she had the chance, but back then she'd been too shocked at the idea of getting married.

By late afternoon, the guests began to thin. Mrs. Melton, the head housekeeper, led Harmony to the second floor, to a suite of rooms as big as the entire first floor of her father's house. She informed her these were *her rooms*. Disbelief battled with delight.

There was an opulent sitting room, a soaring space with large windows for sun. It was furnished in quality carved pieces, soft armchairs and divans, and a desk and side tables weighed down with flowers. Tall shelves flanked one corner, laden with history books of all eras. Emotion tightened Harmony's throat, for she knew he'd had the shelves and books installed here especially for her. The sitting room adjoined a massive chamber containing a wide gold-and-ivory curtained bed, as well as a slightly-less-massive dressing room that would dwarf their largest parlor back home.

It was in this dressing room that she met Mrs. Redcliff, her lady's maid, who told her amiably that she would be available to help Her Grace at all her changes from now on. Morning, luncheon, afternoon, dinner, social events, and bed. At each change, her hair could be re-done if Her Grace wished, brushed and misted and curled in any style she wanted. During the season, she was told, there would be even more changing, for social calls or driving in the park at the appointed hour. Harmony began to comprehend why the duke had commissioned so many gowns.

Disciplining the Duchess

From all corners of the dressing room, embellished frocks flooded armoires and trunks, along with riding habits, cloaks, reticules, fans, shoes, pelisses and shawls of every color and design. All of these items would be replaced regularly, her lady assured her, as they went out of style.

Harmony did not know what to say. It was more clothing than she'd owned in her lifetime. Without being asked, Mrs. Redcliff prepared a bath and helped divest her of her wedding finery. Harmony's ivory and gold-flecked wedding gown probably cost more than the sum of all the gowns in her armoire at home. His Grace had gifted her with a diamond necklace the evening before, and a diamond tiara to adorn her hair. They were hers now, the priceless, garish diamonds, the showy gown, as well as the fine silk stockings she'd worn, and the embroidered, matching shoes of worked leather that did not squeeze or pinch her feet since they had been fitted especially for her. Mrs. Redcliff stored it all away with capable efficiency.

Such grandeur and pomp, such pampering. If only she could believe she was deserving of it.

Harmony sank down in a fragrant, steaming tub of water and let Mrs. Redcliff wash her hair, only because the maid seemed determined to be motherly. The sturdy, middle-aged woman had been selected by her husband from the ranks of his existing staff, and was so much kinder than Mrs. Jenkins had been. This would have been the time to ask questions but she was still a stranger to her, and Harmony was so overwhelmed by her surroundings she doubted she could string together the words anyway. She wondered where His Grace was. Seeing off the last of the guests? Would he come to her now? Or later tonight?

Mrs. Redcliff helped her from the water and dressed her in an embroidered ivory nightgown with a matching dressing gown of ruffled silk. She felt like a package being wrapped for his pleasure, and wondered if he'd chosen these intimate garments himself. They were modest but of the highest quality, and beautiful, so beautiful. She watched in the mirror as Mrs. Redcliff brushed and dried her curls, arranging them in a casual fashion over her shoulders. When she finished, Harmony stared down at the silver-plated hairbrush the maid had used, tracing the swirling C on the ornately etched handle. C for *Courtland*. C for *caught*.

Mrs. Redcliff beckoned her to the sitting room to enjoy a dinner tray and some wine. While Harmony ate, the kindly woman went about the room lighting lamps and rearranging the vases of flowers, and then passed into the bedroom, perhaps to light those lamps too. She suspected the maid was inventing tasks so as not to leave her alone, and Harmony was glad, for she felt reassured by her company. When Harmony finished her meal she went to one of the high windows and looked out at the darkness, wondering if she would have a view of the back or the side yards. She was so turned about in the large house she wasn't certain.

"Your Grace. Your Grace? *Your Grace?*"

Harmony looked over her shoulder at her maid's soft but persistent voice. "Oh! I didn't realize you were addressing me. I have never been...you know...a Grace until today."

Mrs. Redcliff bobbed a curtsy and smiled. "Your Grace, is there anything more I can do for your comfort?"

Stay here with me, so I don't have to face him alone.

Harmony was not afraid of *him*, of course. She was only afraid of *it*. The unknown, and being married, and this wedding night that might be pleasant or disastrous. She inclined her head to the woman. "Thank you, Redcliff. That will be all." She had learned that from His Grace, that she must be cordial and formal to the servants, and call her lady's maid by her surname only. She was a duchess now and must act the part.

The maid curtsied again and moved to the door, then turned back. "I wish you a long and happy marriage, ma'am. I speak for all the staff when I say how pleased we are that you are here. The duke never looked so happy, if I might say so."

Harmony sensed she would have a friend in Mrs. Redcliff, formalities or not. She wished she could go to the woman and hug her. "You are kind," Harmony said instead. "So kind you shall make me cry."

"Oh, no." Mrs. Redcliff's eyes were bright with mischief. "This is not a night for tears." The woman smoothed her apron, abashed. "But I shouldn't go on. I wish you a pleasant evening, Your Grace. Do not hesitate to ring if there is anything you require."

Harmony nodded, and Mrs. Redcliff smiled once more and left with the dinner tray. Kindness always made Harmony emotional, especially the kindness of women. She barely remembered her mother but she still missed her. She longed for her now, when she was so unsure of what would go on. She longed for the reassurances of a mother, a mother's care and concern.

Do not be maudlin on your wedding night, you goose.

She went into her bedroom, taking in a deep breath at the beauty of the flowers and furnishings. She tested the taut surface of the bedclothes. The coverlet was ivory silk with smooth braiding, so perfect and elegant she hated to lie down on it. Mrs. Redcliff had turned down the top and fluffed the cushions. Harmony sat upon the edge, sinking into the luxurious comfort of the mattress. Her bed at home had been a narrow affair, her coverlet and linens worn and sometimes stale-smelling. These sheets smelled of lavender and fresh air.

She was a *duchess*, for goodness' sake.

Harmony rubbed her eyes, which was probably not a very duchess-y thing to do. Then she scrunched up a handful of the diaphanous nightgown she wore. No, she mustn't do that either. She opened her hand and smoothed the garment across her lap. What time was it? She lay back on the very grand bed in the center of the very grand chamber that was now hers, and then straightened up again as a knock sounded at the door.

"Come in." She meant to call out the words, but her voice had shrunk to a whisper. He entered anyway, pausing just inside the door. Harmony gawked. This was not the man she knew. Gone were his fitted coats, his high, starched neckcloths and collars. No trousers and polished Hessian boots. No fine gloves. He wore a long, dark blue brocade dressing gown crossed at his front. From a triangle at the top she could see his bare skin and a hint of dark hair on his chest. He looked even larger now than he did when he was dressed in his tailored garments. He was her *husband*, the tall, powerful gentleman standing across her vast duchess's chambers. She swallowed hard and rubbed her eyes again.

"Dear Harmony," he said in a voice that sounded tender and amused at once. "Shall I stay, or are you exhausted?"

Harmony, not Miss Barrett. She had to get used to that now she was married to him. She was glad to be married to him, even if she'd had to stand in front of a thousand people to do it, worried every moment she would do something wrong. She *did* do things wrong. She'd stammered over words and turned to leave the altar before the ceremony was quite over. He'd had to grab her as he had in Sedgefield village that day. As he'd done the first time they danced, when all she could think about was how fierce and beautiful his eyes were.

"I am not at all tired," she assured him. She *had* been tired and anxious, but now she felt very much awake. She watched him turn and shut the door in his nighttime attire. Beneath that gown was his form and muscle, his nakedness. She was naked too beneath her nightgown. It was marvelous and terrifying beyond belief.

And so she sat in her bed like a lump, though she probably ought to have been doing something. Greeting him, beckoning him. Taking off her clothes? What did wives do? She hadn't the slightest idea, but her new husband made no signs of annoyance. He'd been so kind to her all day even though it was her fault he'd had to marry her. It made her love him, but she was a little afraid to love him, because she was afraid he wouldn't love her back once he realized what it was like to live with her.

Oh, he was all that was proper and kind, pretending to adore her, but she had the feeling he did it because it *was* proper. Because a husband should smile and appear delighted at his wedding, and treat his wife with tenderness. The duke seemed to take extreme pleasure in doing things properly, not just in this, but in everything. *If that is the case*, some small voice whispered, *how on earth could he ever find satisfaction with you?*

"Are you happy with your rooms?" he asked, moving toward her. "And with your new home?"

She watched him come, mesmerized by his warm smile. Everything would be all right, because no one who smiled at her like that could ever mean her harm. "I can hardly explain how happy I am. How beautiful everything seems."

He approached until he stood right beside her bed, then leaned down and took her hands. "A beautiful home for a beautiful wife. It is appropriate." Did he find her beautiful? His tone was not teasing, but earnest. She blinked hard as he sat down on the bed facing her, one leg pressed right against hers. "It was a grand wedding, was it not?"

She nodded. Her chest felt tight. She looked into his eyes and choked with so many feelings she feared she would burst. "Thank you for making them respect me today," she said. "For saving me from ruin. For marrying me. I'll—I'll try to be—to be a good wife for you."

"Oh, my dear." He shifted closer and laid his cheek right against hers. Her gaze darted down as the lower half of his dressing gown parted to reveal a muscular expanse of thigh. She noted dark hair, hard strength.

She swallowed, closing her eyes. "I don't know what to do now."

His hands tightened around hers. "Of course you don't. But being a student of history, you at least know this is normal and natural between spouses, that mankind has done such for centuries, and that you will survive unscathed."

She drew back and attempted to smile, although she didn't quite manage it. "Oh, I never expected you to...to scathe me, Your Grace."

"Courtland, please. Or Court. If you call me Your Grace, it rather dampens the intimacy of the moment."

"Court," she whispered. "Yes, Your Grace. I mean..." When he cupped her face in his hand and leaned to kiss her she sagged in relief.

She had dreamed of this kiss, wanted it, craved it every time she looked at his lips over their weeks-long courtship. She had imagined biting the curve of his aristocratic chin and smoothing her fingers over his cheeks. The first time he'd kissed her, she'd been shocked and even a little frightened by it. But not now. This time she would kiss him back, perhaps even take his face in her hands as he did hers. His mouth was strong and warm against hers, guiding her, encouraging her. He tilted her head and teased at her mouth until she sighed and opened to him. He delved deeper, breathless and a little wild. She did stroke his rough cheeks then, fascinated by their texture. His hands moved down the sides of her neck to tighten on her shoulders. It was so novel, this intimate communion between them.

"Courtland," she said when he finally leaned away from her. "I find that so very pleasant." She touched her lips, traced them, remembering. He stared at her with great intensity in his eyes. Even by the dim light of the lamps, she could sense a rising tension between them she could not understand or control. She leaned toward him, because she knew only he could soothe the agitation she felt.

"Look at me, dearest," he bade her.

She did, drawing in a deep breath. He was so close. The bare skin of his leg and his chest was shocking to her. She'd never seen him without coat and breeches, and boots...

"Don't be afraid of this," he said.

"I'm not afraid." She couldn't hold his gaze. Her eyes dropped to his chest. She wanted to touch him there, but at the same time, she couldn't imagine reaching out to do it. "I'm not afraid," she repeated. "I just don't know what you're going to do to me."

He laced an arm around her waist and drew her close. "I'll tell you, then. First I'm going to kiss you again, and then I'm going to turn you over my lap as I've dreamed of doing for several weeks now."

"Over your la—" Her protest was swallowed by his avid mouth pressed against hers. Her fingers curled upon his chest at last, feeling hard muscle and the tickle of light hair. His lips slanted over hers, bringing warmth to her cheeks and a queer feeling to her stomach. She snuggled against him, thrilled, wanting more. She could feel his fingers undoing the knot at the front of her dressing gown. She barely noticed when it slipped to the floor. She was too caught up in his strength and the spicy, sweet scent of his breath. The more actively she participated, the more deeply he kissed her. He nipped her lips with his teeth and gripped her bottom with a firmness that excited her.

She moaned against his mouth and slid her hands up to his shoulders, exploring the contours of his masculine form with a pleased sound. Her breasts tingled where they pressed against his front. At last he released her and she pushed back from him, all but panting.

"Why are you— Are you turning me over your lap to—"

"Spank you? Yes."

"B-but why? Because I flubbed about so badly at our wedding?"

"No, that is not why."

"Oh." She shifted against him, feeling excited and worried at the same time. "Why are you, then?"

"Because I want to begin as I mean for us to go on." As he said this, he ran a hand up her back and lightly squeezed her nape. Perhaps he tried to soothe her, but her body was shaking with quiet tremors that would not subside.

"But..."

"But?" he asked patiently. "You asked me if I would spank you in our marriage, and I said I would. You agreed it would be appropriate, remember?"

"But—" Harmony tried to untangle the muddle of her feelings. "I thought you would only spank me when I've done something wrong."

He considered that. "Sometimes I will spank you for disciplinary purposes. Other times, like tonight, I'll spank you to foster a sense of closeness between us. If I only ever spanked you when I was cross, you would come to hate it, and perhaps even hate me. And that would sadden me greatly."

Somehow Harmony couldn't fault the logic in that. "But— But—" He waited for her to collect her thoughts. "But how can it make us feel closer?"

He kissed her again, just a light brush across her lips. "It is easier to show you than explain."

With those words, he guided her body forward until she was draped across his legs. Harmony did not resist, although she felt exposed and

115

awfully endangered. He smoothed the skirt of her nightgown over her bottom and pulled her flush against his body, so she felt more secure. A little more secure.

"But—"

He paused in arranging her. She looked back at him, wishing this made more sense.

"I am afraid you will hurt me." She still remembered the spanking in Newcastle. The pain of it had been quite surprising. She wasn't sure this wedding night activity would result in the closeness he sought.

"This will not hurt much, this spanking," he assured her. "You are not being punished. You'll come to know the difference between the two."

"So you are not at all angry with me?"

"No." He stroked his palm across her bottom. "Merely enamored. You are my duchess. My wife. Now, put your hands on the floor and keep them there."

She very nearly said no. She would have said no if he hadn't asked with such politeness, and if his palm upon her bottom hadn't felt so pleasantly warm. He began to push up her nightgown, and then she really felt she must stop him. But she didn't.

He bared her right up to her waist and she let him, keeping her hands on the floor as she'd been told, even though her face burned and her mind was spinning from this new state of affairs. It was her wedding night, but rather than kissing or having marital relations with her, he was arranging her over his knee. He was spanking her simply because he wished to spank her, because he was her husband now and had the right to do it.

This wasn't what she'd expected at all!

She told herself she would stop him as soon as he began, explain to him that she did not agree with being spanked at his whim, whenever he wished it. The very idea! She let him give her a few light smacks, only because she was trying to think of exactly what to say—but it became increasingly difficult to think. The spanks were not too hard, but hard enough that an excited, hot feeling bloomed in her pelvis where she bent over. Her body began to anticipate the rhythmic blows, to enjoy them, even.

She tensed her buttocks, distracted and confused. Part of her wanted to rebel against this patently unfair treatment, but a larger part of her wanted to continue to submit because the pain felt pleasurable in the strangest way. After a time, he spanked her harder. Not painfully hard, but harder, and still she didn't resist. She understood the difference, just as he'd told her. He was not smacking her as sharply as he'd done in Newcastle, when she'd felt punished indeed. This was different. The pain was not bitter, but sweet.

She wasn't sure if she was supposed to feel such pleasure from what he was doing, but she did. She stopped thinking about halting him and protesting this treatment, and gave herself up to experiencing it instead. The sounds of each spank, accompanied by the soft intake of his breath, the size and pressure of his hand against her bare skin... It ought to feel scandalous to her, being naked to his gaze, his hand smacking away at her bottom, but he did not make it seem that way. *I want to begin as I mean for us to go on.*

She shifted her hips, but didn't attempt to get away from him. His large hands heated not only her cheeks but the side of her flanks and the tops of her thighs. Her entire bottom grew throbby and tingly, and she began to feel a restless need for more. Either harder spanking or something else. She moaned, confused, wanting to touch him, wanting him to hold her close and explain these feelings to her.

"What is it?" he asked, pausing.

It is that I cannot tell if you are hurting or pleasing me just now. This was nothing at all like the spanking he'd given her in Newcastle. Then, she had cried and wished for it to end. Now she only wanted more.

He gave her more. Sharper slaps that heightened the tingling to an aching pain. She threw a glimpse over her shoulder to find him watching her with a dark, assessing gaze. She was aware of his hard thighs beneath her belly and his other hand braced at her waist. She was aware of his brocade dressing gown against the underside of one arm, and her flimsy silk nightgown whispering across her nipples as she shifted. His blows didn't hurt much in isolation; it was the continued assault that made her feel curiously close to some edge. She wanted to cry, not from pain, but the sheer intensity of their interaction. He had been correct. Spanking could bring them closer. This realization resulted in a small, shocked sob. Upon hearing it, he ceased spanking and caressed her burning bottom.

"Good girl." His voice was a caress in itself. She was lifted, righted. She felt loose and floppy, like a doll he manipulated with his great hands. He stood her before him, letting her nightgown fall back down to her ankles. His face looked severe, but not in a cruel way.

She gazed back in a kind of stupor, beyond explaining the way he'd made her feel. The way he still made her feel, just by looking at her that way. "I understand now," she finally said. "I understand what you meant. About…about the closeness."

His fingertips strayed over the curves of her heated bottom. "I'm glad."

She shifted, his desultory caress increasing the taunting ache in her center. "Will you do that to me every night?"

"Spank you? Not likely. The other, perhaps." His lips widened in a slow smile. "Every night would suit me very well."

Harmony thought she knew what he meant, but she wasn't taking anything for granted on this night of such surprises. "What other?"

His smile disappeared as his expression turned intent again. "Lie down and I'll show you, my love."

Chapter Eleven:
The Best Part

He will not hurt me. He is kind and caring. Harmony repeated that to herself as he guided her back on the bed and slid under the covers beside her. He shrugged out of his dressing gown, carelessly, impatiently, and Harmony thought he would fall on her and strip her next. She feared roughness and abruptness, but he was gentle. He touched the neckline of her nightgown, traced the delicate ivory ribbon that drew it closed. Only then did he slowly untie it. She stared transfixed at his broad naked chest, his shoulders so different in form and breadth from hers, and his taut stomach below, a compelling ladder of muscles. She wanted to touch them so badly her fingertips ached.

"I— I never thought I would marry," she whispered as he parted the collar of her gown. "I never really thought much about...what we are to do."

He leaned close and kissed her just beneath her ear. "Very little thinking is required."

"Oh." She sighed as his lips brushed across her neck, followed by more lingering kisses. He plundered her mouth, then licked beneath her chin as his hands came to rest at the base of her throat. With a smooth, easing movement, he brushed his palms down over her breasts. She leaned forward into his hands, needing his touch, his contact. He pressed

119

her back instead and kissed her again. As he did, his hands opened over her nipples. His fingers sought and traced them, and Harmony's whole body reacted with flaring, racing…desire.

That had to be what this was. Desire, arousal. Wicked cravings. "Oh…" she whispered.

"Oh," he echoed softly, stroking her again. He was so calm, his touch so deft and practiced. She stared at him in a kind of shock. His manner of touching was like no other touch she'd experienced before. It was gentle and yet so powerful. She didn't only feel the contact in her nipples, but in the ache of her bottom and the heated throb between her legs. She grasped at his hand, halting him.

"Please…what are you doing to me?" she whispered.

"Pleasuring you, darling."

It was not a fit enough word. It was more than pleasure she felt, more than mere enjoyment. He teased her nipples until her legs tensed and her hips started to move of their own accord. She wanted to tell him to stop but at the same time she never wanted him to stop. Her gasps turned to groans, wordless pleas for more. Through all of this he watched her with intense concentration. In some way, she knew she pleased him with her reactions, even though his face was rigid with control.

When she thought she couldn't bear another moment of his teasing caresses, his fingers left her breasts and traced lower, warmly, inexorably toward the place he made her throb. She drew her legs together out of some sense of decorum, but he would not allow that. He eased her thighs apart, stroking her, murmuring soft and reassuring words. She forced herself to open to him. *He will not hurt me. I know he will not hurt me.* He slid her nightgown out of the way, then pulled it up over her head and off to join their dressing gowns on the floor. He turned his attention back to her, cupping her breasts, bringing them to his mouth. When his lips closed over them her pelvis arched in response, and she felt some hot, thick hardness against her front.

She forgot all about the heady sensation of his mouth in the shock of discovery. It was him, his male organ, but swollen to grotesque proportions. She didn't want to be afraid, to be some silly, shrinking miss, but she felt a moment of pure terror. He paused and took her face in his hands.

"You mustn't fret," he said. "It is my body's natural response to you. Touch me if you like. Explore how I feel."

He pressed her hands down so she didn't have a choice. He felt...large. Unyielding and stiff and...very hard. *He will not hurt me. He wouldn't.* But what if it couldn't be helped? One of the few things she knew about the marital act was that he had to go inside her, and that it hurt to accomplish it the first time. Her husband was larger in stature than most men. Perhaps that meant he was larger...all over. Why hadn't anyone warned her of this before?

"What if it doesn't fit?" she whispered, circling his width with her fingers.

He drew in a halting breath. "It will fit."

She wasn't sure she believed him. She moved her hand in a tentative way, up and down his length. He gasped and she let go.

"Did I hurt you?"

He shook his head. "Not in the way you think."

She tried to figure that out but she couldn't, not when he resumed kissing and suckling her breasts. He stroked a hand up her thigh, gripping her sore buttocks and kneading them. He set that spot throbbing harder, that tightening, tingling place between her thighs, and then he moved his hand right to the veriest point of the sensation. He parted her and placed the tip of a finger just over that apex. Harmony grasped at his shoulders as he pressed it gently. "Oh, no. Oh, *no*."

"No?" He chuckled, stroking the delicate place again.

She didn't mean no, she only meant that it felt too wicked, too deliciously wonderful and frightening to be borne. Now she felt sensation all over her body, in her lips, her breasts, her bottom, and deep within herself, in places she didn't even think about before now. She tightened her fingers against his skin as he persisted in tormenting her with her body's reactions. She watched his face, still tight in concentration, then stared at the mat of hair covering his chest. His body was so unlike hers, and yet the things he knew about her... The things he knew to do to her with those agile hands...

"Is this very proper?" she whispered, clinging to him.

"It is proper enough between husband and wife." He studied her with curiosity. "Have you never touched yourself here? Never in your life?"

She shook her head, letting out another gasp. "No. But I would...I would have...if I had only known what it felt like."

"You may touch yourself now," he said against her lips. "Whenever you like, as long as you are in a private place. As long as you think of me while you do it."

Harmony didn't think she could touch herself and make it feel the way he did. He amazed her. Could all gentlemen perform this magic? But of course, she realized in a moment of clarity. This was why young ladies were warned not to be alone with a man, ever. Because of *this*.

"All gentlemen can do this," she said aloud with a kind of shock.

Her husband stiffened above her. "What?"

"This is why…this is why ladies must have a chaperone. Why they must not be alone with men." Her eyes flew to his. "This is what they all believed we did, at the inn in Newcastle." She understood now why they had to marry. Once you did this with a person, how could you do any other thing than spend your life together? "It's amazing that gentlemen can do this thing," she said.

"For your purposes, only one gentleman can 'do this thing.' That gentleman is me."

She smiled up at him. "Yes, sir."

"I am serious, Harmony. You will take no other lovers."

She felt confusion. "Why would I want other lovers? You are exceedingly good at this."

He made a strangled kind of sound and she began to regret bringing it up in the first place. She wanted him to touch her again, touch her forever. She felt a most pressing need for *more*. "There is more, isn't there?" she whispered as he teased her nipples again.

"Yes, there is more." He seemed agitated and pleased at the same time. "This next part is the best part."

"It cannot possibly be better than this."

He came over her then, the full, tall bulk of him, and settled between her thighs. He drove her legs wider, sliding his knees between them. His warmth assailed her. His whole body covered her and bore her down, the heavy evidence of his arousal nestling just below her aching, needy spot. There was a humid wetness there that came from her body. She knew what would happen next, that he would drive into her there, where she was hot and wet. She felt another fluttering of fear. *He will not hurt me. He would never hurt me.*

"This may hurt a little at first," he said against her ear. "Hold onto me."

She put her hands on his shoulders as he nuzzled kisses upon her neck. He moved over her, positioning himself against her down there, and it felt pleasant, not painful. But there was more... He reared back and moved forward in a convulsive movement.

Harmony stiffened as he drove deep, too deep. There was sharp pain and uncomfortable pressure. He held her still and trapped, and she felt panic.

"Please," she gasped. "You do not fit me."

He stopped, bracing his elbows on either side of her. His whole body tensed, his face a tormented mask.

"It is hurting you too," she said. "Please stop."

He let out a harsh breath. "It is not hurting me, dearest. It is only that— If you will be still—"

She wriggled to evade him. "This is not the best part at all!"

"Harmony!" His sharp tone stilled her. She lay beneath him, panting as quietly as she could.

"Please," she said. "Please, you must get out of me before I'm injured."

He took another deep breath and trapped her chin between his fingers. He kissed her, tenderly, slowly, as if he did not still hold her full and impaled. "Give me a chance," he whispered against her mouth. "You'll get used to it."

She imagined weeks, months, before she could adjust to such discomfort. "Must we...must we do this part?"

"Yes."

"I liked the other part better."

"You will come to like this part very much too."

"When?" she asked with great skepticism.

"About five minutes from now." He bared his teeth and withdrew from her. She felt some relief, but it was erased by the sensation of him sliding right back in.

"Oh!" she protested—but it didn't hurt as much this time. He held her hips and did it again, and yet again, a slow withdrawal and another press forward from which she could not escape. It felt uneasy, uncomfortable, but no longer painful. Her hands relaxed on his chest and slid up to his shoulders as she grew used to the novel sensations. His hard belly moved across hers as he surged inside her, quite deeply and firmly this time. It was amazing the way her body now accommodated him. The sharp pain was gone as if it had never existed, and the moisture of her body eased his movements despite his large size. The only uncomfortable thing, she supposed, was that he was inside her, deep inside her, and did not seem inclined to leave anytime soon.

"Does it still hurt?" he asked.

"Not exactly."

He gave a huffing sort of breath. "What does that mean?"

"Now it only feels…odd."

"Does it?" He pressed his hips against hers as he kissed her. "Let me see what I might do about that."

He moved again, a bit more intently, and rubbed one of her nipples at the same time. For a moment it was too much, too much to process, too much to concentrate on. How could she remain in control with him doing these things to her?

"Just let go," he said against her skin. "Your body knows."

Your body knows… He kissed her breast this time, caught her nipple between his teeth and worried it until it ached. She felt it not just in the one place, but everywhere. The sheath that contained him tightened around his length. He groaned and that groan triggered some instinctive response in her. She squeezed around him again, having a sudden and clear sense of her own power in this encounter. She slid her arms down his muscled sides to his hips, feeling him work his body against hers. He arched over her and moved a little faster, the base of his shaft rubbing right against the spot he'd teased earlier.

None of it felt like teasing now.

"Oh, no," she said again, caught up in a blazing dance she'd never known existed. She felt his lips, his teeth at her neck, at her breasts. He stroked her hair and nipped at her ears, never stopping his forays in and out. It didn't feel uncomfortable any more, his presence inside her. It felt rather grand, his long, thick shaft driving her closer and closer to some apex. There was more. More, more, *more…* She struggled for it, her body tossing and arching under his.

"Tell me. Show me," he said, cradling her. "Teach me what feels good to you."

She taught him with her moans, her rising whimpers and pleas. When his fingers pinched or stroked the perfect spot, she gripped his shaft within her and felt her own heightened pleasure in return. She was so close, so close to reaching the place he tried to bring her. He was a force above her, a power encouraging her when she started to feel lost. When he moved in her just right, at the perfect pitch, she cried out loud hoping he knew what she meant, for she couldn't make words, not then. *There, there, there, there, please, there...* She clenched the sheets and then dug her fingers into his straining arms. "Please, don't stop!"

The waves crested and seemed to converge in one great pool of pleasure, and then the pool overran its bounds and washed over her entire body. It was not like a clap of thunder, or an explosion, but a writhing thing that unwound and unwound until she thought she might lose herself in the release. She clung to him, the lofty Duke of Courtland, her new husband who had known how to do this thing to her *all along*. He drove in her hard and made a sharp, exultant sound. She understood he was reaching his own peak along with her, his own unwinding as he jerked between her legs. His knees braced against the bed as he lifted her and shuddered through one last thrust of his hips. She collapsed back, spent, exhausted. Astounded.

When she opened her eyes he was still hovering above her, watching her with a grim intensity that frightened her a bit. She reached up to touch his face, to soften it. "Court," she whispered, testing the name on her tongue.

He turned his cheek into her palm and kissed her just above her wrist. "I told you you would like that part."

Like it? She couldn't believe it, that he could do these things just with his body and hers. At last he pulled back from her, out from that place she hadn't wanted him to be. Her disappointment must have shown on her face.

"We'll do it again, my love," he said, stroking her cheek. "Never fear."

"When?"

"Soon," he said. "After you rest. After I recuperate and regain my wits."

She craved for him to start all over, to do all of it once more immediately, but at the same time she was overtaken with a drowsy sense of satiety. Her eyes began to close. She didn't want to sleep, for she didn't want him to leave her. She forced her eyes open and reached for him, curling her fingers around his arm where she could still see the half-moon marks of her nails.

"Don't go," she sighed, huddling close to him. "It is a big bed."

"I won't go if you don't wish me to."

"Stay with me, please." He ran his fingers up her arm and over her back in a slow, repetitive caress. His body's warmth soothed her to a near-stupor. "You were right," she said as she drowsed. "That last part was the best part."

His caresses paused a moment, his fingers tightening against her. "The last part was magnificent, but I enjoyed all of it very much."

"I did too. All of it was magic, really, wasn't it?"

She felt his chest rise and fall against her cheek. His arms came around her to pull her closer, right against his body. "Yes, dearest. Magic indeed, but you are very tired now. We have a lifetime to make love. Close your eyes and sleep."

"But—" She mustered up the energy for one last question. "Where did you learn to do that magic? Have you always known how?"

He didn't answer. Or perhaps he did. Just before she drifted off, she thought perhaps she heard him say, "The magic came from you."

* * * * *

Benedict Thomas William Hawthorne. His Grace, the Duke of Courtland. He kept repeating his names and titles in his head, trying to remind himself who he was. *His Grace, the Duke. Benedict Thomas William Hawthorne*, a man of duty who never cared to be loving or emotional or affectionate. The Duke of Courtland, who would never become a lovestruck and ridiculous man.

Ah, well.

He would allow himself this temporary insanity. By God, he'd earned the right after this last couple of months. While the rest of the *ton* speculated and snickered behind their hands about what might go on in the Duke of Courtland's marriage bed, here he was lying beside his wife in a state of exhausted bliss. Bugger the lot of them. He would allow himself to adore her because she deserved to be adored.

What courage she'd shown at their wedding. The pomp and crush had been intimidating even to him, although he'd always known he would go through it. A few months ago Harmony had been the reclusive daughter of a lesser viscount, and surely never imagined such a grandiose wedding in her future. His mother had alternately scowled and sobbed through the ordeal. She was disappointed in Court's choice, like so many in the *ton*, but it didn't matter now.

From the start he had wanted Miss Harmony Barrett, but never would have allowed himself to have her. Never. Which made all of this so much sweeter. Forbidden fruit.

And he had partaken of his forbidden fruit with the fervor of a man starved. He had never slept with a virgin before, but was aware there was an art to it. He had intended to be steady and reassuring, hoped only to complete the marital act without disgusting her. Somewhere along the way that strategy had changed to taking whatever he wanted, however carnal, and making her like it. How bacchanalian he'd been, spanking her, groping and kissing her, urging her to a frenzy of arousal. He hadn't been satisfied until she'd tossed beneath him in the throes of ecstasy.

When she awakened and turned to him the following morning, Court prepared himself for withdrawal, for blushes and regrets, and her terrible realization that she was wed to a man of perverse lusts. She was warm and naked beneath the covers and he—he was stiff enough to bore a hole through iron.

He drank in her beauty as she yawned and stretched. *Lovestruck. You are a lovestruck fool.* She smiled at him, sheepishly perhaps, and her eyes sparkled. There was no recrimination to be found.

"How different you look this morning," she said.

He put a hand to his face, felt a night's worth of stubble. "I have not yet— My valet—"

"No. I mean you look different...because of last night." She blushed and slid closer, snuggling against his very front. He moved his hips back but there could be no disguising his aroused state.

"Oh my." Her eyes met his. "I never knew men were fashioned so. I never imagined that...well..." She sighed, clearly flustered. "I can't believe I never knew."

Only Harmony would become indignant over it. He smiled to soothe her. "Now you know. For better or worse."

She laughed and moved closer still. "How on earth could it be worse?"

I could never let you out of this bed again. I could become obsessed with you. I could never stop thinking about sex with you. "Harmony," he said instead. "I want you again."

She drew in a breath just before he kissed her, his hand curling possessively around the curve of her neck. He pressed his hips to hers, pressed the rude evidence of his words right against the loveliness of her belly. She clung to his shoulders, so open and trusting, which only made him want her more.

"Are you tender from last night? I don't wish to hurt you," he said, easing her onto her back. "I'll try to be gentle." He should have taken

127

more time as he had the night before, lingered and caressed her, but he found himself touching her instead in all the places he knew would bring her immediate arousal. Her saucy, thrusting nipples, the heat between her legs. She dragged her toes along his calf and held his shoulders tighter. "Oh," she breathed every so often. "Oh, no."

Oh, yes, he thought. *Yes, yes, yes.* He positioned himself and moved into the tightness of her, through her warmth and heat, dying every moment. "Oh, Harmony," he said, or perhaps he only growled. He slid a hand beneath her hips and held her so he could thrust deep. There were no gasps or squirms of unease.

"Does that feel good?" he asked. "Better than yesterday?"

"Oh yes." She sighed, moving against him. "I believe I love this part. I truly do."

She was a more avid participant this time, meeting him thrust for thrust, giving herself up to the abandoned heat of lovemaking so Court felt free to abandon his inhibitions too. He grunted, he grasped, he wove a hand into her curls and forced her head back for his kiss. He nipped at her neck and her delicate jaw, all the while burying himself inside her with the passion of a love-maddened man.

"Yes, please, more," she whispered against his lips. "How strong you feel inside me. Court..."

That breathless *Court* nearly undid him. This luscious, unbridled creature was his very own wife to lie down with whenever he wished. No courtesan had ever pleased him like this, not from the time he'd lost his virginity at the age of fifteen. He urged Harmony on, reveling in her wildness until the intensity took both of them. Her arms tightened around his neck, pulling him down and drowning him in the splendor of her release. He reached fruition to the music of her whimpers and pants, and cradled her like a treasure beneath him. His stones tightened almost painfully, the pulses of his orgasm blurring all thought from his mind.

He collapsed atop her, nestling his rough cheek against her soft one. His entire world in that moment was her scent and the soft tickle of her curls. She trailed lazy fingers at his nape until he collected himself enough to withdraw from her, and settle beside her so she had room to breathe. Again, the bright smile, the gaze that communicated delight rather than disgust.

"How remarkable you are," he said, stroking her cheek. "How fortunate you make me feel."

"Fortunate?" Tiny lines, a little frown. "Why?"

"When I imagined how my wife would be, I never imagined someone like you."

She gave a pleased little laugh. "Shall I take that as a compliment?"

"I wish you would."

"I thought maybe, last night, that it was one special moment," she said, gazing up at him. "That it wouldn't happen again."

"I have a feeling it will happen every time we are together."

"That would be wonderful," she said, snuggling back into his chest.

Wonderful was not a good enough word for it. Not nearly good enough.

Chapter Twelve: Naughty

The Duke of Courtland sat at dinner with his new duchess thinking about sordid, lascivious things. This created a rather uncomfortable situation, since his mother the dowager sat at his other side. He and Harmony had been wed a week now, and still the briefest glance at his wife awakened the savage in him. The smallest movement or casual touch made him want to rip off her clothes and press her back on the table and rut on her wildly. His mother would not have approved.

Court had intentionally limited contact with Harmony in the weeks before their wedding for this reason—she stole his control. Not maliciously, of course. She drew it away from him with glances and stares, with smiles and the charming, exuberant things she said. Their wedding night had nearly killed him. The blood on the sheets might have come from his own uncivilized heart beating so hard for her in his chest. He had sensed, of course, that his Goddess of Chaos would offer him more pleasure than the typical English miss, and she had. More passion, more questions, more uninhibited participation than he could have hoped.

He had lain with her every night since, and burned for her in the daytimes in between. When he came to her at night she professed to long for him, and afterward she clung to his shoulders so he could not leave her bed. His whole life had become those naked hours, her warm, soft body beneath him and beside him. Her kisses, her touches. Her sighs. At some point, he would have to regain control over his behavior. When he grew used to her, perhaps, inured to her charms.

But he had the terrible suspicion he would never get used to her, and never really have enough of what she gave. He had a feeling she was going to move him from lust to veritable voraciousness, and what then? He would behave shamefully, doing things to her no proper man should do to his wife. Worse, she would probably urge him on with her little moans and groans.

Then there was her unconcerned acceptance of his need to spank her, to play with her bottom and wallop it scarlet. All along he had nurtured some desire to spank his future wife, but he'd never believed it might actually happen without Gwen fleeing back to her papa's arms. Harmony showed no intention to flee. Of course, he had not really punished her yet, aside from the episode in Newcastle which had been an abrupt, flustered kind of session. He wondered how she would react the first time he truly punished her for some offense. He wondered if he would be able to punish her at all.

He fumbled his silverware with a clatter. His mother made a harrumph of a sound as Harmony glanced up at him. He looked back at her, appreciating how much she'd already changed in the short course of their marriage. She was dressed formally for dinner in an ice blue silk gown, the muted hue bringing out the depth of her eyes. His family's diamonds glittered at her neck. The sparkle forced his gaze down to the tempting expanse of her décolletage before he managed to snap it back up to her pretty face.

Yes, he could. For her benefit, he would punish her if he had to.

His mother's tsk reminded him he was staring at her like a besotted swain. Harmony cleared her throat and put her hands in her lap.

"Is the dessert not to your liking?" he asked.

She sighed and lowered her voice to a whisper. "I misused the utensils at some point." She gestured to her setting. "I have nothing left with which to eat."

Court felt some sympathy for her. Formal dinner involved a boggling array of silverware. He beckoned a footman with a glance and an arched brow.

"Her Grace requires an additional dessert spoon."

If his servants were at their best, they would have noted her lack of spoon and rectified it silently. He would have to speak to the head butler later, he thought, rubbing his forehead whilst staunchly ignoring his mother's glare.

"It is of no consequence whatsoever," he murmured to Harmony as the footman returned with a single silver spoon on a tray. Harmony took it and stabbed at her pudding.

"You needn't slaughter it," his mother said. "Just eat it now that you have your spoon. Or leave the table, if you cannot be civil."

Court held up a silencing hand to the dowager. His wife stared at the pudding, her face like stone as he reached and patted her hand. "If you are finished eating, you may be excused."

She pushed back and remembered almost too late to turn and wish them good evening. She held her back stiffly as she walked out. As soon as the doors were closed, he turned to his mother.

"I would appreciate it if you would refrain from scolding my wife. She is a duchess, not a child."

"She was poking at her pudding like an ill-mannered infant."

"Like a frustrated dinner guest. Must you glare at her and make her feel uncomfortable? This is her home now. Her table. Her family. If you cannot soften your heart toward her then perhaps you should take dinner in your room with Mrs. Lyndon."

His mother narrowed her eyes. The battle lines had been drawn; this was only another skirmish in the series.

"Perhaps I shall dine in my room," she sniffed. "She disturbs me so I cannot digest my food properly. And the way she stands up and leaves when she is finished! I cannot imagine how she was raised."

"She stood up and left because I excused her. She was not feeling well."

The old woman blanched. "Tell me she is not already increasing. She could not be so gauche."

Court coughed into his napkin until he could compose himself, then scowled at his mother. "You've begged me to provide an heir for nearly a decade now, and now you complain?"

"If a babe arrives too soon after the wedding there will be talk."

"There is already talk. There has been talk since the beginning. At any rate, she did not flee the table because she's increasing. She fled because you persist in being rude to her."

"I, rude? You will call me rude when you ogle her throughout dinner each and every night? It is sickening to witness, if you must know the truth."

"Can you not find it in your heart to be happy for us? To be pleased that we suit so well?"

"How can you believe that you suit well?"

"We suit, mother. As much as that galls you, it cannot be changed."

His mother desisted, stabbing at her pudding in much the manner Harmony had. "I wish I could be happy for you, but all I see is the Courtland name attached to that...that...oddity. I only wonder why you allowed yourself to be trapped by a prospect so far below you."

"She is not a prospect, mother, she is a person. And it makes no matter now if she is a prince's daughter or a commoner's—I wed her. She is my wife. She is charming and intelligent in conversation. I find her beautiful and kind of heart."

"Beautiful! Kind of heart!" His mother spat the words as if they were condemnations. "My son, are you so besotted you cannot see? What you feel for her is infatuation. Inappropriate fascination which shall fade and leave you with a very unsuitable partner for the rest of your life."

Court wanted to argue, to set her down with a few choice words, but some part of him feared his mother was right. The intensity of lust and desire for his wife was not the stuff of steady marriages, but rather the way a man might go on with a torrid *affaire de coeur*. He tried to picture Harmony at state dinners, at society gatherings where sharp eyes and ears watched for every gossip-worthy shortcoming. He pinched the bridge of his nose and slid his hands down his face.

"She is my *wife*, mother." He kept repeating it, because it was the only thing with which she couldn't argue.

"I am aware she is your wife. There has been enough mockery and laughter to remind me of that."

"What matter if people mock and laugh?" he said, straightening up again. "She is a duchess, and must therefore be shown respect."

"Society will show her respect as far as they must, but she will never win their true consideration. I promise you she won't."

"I promise you she will," he countered stubbornly. "In time."

"Bah. There is no time. She must be brought up to standard by spring, or I swear we will not host the ball. I shall not blush and apologize all evening for her antics. I will not subject the Courtland name to the derision of the *ton* just as the season gets under way."

"We shall open the house as we do every year," Court said, standing with temper. "And Harmony will play the part of my duchess perfectly. She shall be transformed into the picture of civility. Even you will be obliged to say so."

"Hmph."

"And you will apologize to me then, mother, for speaking of her so unkindly, and to Harmony too."

"Hmph," she said again. "You have less than five months to enact this transformation."

Court shrugged. "She will take but a month or two to learn the way of things. She is exceptionally bright. And she loves me," he added a bit childishly. "She will wish to please me."

"Love," his mother muttered.

He bowed to her. "Good evening. Enjoy the rest of your dinner."

An unmannerly exit, but it was better than staying to argue with her. From the dining room, he strode to his wife's room. Her lady's maid answered his knock, curtsied and let him in. He looked about for Harmony and found her settled in a chair in the corner with a book.

"Leave us," he said to the servant, his gaze fixed on his wife.

The woman mumbled some niceties and took herself off. At the sound of his voice, his wife sat up straighter and closed the book in her lap. It was a large volume, some historical tome, no doubt, but it hadn't yet worked its necessary magic and erased the tight expression from her face. Her dinner finery was gone, replaced by a pale yellow velvet dressing gown. Her hair was loose, a halo of flaxen locks around her head. She stood to face him with the book clasped against her front.

"I apologize for giving up," she said. "Was the duchess put out that I left?"

He crossed to her with a sigh. "You are the duchess now. You mustn't worry what she thinks." He closed his eyes and shook his head. "No, you should worry what she thinks in some matters, but there is no cause to come undone and storm away over mismanaging your dinner spoons."

"It isn't only the spoons," she said. "It's everything I do, every day. Wearing the wrong dress for luncheon or bringing up the wrong topics of conversation, or speaking out of turn to Lord Galvin in the park."

"Lord Galvin will recover," Court said with a frown. "In my opinion, he is far too tightly wound."

"But don't you see? It's always something. Can I not just hide away from everyone? Then we could all be content." She reached to stroke his starched cravat. "Can I not just stay here in your home and make *you* happy?"

Oh, the images that brought to mind. He arrested her softly tracing finger before he lost his ability to think. "You know you cannot. It would be enough for me...God help me...but..." He gritted his teeth against the longing in her gaze. "I should like nothing better, but I am a public figure and you are my duchess. You cannot hide."

"But I'm not what they want," she cried, covering her face with her hands. "I never will be."

"Who says so?" He drew her hands away and forced her gaze to his. "You are too stubborn to be intimidated. You must not say 'I cannot.' You must try. You know, there was a time I believed I would make you the world's worst husband, but I married you anyway."

"Because of my muddling," she interjected morosely.

He silenced her with a finger to her lips. "The matter of 'why' no longer signifies. I had to become your husband, and I decided to try very hard to make you a good husband, to provide security and comfort to you. I didn't wish you to be disappointed in me."

"Oh, Court," she said, her mood softening. "I don't want to disappoint you either."

"Then you must set yourself to the task of this marriage and do your very best. Certainly you will have a lot to learn to be a proper duchess, but I daresay you will come to be quite excellent at it. You shall be so lofty and shining I'll be a mere shadow at your side. 'Where is the duke?' everyone will ask. 'He seems to have disappeared completely.'"

She laughed at his animated portrayal of the scene. "You could never be in my shadow," she said. "Even if I were the best duchess ever. You are too grand and tall, anyway." As she said this, she clambered up on her reading chair and placed her arms on his shoulders. He ought to chide her and tell her to get down. The chair was a fine Welsh piece, one of his mother's favorites. But he did not tell her to get down. She moved her hands up his shoulders and back down to his upper arms, boldly taking his measure. Her eyes grew warm and languid, as if she found his measure pleasing indeed.

135

"Grand and tall, am I?" he said, his fingers teasing at the curve of her waist.

"You know very well that you are. You make such a fine figure when you are all dressed for dinner in your handsome coat and neckcloth." Her hands traced up again to rest on either side of his collar. She studied his neckwear, her forehead crinkling with those familiar lines. "Is it you who ties them so beautifully, and puts in these little pins?"

"No, it is my man," he said, his voice gone slightly raspy. "My valet."

"Would he teach me how? I should like to be able to do such a thing, to arrange your collars and cravats." She leaned to brush her cheek against his neck and almost lost her balance. His arm came around her waist to steady her, though he himself was quickly losing grasp of his control. The savage was awakening, beckoned by her slightly parted lips, the possessive approval in her gaze.

"You are not to fraternize with my valet," he managed to say. "Duchesses do not need to learn how to tie cravats."

She frowned. "Even yours?"

"Stay away from my valet. You are far too curious. Next you would be asking how to shave me and how to polish my boots."

She scratched her fingertips through his evening stubble. "I should love to shave you, Court. I really should."

"I'm afraid that is an absolute no." He kissed her on her pout, tightening his arm around her waist.

"But I love this part of you. Your rough, strong jaw and your neck." Her fingers traced down to the sides of his collar, just below his ears, then up to linger beneath his chin. He had never imagined marriage like this, with teasing talk and affectionate touches. "I remember the first time I saw you in your formal clothes," she said, staring into his eyes. "You walked into the Darlingtons' drawing room and stood and looked around, and you appeared so steadfast and haughty."

"Haughty, Harmony?" He struggled to swallow. "I am not haughty."

"Sometimes you are. That night, you were haughty and dark and tall, and so very handsome, and very forbidding. All the ladies noted it. When you dress for dinner I always think of that night. When I see you like this..." Her hands were back to teasing at the folds of his cravat.

"I…I do not know what comes over me. I have the most…unladylike… thoughts."

Court came to a slow and bemused realization. His wife was trying to seduce him—whether intentionally or innocently, he did not know. He did not care.

"Untie it," he said in a low voice.

Her steady gaze flickered for a moment. Innocently, then. It did not change his response. She paused, then he felt her fingers working at the linen. "I hate to disturb it, it looks so lovely," she said as she placed the sapphire-tipped pin in his palm.

He slipped it into the pocket of his coat for his valet to find later. "Tell me about these unladylike thoughts."

She drew a deep breath that made her breasts rise and fall beneath her velvet dressing gown. A narrow sash held the garment closed. As she worked at his cravat, he tugged her sash open and drew off the gown to reveal a filmy nightdress. He could see the merest hint of her breasts beneath the silk. "Tell me," he repeated, as he caressed over one and then the other with his thumbs. "What unladylike things do you think about when you see me dressed this way?"

She gasped as he touched her. Her eyes fell closed a little. "I am… I am too ashamed to say. Wicked thoughts. That night at the Darlingtons', I could think of little else but—but—" He brushed over her nipples again through the thin fabric. She abandoned untying the cravat, clutching his shoulders.

"But what?" he prompted.

Her eyes refocused slowly. "Well. I hadn't any point of reference, but…" She resumed her task and managed to tug one tail loose. "To be honest, I tried very hard to imagine what you might look like without your clothes on."

He seized his cravat as she pulled it free of his collar. "You ought to have been spanked for that."

"Yes, I ought, but there was no one around then to make me behave."

"Wasn't there?" He stroked the lacy edge of the neckcloth down her cheek. "How fortunate I am here now." He draped the crisp length over his shoulder and unfastened the front of his wife's nightgown, pushing it over her shoulders and down to pool at her feet. She stood naked and lovely before him, still perched upon his mother's esteemed Welsh chair. When she moved to cover herself he stopped her, catching her hands. He nuzzled his cheek into hers, aroused by the way she trembled beneath his touch.

"Do you wish me to make you behave, naughty girl?" he whispered. "Punish you for your wicked thoughts?"

She made a small, excited sound and buried her face against his neck. "I am ashamed," she whispered.

"Yes or no?"

She leaned into him a little more, right against the front of his coat. "Yes. If you think it would be best."

He pulled his cravat from his shoulder and took it between thumb and forefinger. With his other hand, he caught her wrists. He began to circle them with the linen, putting her under his power and authority. She watched for a moment, biting her lip. Such beautiful anxiety…but he did not want her to be confused.

"This is not for the spoon incident, you understand." He watched her until she nodded. "What is this punishment for?" he prompted.

"For…for having lurid thoughts about you when you're in your fine dinner clothes, with your neckwear tied just so."

"Exactly," he said, easing comfortably into his role of disciplinarian. "Lurid thoughts are never becoming in a lady. Particularly a lady of your esteem."

"I have esteem?"

He knotted her bonds with a sharp glance, leaving a small length free. "You are the Duchess of Courtland. I shall not remind you of that fact again." At that, she gave him an impish grin that nearly set him laughing. "Behave yourself. Or this jesting punishment will become all too real."

"Are you only jesting?" She looked down at her bound wrists and back at him.

"I am half-jesting." He placed a hand beneath her elbow and helped her down from the chair. "You are very naughty, climbing on chairs and thinking lurid things, and doubtless deserve a spanking whether it is in jest or not. Come."

He drew her across the room and positioned her so she faced the front left post of the bed. He looped the cravat around the post and tied it so her wrists were trapped, then stood close behind her and stroked her hair. "Now, naughty wife, you shall stand still and await me until I return."

She looked over her shoulder in alarm. "Where are you going?"

"To get a birch," he said, thrilling at her wide-eyed gaze. He crossed to leave, then turned back at the door, taking in the sight of her tied naked to her bed, awaiting his punishment. "Take care not to tug on that neckcloth," he added as an afterthought. "It is my second favorite one."

Chapter Thirteen: Happiness

Harmony pressed her forehead to the bedpost, wondering why she was so raving mad.

She had recklessly teased and flirted, inspired by his gaze and the beauty of his smartly attired body. She had played with something she'd never known she possessed before she married—feminine power. Power over her handsome, towering husband, who reacted to her touches with an intensity that thrilled her.

But he'd turned her antics back on her and now here she was, fixed to her own bedpost by his lace-trimmed neckcloth. Somehow, as she'd become lost in their interplay, she'd forgotten her husband knew how to wield power much more deftly than she.

A birch, God help her. He kept a birch rod in the house?

Of course he would have them in the house, "uncomfortable habits" and all that. For all she knew, he kept a collection of flagellatory mistresses in far-flung rooms. His home was such a vast property, she would never know if he did. She could not be so spoiled as to say she was unhappy, but she was not at ease in this St. James mansion or in her new role as his duchess. There was so much to learn, from how to dress, to making calls, to navigating around the obsequious house staff and prickly dowager. It was all so complicated, except for this—being alone with her husband.

He had come to her every night since they'd wed and stayed with her for many hours, touching and exciting her beyond decency. She wasn't sure if this was normal or excessive marital behavior, but she didn't want to ask anyone. The great amount of time they spent together suited her just fine.

But this was the first time he'd spanked her since their wedding night. She turned her head at a distant footfall. Was that her husband in the hall or was it a servant? What if someone entered and caught sight of her in this ignominious position? Dear God, what if her husband had sent a servant to assemble a birch rod, and some footman was even now delivering it to him at the door to her bedroom? After all, she couldn't picture His Grace lowering himself to stroll out to his own woodlands and collect the switches to bind together. Would all the servants know?

Of course they would know, you ninny. Of a certainty, they knew his proclivities before you showed up.

Everyone in the *ton* knew, she realized now. A couple days before, while visiting his library, Harmony had glimpsed a newspaper on his desk with a caricature of a scowling old gentleman taking a switch to a kicking, becurled young lady, her skirts tossed in the air. The caption read, *The Esteemed Duke At Last Finds Wedded Bliss*. Court covered it with other papers as soon as he noticed her looking at it, and that was when she'd realized with shock that it was a cartoon of them.

She didn't care. She *didn't*. She didn't care if people snickered behind their hands at them. She wanted to do what excited him, because it excited her when he became so lustful and wicked. But now that the price was about to be exacted, she was reconsidering her choice to play at this game. She had never been birched before, although she knew her father had lit into Stephen a time or two when he'd done something particularly bad. Afterward Stephen had moped and sat quite uncomfortably. *My husband will not hurt me.*

I don't think he will hurt me.

At least not too much.

The door opened and Court returned. He crossed the room in stealthy silence until he stood just a few feet away. She wanted to hide and cover herself, but with her hands confined she hadn't the choice, so instead she huddled right against the post. Her eyes dropped from his forbidding stance and his steady gaze to the birch rod in his hand. It did not appear freshly cut, which was a relief. In fact, it looked not much larger than a nursery birch. She let out a breath.

"Sir...I think... I am quite certain... I believe a stern lecture might do as well to teach me the needed lesson."

One corner of his lips quirked up. "You believe that, do you?"

"Yes, sir."

He tapped the birch against the side of one polished boot. "I am not inclined to let you off with a lecture."

"Oh." She imagined even a smallish birch hurt a little. "I see."

He tossed the implement on the bed and took off his coat, then his waistcoat, never taking his eyes from her until he turned to set them aside. He pulled his shirt over his head and tossed it over the other garments, then turned to her in only his trousers and boots. He looked dangerous. Daring. Sexy. He smoothed a hand across the front of his falls. She could see the outline of his shaft there, pressing against the material as he rearranged it. When she looked back up at his face, his half-smile had widened to a grin.

"More lascivious thoughts?" He reached for the birch rod on the bed. "How needful of punishment you are." He paused. "The correct answer to that is 'Yes, sir.'"

"Yes, sir," she forced out through the tightness of her throat.

"Dear, you are already flinching. You must not flinch and tense, or you'll bruise." He inspected the slim switches that comprised the birch rod. "At some point I may need to make use of a ginger fig."

She was nearly afraid to ask. "A ginger fig, sir?"

"To prevent you clenching your bottom when I spank or whip it." He seemed about to explain more, but then shrugged his shoulders. "You'll learn about it later. The technique is most quickly understood in the course of its use."

That thought did not soothe her at all. He approached and stood behind her, one hand on her shoulder, and her body felt like one great cringe.

"Bend forward," he said. "Just a little, that's right. There will be ten strokes. I would like you to count each one."

"Yes, sir." *Oh, my. Oh, my!*

Harmony leaned forward, clutching the bedpost. He pushed her down a little more until she was posed to his liking—but not hers. She felt too vulnerable, with her backside stuck out and about to be punished. She was not at all sure she liked this game. She shut her eyes tight until she heard the faint sound of the implement swishing through the air. The birch connected with her bottom, bringing a sting but not unbearable pain. If it was only this discomfort, she believed she could bear it. "One," she said, taking a deep, centering breath.

He rubbed the birch rod along her bottom and she shivered a little. Then it was gone and she braced for the next blow. "Two!" This one was a bit harder. It stung very uncomfortably, like a hundred tiny pricks. The next came before she'd sorted out the effect of the second. "Three!" she cried, gripping the post. He stopped for a moment and she realized that the sting left behind was not lessening, but growing worse. The next blow made her go up on her toes. "Four!"

Five was the hardest yet. Harmony counted, then whimpered softly and shifted from foot to foot. Her husband's broad hand spread upon her bottom, massaging, caressing.

"We are halfway there," he said. "As I punish you, you must think about how to be better."

"Yes, sir. I have been thinking. I think I have...I have already learned my lesson—"

The birch came swishing against her bottom mid-sentence and she cried out "Six!" "Seven!" "Eight!" He paused but a second or two between each one. They were not any harder than the ones that came before, but the pain rose and rose, burning ever hotter. She clenched and twisted and on the eighth she straightened up and turned to him. "Please. You're hurting me awfully."

"Awfully?" His eyes were mild, as was his voice. "You are not even crying, so I believe you can survive two more strokes."

She frowned at him and turned, and pressed her body to the bedpost. Just as during the wedding-night spanking, she felt aroused as much as she felt pained. She wanted to take two more to please him—oh, but it was so hard to bend down and accept them. He was right that it wasn't really awful. She hadn't yet felt such agony that she must beg him to stop. It just *hurt*. He waited, watching her. Finally, she took a deep breath and forced herself to bend and offer her aching bottom for more punishment. He made a soft, pleased sound and she was glad she'd been so brave.

"Only two more," he reminded her. "Count them aloud."

The birch whipped against her bottom, erupting in a bloom of pain. "Nine!" she said a bit truculently. Surely he needn't hit her that hard! Just one more...

143

The last was the hardest, a stiff, sharp whack that did, finally, bring a haze of tears to her eyes. "Oh...ten! Please! No more!"

His hand smoothed over her sore, stinging cheeks. "There will be no more."

Harmony fidgeted at his touch. In a way it soothed her, but in another way it made her wish for a different sort of caress. He guided her upright and said, "I'm pleased you were such a good girl during your punishment."

"Oh, but I wasn't." She pressed herself against the bedpost again. Behind her, she could hear him undressing the rest of the way. Boots pulled off, trousers pushed down in a whisper of cloth. "I tried to think about being better..."

"Did you?" His warm body pressed to hers from behind.

"But it didn't do any good. I am still having those...those wicked thoughts about you."

He moved closer, pushing his stiff rod right against the heat of her bottom. An answering pulse throbbed between her legs, in that spot where he could make her cry out and yearn for him. "Hmm," he said. "How intractable you are."

She shuddered as he pressed a palm against the heat at her center, then nipped at the curve of her neck. Harmony leaned back against him. "I am intractable," she sighed, "because I don't think I can make those thoughts stop."

He didn't answer but started to work at the piece of linen that bound her hands. He pressed his cheek against hers as he tugged the knot apart, although he didn't release her wrists yet, just the bit that held her to the bed. His nearness felt hot and branding against her skin. "God help me," he said. "I cannot punish you without wanting to possess you afterward."

She closed her eyes at the raw longing in his voice. "Is it not supposed to work that way?"

"It can work any way that pleases us."

Oh, she felt very pleased at the moment. He turned her to face him and wrapped his fingers around her wrists. Her hands were still bound together and she had the feeling they were going to stay that way a while longer. She clasped them to the front of her chest as he leaned to kiss her. His grip tightened on her wrists and she felt a breathless excitement at his passion, his ungentlemanly force.

She whimpered with longing as he let go of her wrists to brush his hands down her hips. He grasped her bottom, not cruelly, but very

144

firmly, and drew her hips forward against his jutting length. The sting and soreness of the spanking still hadn't gone away, so she felt the double sensations of discomfort and desire. His rod was so grand, so very thick and hot. He called it a "cock" when he whispered licentious things to her in the midst of their play. He had taught her many naughty things in the course of one week, and she wondered what she would know by a month or a year hence. She would be a complete wanton!

She wasn't sure if that was a good thing, but she didn't care so long as it pleased him. When Court walked her nearer to the bed, pushed her back on it and came over her, she reached out for him with her tethered hands. He took them in his and pinned them over her head and told her she was not to shift them away.

"What shall I do with you now?" he said, gazing down at her. "My helpless wife, with her naughty, unladylike thoughts?"

She arched her hips and brushed boldly against his hard length poised at her most private place. It was an invitation to do what *she* wanted.

But he did not, not right away. He drew back, making her lay as she was so she was bared to him, hands still trapped and stretched over her head. He traced his fingertips over her body, over her breasts and nipples in a clever touch, then more firmly at her belly and waist. "I think I'll take some time to admire you first. You know, I had my own wicked thoughts, staring at you across Lady Darlington's drawing room."

Her mouth fell open. "I don't believe you. You didn't."

His hands slid lower, parting her thighs. "I most certainly did. I thought your hair was so shiny and soft looking, and your body so beautifully voluptuous. I thought how lovely you must be beneath your dress."

"Oh, no." This was a shock to her. She remembered him staring at her that evening, but she never would have believed… "You thought about me with my dress off?"

He looked up at her, his thumbs poised at either side of her quim. "Oh yes, my sweet. I thought about how lovely you must be down here. I wanted you."

With those words, his thumbs parted her sex and quested to the tiny, aching button he called her pearl. "Oh, my word," she whispered. "I can't believe it."

He neglected to answer with words, only caressed and explored her until she shivered in pleasure. A moment later he dipped his head to her center and stroked her with his tongue. Her hands came flying down to stop him from this scandalous course, but he pushed them up again.

"Let me do as I please." Spoken like a true and imperious duke of the realm. Harmony lay back and closed her eyes. So carnal, so corrupt. So...astonishing. He was doing with his mouth what he normally did with his fingers, teasing and drawing shivery pulses of pleasure from that sensitive place. His breath was hot against her skin, his hands nudging her legs open when she clenched them closed against the sensation that devastated her. "Oh, Court...this is wicked. And wonderful!"

He hummed against her as if to agree. She writhed upon the soft, fragrant sheets, gazing up at the pleated canopy above her as her ecstasy climbed to a higher and higher peak. She longed for completion, but he kept it just out of reach, making her burn and crave all the more. If she could only touch him. If he would only come inside her and move in her and drive her down into the bed, she knew she could reach that place of unbounded pleasure.

"Please," she cried out. "You will kill me like this."

"Perhaps," he murmured. "A momentary death."

She stared down at his glossy dark hair, the breadth of his shoulders holding her open and vulnerable, as vulnerable as she'd been during the birching, but now he was tormenting her with pleasure, not pain. Her hips moved, seeking more. "Courtland. Court. My love..." She was begging now.

He made a rough, wanton sound. His lips and tongue left her, replaced by a groping hand. One finger, then two slipped inside her, his large hands priming her as she pressed her "pearl" against his palm. His gaze raked over her, over her heaving breasts and her arms cinched above her.

"Did you really want me?" she asked. "That first day you saw me? You wanted me like this?"

"Dear girl," he said through gritted teeth. "If I knew about you then what I know now, I would have laid siege to you there in the drawing room. Stripped you bare and taken you in front of everyone."

Harmony laughed as he withdrew his fingers and pressed his lips to her neck. "That would have been terribly impolite."

He growled. "You do not inspire politeness in me."

She tensed as he drew her legs over his shoulders and positioned himself at her entrance. He looked down at her, her conqueror, her master in this. She wrapped her fingers in her hair to keep her hands where he'd told her to—otherwise she would have clutched him to draw him inside. She was still aroused from his earlier lovemaking, his miraculous mouth. Now, as his length pressed into her, she shuddered from the fullness and satisfaction of accommodating him. At her groan, he began to move, clasping her thighs and holding her firmly for his ever-deepening thrusts. She felt her powerlessness...and his power. A restless tightening built in her middle, and between her legs where he took her as hard and fast as he pleased.

Her wrists strained against their bonds, her whole body stretching and opening to encompass him. She was his captive, pleasured and now given to his use. She let go as he'd taught her to, let go of politeness and manners and ladylike behavior and snapped her hips against his. She heard a cry as if from a distance, her own cry of release buried in the side of his neck. His hands were on her wrists again, bearing them down, grasping them in a spasmodic grip as she lost herself to all else in the world.

Her husband collapsed atop her with a groan, his scent and the weight of his chest so familiar now. The tension in his body slowly dissipated. He let go of her wrists and she lay beneath him feeling exhausted and very, very safe. He kissed her, deeply, sweetly, then nuzzled her face with a sigh. "I suppose I should untie you. Give me your hands."

He rolled away and she offered her wrists, watching as he unwrapped them as tenderly as they'd been wrapped. She studied his face at the same time, mesmerized by the combination of his stern "duke" expression and the softer emotion underneath. She hadn't recognized the emotion before, had never expected it to be there. It was subtle, another mysterious layer to the man she'd married. When her hands were free she held his face between her palms, staring, feeling a connection to him that went beyond marriage and propriety and titles.

He gazed back at her, his lips curved in an ironic smile. "To think— you worried you would not bring me happiness."

She smiled too, letting go of his stubble-roughened face to hug him close. "I'm glad if I do. You are deserving of it."

"I hope you will always believe that." He drew back and dropped a line of kisses down her neck. "There will be difficult times between us. Times you will wish me to the devil."

She shook her head, but he remained pensive. With one last kiss, he released her and reached to retrieve his now-wrinkled neckcloth.

"I didn't damage it, did I?" she asked.

"If you had, I would have forgiven you after such a delicious tryst. But it seems to have survived." He stared down at it, worrying the trim in the palm of his hand.

"What's the matter?" asked Harmony.

"Nothing," he sighed after a moment. "The rest of them be damned."

"Is this about…those…those drawings in the paper?"

He grimaced. "I did not mean for you to see them."

"I'm sorry I cause you such embarrassment. I'm so sorry."

He silenced her with a kiss, then leaned back and cupped her cheek. "I am not concerned. The *ton* will eventually move on to new scandals and gossip. Spring will bring a new season with plenty of fodder for idle tongues."

"I am glad to be married now," said Harmony. "I'm glad I won't have to participate in all that society nonsense."

One brow rose as he looked at her. "You'll still have to participate, but yes, you won't have to be courted any longer, or seek a match." His face softened as he drew her back into his arms. "You've already made a stunning one."

She giggled as he nibbled beneath her ear. "I won the hand of society's most eligible bachelor, didn't I?"

"The most eligible bachelor no one wanted. Yes. Aren't you fortunate?"

He was jesting, but she could sense the hurt underneath. She thought of beautiful Lady Wembley, how she had jilted him and hurt his feelings. Harmony could tell he had wanted the lady very much, although she was sure he'd deny it if she asked. She stroked his neck and threaded her fingers through his hair.

"Yes, I am fortunate," she whispered. "Because the most eligible bachelor was also the most wicked."

He let out a soft breath, gripping his neckcloth in tense fingers. "I think I am not the only wicked one in this union. What shall I do with you?" He shook his head, as if to bring himself from a stupor. Harmony could see the dutiful duke emerge, pushing the lover aside as he sat up on the side of the bed. "Speaking of the season, there is a huge rout of a ball here every year in the spring. It is a great tradition of the *ton*, a bash to kick off the social whirl. My mother wishes to cancel it this year."

148

"Because of me?" Harmony's heart fell to some place near her feet. "Because she believes I'll ruin it," she realized.

He shook his head and waved a careless hand. "It won't be cancelled, of course. I told her the ball would go on as planned, and that you would be an unprecedented success. A perfect hostess for the event."

Sadness and embarrassment were replaced by sputters of alarm. "Unprecedented? A hostess? Me?"

"You are the duchess now. It will be your ball in name at least, not my mother's. I told her you could very well handle it, and you shall."

Harmony felt out of breath. Panicked. She flinched as her husband touched her brow.

"I will help you," he said. "My mother and the household staff will help you. I know you will make me proud."

He could not have used more intimidating words. She must not only succeed at a bare minimum, but she must make him *proud*. "I will not be able to do it."

He waved the folded-up neckcloth at her. "Words like that will only find you tied to the bedpost again. You can do it, and you will. You must do it, for I've entered into a battle of wills with my mother over it. I should dearly love to show her up, and I think you would too."

All the relaxed happiness of their intimate encounter bled away with talk of this ball. The cursed thing would be hanging over her head from now until April. She didn't know what upset her more, her inevitable failure as a hostess or the dowager's enduring disdain.

"I wish she did not despise me so," Harmony said. "I can change my behavior if I try but I cannot change my origins, my 'low' birth. She will always keep me at arm's length, won't she?"

"Perhaps," said Court. "It is impossible to know how time will change things. She is an old, bitter woman in some ways. Perhaps you are not meant to be close."

"But she is your mother." *And until I win her over, I can't make you proud.* Perhaps he didn't realize that but she did. Without the dowager on her side, any attempt to fix her notoriety was useless.

Her husband kissed her again, stroking her bottom cheeks in a tender, possessive way. "So, what did you think of your first birching? It was your first, was it not?"

"Why do you say that?"

"Because if you'd been routinely birched as a child, you wouldn't be so incorrigible now."

149

There, he was doing it again, joking and teasing her with the driest expression on his face. She swatted his chest. "Yes, it was my first, if you must know. And it hurt. I should not like to endure a more severe birching."

He raised an eyebrow. "Then, my dearest Harmony, you must endeavor to be very, very good."

Chapter Fourteen: Spectacular

She was impossible. Absolutely impossible.

The holidays came and went, and his Miss Chaos...now Duchess Chaos...showed little progress in the way of refinement. At her brother's wedding to Lady Meredith, she made a cake of herself by...well... knocking over the wedding cake as she was staring up at the frescoes on Needham's ceiling. At the Hawthorne family's intimate Christmas dinner, Harmony managed to both spill wine on his cousin, the fastidious Lady Runnenbarth, and bring up Mongol hordes, this time before the entire group.

It was not that she did not try. She did, but there were a regrettable number of lapses, all of which she paid for upended over his knee.

"But one cannot rightfully discuss the history of the Jin Dynasty without bringing up the Mongols and Genghis Khan," she'd wailed as Court turned up the skirt of her gown.

"A lady does not discuss hordes of any type at the dinner table, nor Genghis Khan. Ever," Court had replied firmly as he meted out a spanking commensurate with the degree of her crime. Afterward she'd apologized very prettily and tearfully, and sworn up and down that she would never, ever utter the word "Mongol" again, and then she'd gone to the library and buried her nose in a book about the Mongol Empire like the stubborn, obsessive creature she was.

151

Mere months to the ball, and all he had to show by way of progress were a surfeit of spankings that accomplished nothing aside from inflaming him to greater and greater heights of lust. In the short, dark days of winter, Court called reinforcements to the house. Lady Renfrew-Burress, to improve Harmony's deportment. Lady Archleigh, to teach Harmony how to properly converse in company of all kinds. A dance teacher, Mr. Lightmore, to develop her poor ballroom talent. The foppish young gentleman was a friend of his wife's brother, but Court hired him anyway because he was reputed to be the best.

After these lessons Harmony would be cross and withdraw from him, and retreat to the library, losing herself in her books, shrugging off any sheen of cultured finesse her tutors had managed to impress upon her in their limited time. He was heading there to see her now, just after her lesson with Lady Archleigh. She had books in her rooms but she often used his library and he liked having her nearby. She was quiet when he needed quiet and sweet when he needed sweetness. And after her lessons, well…she was a bit of a shrew, but he still loved her more than any sane man ought to.

He arrived at the library, sailing through doors silently opened by liveried footmen. A glance around the room revealed a pair of shapely legs propped over the arm of a chair in the corner.

He cleared his throat as he approached, causing the legs to disappear. By the time he faced her, she sat as primly as any English rose.

"We have discussed that duchesses don't sit with legs strewn over armchairs."

She gave him a *who, me?* look that dissipated into a guilty grimace. "I'm sorry. It's only that Lady Archleigh exhausts me so. After our time together I just want to—" Words escaped her. She drew up and shuddered her whole body in an adequate representation of what she was trying to express. She peered up at him with one eye closed. "Are you going to spank me?"

"No," he said. "Well, not yet. But stop that please. You look like a pirate."

"Arrgh."

"You do not amuse me when you behave so."

Even as he said it, the corners of his lips started to twitch. Damn her. "What are you reading?" he asked.

She flipped over the book in her lap and held it out to him. *"The Culture of Ancient Greece During the Bronze Age*, by Michael Thomas Burgermeister."

"Oh? I do not remember having that in my library, nor buying it for you."

"Mr. Lightmore brought it. He is an acquaintance of Mr. Burgermeister and thought I might like it. Honestly, it is terribly academic, but it was kind of him to think of me, wasn't it?"

Court didn't answer for a moment, shocked by the young man's cheek. How dare he present his wife with a present of a history book? Court could tell from Harmony's guileless expression that she hadn't the slightest idea how inappropriate it was to have accepted it. If Lightmore were an old bewigged nodder with creaking corsets, maybe, but he was not. Decidedly not. He was of an age with her brother, with all the dandies of Barrett's set.

"From now on, if Mr. Lightmore brings gifts to you, you are not to accept them."

Her lips drew into a pout. "Did I flub up again? But what should I have done? Refused it?"

"Mr. Lightmore knew it was inappropriate to offer a gift to a married lady. When any gentleman offers you a present, you must tell him you cannot accept it, and let me know about it at once. Is that understood?"

"Yes, sir," she said, not without frustration. "But I thought it was very nice of him. You will not tell him off on my account, and make me have some new teacher? Mr. Lightmore is patient, and he makes it easy for me to remember the steps."

Jealousy flared at the way she defended her teacher. Yes, Court wanted to tell Lightmore off. Yes, he wanted to send him to hell with a boot to his arse. But he wouldn't, not if the man could actually inspire Harmony to enjoy dancing. "I won't confront your teacher this time. But remember what I said. No more gifts."

"Yes, sir. May— May I keep the book?"

"Do you *want* to keep the book?"

"It does contain a wealth of information."

He shrugged. "Very well. But will you put it away and accompany me on a walk? I'm restless indoors and it's not too cold a day. The rain has gone off and I should like to see my flower in the sunshine."

That brought a smile to her face. "Shall I be your flower? Opening my showy petals?"

No! Well, yes, but only for me. What were these feelings of anxiety, of jealousy? For five seasons, no gentleman would go near Miss Harmony Barrett, not to dance or even converse with her. Now Court felt she might be snatched away at any moment by an interloper. But she was different now, more fetching somehow, and not just because he knew her in a carnal sense. Her face was brighter and she was more aware of her feminine power. She used these wiles on him regularly and he knew it.

What if she decided to use them on someone else?

From now on, he thought as he drew on his walking coat, he would be there while she and Lightmore were together at dancing lessons. Then there would be no question that proprieties were being observed. That decided, he gave himself up to the fresh English weather, to a walk with his wife in the bracing and only slightly chilly air of a winter's day. The sun kept the temperatures from offending; in fact, as they sauntered about the impeccably landscaped garden behind the house, Court grew warm and Harmony developed a comely blush in her cheeks. He wanted to kiss those cheeks, and her lips too, but it was not polite to go about making love in broad daylight, even in a private garden.

He talked about the weather instead, pointed out the robins in the trees, anything to stop himself dragging her to some sheltered place and mauling her for the next three hours. "How different the garden looks in winter than in spring," he extemporized at one point.

"Why, yes," Harmony answered. "I imagine it does look different. But why are you conversing like such a stick?"

He raised an eyebrow at her. "It is rude to accuse one's companion of being a stick."

"Arrgh," she said, winking.

"Harmony." His voice held a warning note.

"Well, you looked like a pirate just then, with your eyebrow all scrunched up above your eye. Tell me, did you only ask me for a walk so you might test my conversational prowess? Gauge my progress with Lady Archleigh?"

"If I were, you would be failing miserably. You mustn't be confrontational."

"You told me once I must stick up for myself. You remember, in the Darlingtons' garden?"

"I remember, but that was a different case."

"You also called me stupid."

"I never did such a thing." He took her hand, squeezing it, bringing her palm to his mouth for a kiss. "If you do not learn to converse with more subtlety, the lessons with Lady Archleigh shall continue."

His wife pulled her hand from his. "I don't know why people can't talk to one another normally. Why they must mull over and weigh every word before they utter it. It seems false."

"Most people don't need to weigh their words. But you do, because you have an unusually busy and complicated mind." He put an arm around her and squeezed her for a moment in the waning afternoon light. "It is one of the things I like most about you."

"Then why do you try so hard to change me? If you like me as I am?"

Court frowned. "I am not trying to change you, only improve you. The world is not only me," he said in his defense. "It's not only me you must please."

She looked up at him with the full force of her dissecting blue eyes. "Why not? Why can I not just please you and myself? And our children, if we have them someday?"

She always asked the most difficult questions, and Court disliked being argued with.

"It will please me for you to become more socially adept," he said with an air of finality. "For you to be accepted by our contemporaries. I would like the satiric drawings and gossip of our marriage to cease, and so would the dowager." He took her hand, disturbed by her troubled expression. He wished sometimes the world *was* only her and him. "Tell me what happened at Almack's. Why you were forbidden to waltz."

She shook her head. "I cannot. I cannot even bear to think about it."

"Tell me, or I shall force you to waltz with me right now."

"Please don't. I'm hopeless!"

"Mr. Lightmore has not instructed you in it?"

When she answered that he hadn't, Court felt the gentleman redeemed a shade in his eyes.

"Good. You are not to dance the waltz with anyone other than me. Ever." As he said it, he began to move with her, a slow rehearsal of the steps.

"You are always saying things like that," she said, gripping his shoulder. "How possessive you are."

155

"Perhaps, but I will not apologize for it. I know some couples of the *ton* think nothing of stepping out on one another, but you'll never do that with me."

"Or you with me," she said, narrowing her eyes. "You must honor our vows too."

"I am not the one between us known for making irresponsible and reckless choices."

"And I am not the one between us known for depravity and vice. I have no intention of stepping out on you, as you say," she said, stumbling over one of his feet. "I'm rather insulted to be lectured about it."

"Not a lecture." He arrested her when she would have swayed in the wrong direction. "A warning. Don't, or I will make you very miserable in consequence."

"Warnings and threats don't become you," she said, stiffening in the midst of a 1-2-3 beat. "Haven't I been a good wife to you? I am trying." She raised her voice slightly and took two steps back from him. "Do you know what happened at Almack's? I popped out."

"You what?"

"I was waltzing with the Earl of Havershaw and I tripped and he tried to catch me. I grasped at him and fell and at some point my...my bountitude escaped the bodice of my dress."

He gaped. "Both...bountitudes?" He could picture it far too easily. "Oh, no."

"Oh, yes," she said, her voice gaining outrage by the word. "And Havershaw stood there like a ninny, staring, and numerous other people saw too. I pulled up my bodice but it was too late, and I also scuffed my knee and ripped my favorite stockings, all because I cannot waltz for a prayer. They were right to forbid me, you know."

It explained Lord Havershaw's inability to hold Court's regard ever since the betrothal. He put a hand to his mouth to hide his smile. "Oh, my dear," he said. "A debacle indeed."

She glared at him. "If you snicker, I may do something very unseemly that you will not like at all, and then you will probably punish me for it afterward and it will be a thoroughgoing mess."

"I don't wish to laugh," he said, "but I may not be able to help myself. The Earl of Havershaw, of all people. He wouldn't know what to do with your 'bountitudes' if they landed in his outstretched hands." He gave her a look. "They didn't, did they?"

"No. Although I believe he fainted afterward, which was probably what I should have done. Perhaps then I wouldn't have had my waltzing privileges revoked."

"No," said Court, struggling to hold back the mirth that choked him. "I'm quite certain it was over for you the moment your bodice failed you."

"You see, it wasn't my fault, it was the way I fell!" She began making vague gestures of illustration that finally defeated him. He burst into laughter as she stood with her arms crossed over her chest.

"You're a fine example of a husband," she snapped. "Laughing so hard at my misfortune you can barely catch your breath."

"It is not misfortune," he said, wiping his eyes. "If not for this episode, perhaps Havershaw would have fallen in love with you. Courted you, married you. What a shame that would have been."

"For him," Harmony groused. "Not for you."

He sobered, took her arm and pulled her close. "Despite what you believe, I am glad we ended up married. Even though I try to improve you, Duchess Bountiful, you must remember that I love you just as you are."

She stiffened and pulled away from him. "Oh, Court!"

He spun at her shrill cry, prepared to guard against the attack of some beast, but Harmony was only bounding over to a spindly rose bush. "Do you see?" She pointed as he came to her side.

"It is a rose."

"It is a winter rose. The only flower in the whole garden. How do you suppose it came to be here?"

"Er...it grew on that bush?"

She tore her attention from the downy white flower to scowl at him. "You have no sense of romance. You do not find it spectacular, that this one lone flower thrives here in this icy garden? And so beautifully too."

He gazed back at her for a long moment. "I do find it spectacular." He crouched down beside her to look more closely at the rose, only because he knew she would be upset if he didn't. He studied the bloom as she traced its contours with a gentle caress. The flower was fully opened, its surfaces smooth and pearlescent. "Such showy petals," he said quietly. "What now? Must I make a wish on this spectacular and unexpected flower?"

She shrugged, a little shadow falling across her face. "You might, if you believed in them."

"Will you make a wish then?" he asked.

"I already have," she said. She of the showy petals, and he, dry and thorny and not given to wishes at all.

* * * * *

Harmony came to love the gardens at the St. James house nearly as much as Court's comfortable library. When she had to get away, escape the smothering walls and gloomy portraits and constant watchful eyes of servants, she stole to this manicured expanse and breathed the chill air. It was the one place the dowager never came.

Harmony could almost forget they were in town when she walked deep in the gardens. She could forget about her lessons, about developing pomp and hauteur. She understood that Court had to be close to town to fulfill certain duties, like attending the King's court and taking his seat in the House of Lords. She was proud to be wife to such a lofty person, and truly wished to remake herself as the elegant lady he deserved. A lady more like Lady Wembley, Court's ideal.

He never said aloud that Lady Wembley was his ideal but it was plain enough she was eminently suited to be the wife of an esteemed figure like him. Lady Wembley and her husband were coming to dinner this very night and Harmony was pleased to hear it, for she planned to study the lady and emulate her in any way she could.

Court was not so pleased. At least, he hadn't acted pleased when his mother surprised him with news of the dinner plans. After riding with Harmony in the park, he escorted her back to the house and raced off on his horse in a great temper. Poor Spartan. The stallion was probably accustomed to his master's moods. He probably enjoyed being ridden well and hard now and again. *Like you, Harmony.*

She put her hands over her eyes, horrified by her increasingly corrupt thoughts. How could her husband expect her to become a refined lady considering the things he did to her behind doors? She shook her head and hurried to the house to seek out Redcliff's guidance in what to wear for the dinner party. She would do her best to make her husband proud.

On her way back to the house, she saw a hound limp across the lawn and slink into the cover of some trees. Poor thing. She thought it was too large to be one of Courtland's dogs, but if it was in pain it ought to be seen to. Against her better judgment, she hurried to the stables to tell Jeb to alert the groundskeeper about the unfortunate creature.

Now, running late, she proceeded upstairs to prepare for dinner. Redcliff insisted she bathe, and Harmony enjoyed the warm water after the bite of wintry weather outside. She dried off and regarded her face in the mirror as Redcliff bustled around the dressing room, collecting combs and pieces of jewelry.

"I have to look perfect," she told her lady's maid. "Hair, gown, everything."

"We ought to put you into the silver flocked dress His Grace favors, with the gilded trim. We can use matching silver ribbons in your hair."

Harmony clapped her hands. "Oh yes, Redcliff. It shall be magical. It is not too much for dinner, is it?"

"Not at all, but let's begin," the woman said, moving to the armoire that held the silver gown. "The Wembleys and Tremaynes have already arrived, and the Runnenbarths are sure to arrive soon. Her Grace the Dowager will be terribly cross if you delay her dinner party."

The maid worked quickly, transforming her from regular old Harmony to the refined Duchess of Courtland. The high-waisted bodice of her dress fit like a second skin, while the skirt draped in a perfect silhouette. Matching silver slippers and teardrop jewelry at her neck and ears were understated but pretty. Harmony thought her bosom would always be too ample for true elegance, but all in all, the effect was not bad.

Battling time and the summons of a maid from belowstairs, Mrs. Redcliff curled her hair and pulled it up into a pile of silver-threaded ribbon and jeweled flowers.

"Oh, Redcliff," Harmony sighed, standing to look in the full-length mirror. "How marvelous you are. It is truly perfect."

A smile played around the edge of the older lady's lips. "Wait until His Grace gets a look at you. Now, you must be gone downstairs. Don't delay."

A movement from the window caught Harmony's eye. Oh, the poor creature, the dog, it was positively lame. It must have broken a leg. She could see Merit, the groundskeeper, trying to stalk the frightened hound and corral it away from the trees with Jeb's help. "Yes, I will go down at once," Harmony said.

She would just quickly, very quickly pop outside to be certain Merit had everything in hand.

Chapter Fifteen:
Understanding

Court prayed for calm as his mother shot him vicious looks across the parlor. Their dinner guests milled about exchanging news and pleasantries. Unfortunately, the soup was already in the dining room growing cold.

"Let us proceed to the table," he said. "Doubtless the duchess will join us soon."

His mother's face looked even more sour, if such a thing was possible. She had arranged this dinner as a petty form of revenge for a disagreement they'd had a few days before about whether or not to engage the king's French cook's assistant for the Courtland ball. Court very much enjoyed the work of their own French cook, who was extremely moody and likely to quit if he were thrown over, even for one evening. The dowager was obsessed with King George due to some distant family connection Court suspected was made up, and therefore grasped at every opportunity to bring royal influences to the household.

As for the Wembleys and Gwen's parents, the Tremaynes, she'd invited them to confound him and humiliate Harmony. The Runnenbarths were invited to act as an additional audience to his comeuppance. The dowager's companion Mrs. Lyndon would surely serve in that capacity too. Curse this dinner party and his mother's blasted spite.

She could spite him to hell and back. He still would not allow her to engage the King's cook's assistant, nor even the King's cook himself.

And where was Harmony when he needed her? Why could he not manage these two unruly women in his life, when he managed the complex politics of England, the machinations of the court of the Prince Regent, and his own exorbitant wealth and holdings? Her seat across the table sat empty as the guests enjoyed cook's winter specialty of spiced squash soup. In yet more spiteful glee, his mother had placed Gwen at his right hand. How properly she sat, and how delicately she sipped from her spoon.

Well, Harmony could eat soup with the best of ladies now. She had made fine progress in manners, if not promptness. Where the devil was she? He glared at one of the footmen, enough of a signal to send the man running to fetch the housekeeper and send her personally this time to bring Harmony down to join the group. That, or some indication that she was ill and with regrets would not be joining them. Such cowardice did not seem typical of his wife, but it couldn't please her to be compared to his former *inamorata* in such an intimate and formal setting. He could understand such cowardice, although he couldn't let it pass without some punishment. An over-the-knee spanking at least.

He looked up, realizing he'd barely been following the conversation. Gwen must have asked him a question since she was looking at him intently. To his relief, she repeated her question again. "I wonder if you have enjoyed being married? The duchess seems so very kind a lady. So charming and sweet."

Her words were sincere, not satirical. Bless Gwen, she was never one to sneer at another, which was one of the things he'd adored about her. His mother, meanwhile, puffed out her cheeks in an effort not to scoff out loud.

"She has brought me much happiness," Court said with a true smile. "She's brought a lot of life to the household."

"That's wonderful to hear, Your Grace."

Court heard her reply but beneath her softly spoken words he also heard Harmony. She wasn't coming from the hall. In fact, it seemed as if she was coming from the kitchens. His mother's eyes went wide, hearing her too. "Courtland—" she began, and then all hell broke loose.

The double doors on the far wall burst open, sending one footman flying. Harmony and his groundskeeper entered, chasing a baying, lame hound with wild eyes. Both Harmony and his man's clothes were covered in dirt.

"Catch him," Harmony shrieked, going the opposite direction of his servant. "Help us!"

Everyone at the table gawked but a handful of footmen, fine in their dinner livery, stiffly joined the chase.

"Is it not Sir Radley's old dog?" Gwen asked in bewilderment from his side.

Court was too flabbergasted to reply. The panicked cur limped under the table. The ladies screamed in unison while the gentlemen grunted and pushed back their chairs.

"Courtland, *do* something," his mother wailed, fanning the prostrate Mrs. Lyndon, who had fainted back in her chair.

But he felt frozen. He could do nothing. He watched Harmony dive beneath the table along with the groundskeeper. "He's scared," she called out. "Don't hurt him."

"Yes, ma'am," his man replied respectfully, as if he was not under a table with the duchess struggling to catch a dirty, injured dog.

"There," came Harmony's voice. "Push him this way, and I shall guide him out. Oh!"

The mass of brown and black fur exploded from beneath the table right into his mother's lap. Her chair tipped back and she grabbed for the tablecloth. Court watched orange spiced soup explode over Lady Runnenbarth and the Tremaynes' laps and then onto his mother as her chair finally upset, dumping her on her side. She let out a scream and he jumped to his feet. The entire room was a tangle of flailing men and screeching women, orange soup, a panting dog, and a flash of silver that was his wife. The dog, wife, and groundskeeper flew out the way they'd come, leaving him to collect his shrieking mother from the floor.

Maids and footmen streamed in, dabbing at the guests, cleaning spills and soothing the ladies. His mother gazed up at him in pain, her hand twisted at an unnatural angle. "My wrist," she cried. "Please, send for my physician." With those words, she promptly joined her friend Mrs. Lyndon in passing out cold.

* * * * *

Harmony hid in the stables, behind a pile of straw in the farthest corner. She heard carriages come and go, saw Jeb lead out horses and take in new ones. A doctor came. That made her shake. What had she done? What would Court do to her when he came for her?

He would have to come get her. She could not make herself go to the house and face the chaos she'd wrought there. At least Sir Radley's dog was okay, caught and splinted and returned home. Just a sprain, said one of the men who helped her. The poor dog had been so afraid. Now she was the one afraid, and cold and miserable. She wanted to burrow into the pile of straw and hide forever.

For two hours she cried into her hands and worried at every sound. What would she do when he came for her? What if he didn't come for her? What if he finally washed his hands of her? She wasn't improving, she wasn't growing more refined, she wasn't even falling pregnant with an heir. She was failing him in every way. What if he was so angry he sent her back to her father in disgrace, to live apart from him the rest of her days?

Why hadn't she let the dog be? Why hadn't she let Merit handle everything and gone downstairs to dinner? She'd had a dog that looked a lot like Sir Radley's dog when she was a young girl. She still remembered the way he followed her around. She remembered burying her face in his fur when she felt sad or alone. Sobs racked her as memories crowded in. She'd felt so sad and alone her whole life, but never more so than now.

She heard low voices, Jeb and her husband. She inched farther back into her dark corner, her only light that of the mournful moon. It reflected off her pale silver gown until she practically shone. So much for hiding. She closed her eyes as his footfalls drew nearer. She didn't want to see his expression, his anger. His voice, when he spoke, was not gruff nor gentle, only very cool. "You cannot hide out here all night."

Tears squeezed from beneath her lids as she spoke against her palms. "You can't want me in the house."

"If my mother had her way, you would never be let back in the house. You broke her wrist. Well, that confounded dog that knocked her over."

She huddled into an even smaller ball. "I'm so sorry."

"Look at me."

"I can't."

"You have no problem acting the crazed hoyden in front of a roomful of people but you can't look at me now? Look at me," he said again, and this time the command in his voice had her head whipping up, her eyes focusing miserably on his. He drew a breath, another, not a trace of softness in his stance or features.

"Normally I would give you a chance to explain yourself, but I can't see any plausible explanation here except that, rather than join the dinner party as you were told, you went chasing after a damn stray dog."

"He was injur—"

"He was not your problem. Are you in charge of the neighborhood animals?"

"I was helping Merit. I was trying to help."

He reached down and hauled her to her feet with a vehemence that had her babbling in fear. "I'm sorry. I was wrong, I know. I'm sorry—"

"Sorry changes nothing. You must be taught a lesson. You must be punished for this."

He didn't say it with any of the usual care or affection evident when he punished her. She felt afraid. Her gaze shied from his hard eyes to his tense lips. "I'm sorry," she whispered. "I'm so, so sorry."

"You are always sorry," he said, drawing her through the stables and out into the courtyard. "You are always sorry after the fact, but that's not enough anymore. I've been patient, Harmony, but as of this evening, my patience has run out."

It was true. He'd been so patient, given her all the tools she needed to please him, but too often she still did as she wished no matter the consequences. She'd known earlier she shouldn't have gone out to help Merit with the dog, but she'd done it anyway, trusting that Court would understand even if he didn't approve. She'd thought he might give her a curt reproach for being late to dinner, perhaps a bit of a spanking. She'd been so headstrong and foolish. She knew, beyond a doubt, she was going to receive much more than a bit of a spanking over this.

Footmen held open the front doors as he steered her inside. The house was quiet, all the guests gone home. He hauled her past the darkened dining room, the scene of her crime, now cleaned and set for tomorrow's breakfast. She wondered if this house had a dungeon. If it did, he might lock her away there for a week. A month.

He didn't take her to a dungeon, but a room very like one. He opened the heavy door and escorted her through into an echoing space that smelled of must and disuse. She saw half-filled shelves and an old desk larger than the one in the library upstairs. This was a study, but not his study.

He turned and stared at her. She put a hand to her hair and then tried in vain to smooth her mussed silver skirts. This beautiful, magical dress, ruined. She could never bring herself to wear it again. A piece of straw dislodged itself and fell onto the wood floor.

"It pains me to do this," he said. He seemed about to say more, then clamped his lips shut and pointed. "Approach the desk and bend over it."

She would have liked to say no, to run out the door screaming for help, but she knew she couldn't. She'd earned this punishment. She'd earned it by causing havoc and breaking the dowager's wrist, and shaming him in front of his company. In front of prim and perfect Lady Wembley, who should have been his wife.

She forced her legs to move and carry her across the room to the desk. The top was dusty, its hard surface offering nothing to comfort her. She couldn't bear to bend over it. She looked at her husband, her support, the one ally in her life who usually defended her.

"I'm so sorry. Please! You must understand I didn't mean any of it to happen."

Nothing changed in his face. If anything, it grew harder as he removed his coat and waistcoat, stripping down to his ivory linen shirt. "You caused my mother grievous injury. You humiliated me in front of my closest family and friends."

"In front of her," Harmony said bitterly. "If she had not witnessed it, would you be so angry?"

He scowled, not condescending to answer her. He crossed to a corner, to a rack containing canes of various length and thickness. While Harmony's insides roiled with anxiety, he inspected them, selecting one of middling size. He turned back to her, his eyes, once warm, two chips of ice.

"I instructed you to bend over."

"I don't want to." She sounded like a whiny child but she was too frightened to come up with dignified words. "Please, I'm sorry. I don't want you to whip me with that."

"What you want does not signify at the moment." He crossed to her, the wicked cane clutched in his hand, and forced her down over the desk.

"Please!" she cried out.

"You can make all the noise you wish but no one will come. This was my father's study. It is removed from the rest of the house for a reason."

165

"Stop, please!" She struggled against his hand pressing her down. "I will become like Lady Wembley, I swear. I'll be just like her if you but give me one more chance."

"This is not about Lady Wembley."

"You wish you had married her," Harmony sobbed, fear making her lash out. "I want to be like her. Do you think I don't? I know you would be happy then. You wish I was her! So do I!"

He pulled her up, his arm around her waist nearly robbing her of breath. "Do not shriek at me, Harmony. Do not engage in emotional games. You sound childish and mad, which is exactly why you're about to be caned like a naughty pupil."

"If I was her you would not do this!"

He raised one haughty brow. "If you were her, I doubt I would need to do this. However, before we wed, you agreed that I might improve your behavior through a program of physical consequences. What do you believe you deserve for your actions this evening?"

Harmony shuddered in his arms. He was right. She had agreed to a marriage where he might spank her if he wished, if he thought she deserved it. And if she ever deserved it, it was now.

"I suppose I deserve a spanking," she said sullenly. "But I don't think I need to be caned."

"Something lighter then? A few smarting slaps with my hand?" He raised the cane so she could see the thin, rigid menace of it. "Unfortunately I do not agree. I think you need ten strokes of the cane across your bottom and then I expect to hear a very handsome apology for your behavior at dinner. I am your husband but I am also your disciplinarian, and it is for me to judge how best to guide you."

Ten strokes of the cane. She didn't hear any of his lecture after that. She knew everything he said was true but she really didn't want to be in this horrible, dark room. She didn't want to be in disgrace and she didn't want to be caned.

"I promise— I won't— I'll never again do anything so—"

He placed a finger over her lips. "Enough. You know that isn't going to work. It is time to receive the discipline you have earned."

How cold he was. How businesslike. When he spanked her in the bedroom it was so much less traumatizing. Harmony let him bend her over, burning with humiliation.

"Reach forward and grip the edge of the desk," he instructed her. "Every time you choose to let go, I shall add an additional stroke."

"Yes, sir." She was already in tears. As her fingers closed around the wooden desktop, Court moved behind her to lift the skirts of her gown and drape them over her back, out of the way. He had spanked her on her bare bottom before. He had even used implements, but not like this. Not with this cold and detached demeanor. She stared ahead of her, biting her lip, tasting her own tears.

He braced a hand at the small of her back to steady her. She heard the cane whistle through the air and then felt the impact. Oh no! Sweet mercy. The fiery pain was a shock to her very core. She cried out and flung a hand behind her. Her husband tsked and tapped at it with the tip of the cane.

"I suggest you find some self control or you shall end up very punished indeed. You have just added an additional stroke."

"I can't—"

"Can't what? Can't bear the pain?" *Whack!* "Perhaps you will remember that next time you decide to go after stray dogs rather than attend the dinner you were supposed to." *Whack!*

Harmony sobbed into the surface of the desk, gripping the opposite edge for dear life. She could not let go again, she simply couldn't. He delivered each stroke with an exacting and excruciating force, occasionally pausing between them to let her catch her breath. There was no playfulness about it, only firm resolve. *Whack!*

What was that? Six? Seven? "Oh, please," she wailed. "I'm sorry."

The cane came whistling again, a whipping smack of a stroke that hurt so much more than seemed humanly possible to endure. "If you dislike this—" *Whack!* "Then perhaps next time you will choose to behave as a duchess—" *Whack!* "And not an impulsive girl."

Her bottom was burning up, on fire. Her whole body trembled but he held her down, preventing any movement or escape. He delivered another stroke, and then a final one that burned across the others like a crowning lash of fire. Her knuckles were white with the effort to remain in position. She prayed he was done. But oh, what had he told her? *I expect to hear a very handsome apology.*

She would not be able to talk with the tears choking her. He lifted her from the desk and she faced him as her skirts brushed over her sore cheeks and fell to her ankles. She couldn't stop sobbing. It wasn't just the pain of being struck with a cane ten...no...*eleven* times at her husband's hand. It was that she would never be completely at ease in his company again, not now that she understood the cold and effective discipline he was capable of. His over-the-knee spankings, mild paddlings and lectures seemed like child's play now. All of it, of no consequence. This study, this desk had opened her eyes.

"I am so sorry," she choked out in misery. "I must be such a bitter disappointment to you."

He watched her, unmoved. "Try again, without the self-pitying melodrama. I suggest a simple 'I'm sorry' with a promise to do better next time."

Harmony took a deep, shuddering breath. "I'm sorry. I promise next time I shall come to dinner when I'm expected and not...not run off doing other things."

She wished he would hug her and tell her she was forgiven but he launched into another lecture.

"I will accept your apology, Harmony. But only if you mean it. I think you believed you would only be required to submit to discipline that agreed with you. It is a common misconception in relationships like ours, but going forward you will be held accountable like for like. Mild behavior will bring mild consequences. Severe behavior will result in severe consequences, as you have just experienced. Do you understand this?"

Four simple words, and yet for Harmony they illuminated the two parts of their marriage. The part before she had understood, and the part to begin now as she stared into his hard gaze. "Yes, sir. I understand."

Her own four words, and no need to say more. How couldn't she understand with the sore pain of her bottom cheeks? How couldn't she understand when the cane still dangled from his fingers? When the rack across the room held at least a dozen more of the wretched instruments of torture?

Finally he moved away, walked over to the rack to return the cane to its place. He put his waistcoat and coat back on, taking care to fasten every one of the numerous buttons, adjust his cuffs, and straighten any wrinkles in the pristine garment. That finished, he crossed back to her, standing with his arms behind his back. He put her in mind of that dark, haughty aristocrat she'd first seen in the Darlington's drawing room, but it didn't excite her this time.

He held out a hand to her from four or five feet away. "Come here."

She approached him and took his outstretched hand. He drew her into his arms and settled her against him, but she felt no comfort. He seemed a stranger to her, which frightened her to more tears. With a flick of his wrist he produced a handkerchief and used it to wipe her face. There weren't only tears, but undignified rivulets of snot dripping from her nose. She let him wipe it all away, beyond humiliation.

"You understand I don't enjoy punishing you so severely," he said as he worked. "It's difficult to hurt the ones we love. I do love you, Harmony."

She couldn't speak, couldn't have returned the words to him anyway, not when she knew them for a lie. Perhaps because she held herself so stiffly, he released her, pocketing his handkerchief. He tilted her head up and looked into her eyes. She saw a little of the old Court there, but the other Court too, who was still not well-pleased with her.

"I would say you are forgiven, but you have injured others who may not yet feel inclined to forgive. I expect you to apologize to my mother and do what you can to assist her as she heals. I also expect you to call on the Wembleys, the Tremaynes, and the Runnenbarths and apologize for your reckless behavior."

"Yes, sir," she said wearily.

"But for tonight, I'll leave you alone to rest and reflect. Come."

He escorted her up to her rooms. Dear Mrs. Redcliff was there to meet her at the door. Without words, she drew Harmony's second bath of the day, filling the tub high with water that was not too hot, but warm enough to soothe her. She frowned when Harmony asked for privacy, but obeyed her mistress and waited outside the door.

Harmony dried herself afterward and crossed to the mirror. She stared at the red stripes emblazoned across her backside, marking her as a very bad girl, then reached for the soft silk nightgown Mrs. Redcliff had laid out for her. She pulled it quickly over her head, wanting to hide them from her sight, but she could still feel them.

She was so tired, so drained she could barely make it to her bed. She cried once more, just a little bit as Mrs. Redcliff patted her shoulder and murmured, "There, there. There, there." But even Mrs. Redcliff couldn't soothe the hurtful memories of the evening.

She was not yet forgiven. What if she was never forgiven?

He had told her once on the banks of the Darlingtons' lake that she wasn't beyond help, but Harmony feared he didn't believe that anymore.

Chapter Sixteen: Chill

Court relaxed in his chair, watching Harmony with a half-lidded gaze. His wife was at work with the dandy Mr. Lightmore, stepping through country dance formations and attempting to improve the gracefulness of her steps. He was pleased to see that she applied herself to the task. If she was aware of his presence at the lesson, she gave no sign. A week had passed since her punishment, a week during which she avoided him as much as the bounds of courtesy allowed. At night, rather than lie with her, he kissed her on the forehead and let her retire alone.

It chafed to forego his marital rights, but he knew he must permit her the necessary time to sulk and shrink away from him. It had been a severe correction. He felt guilt over it, yes, but he had examined his motives and found them pure. That night, he had purposely waited until the worst of his anger dissipated, lest he flail away at her without the necessary control. He had not broken his wife's skin, nor injured her or drawn blood. It was perfectly legal and respectable for a husband to discipline his wife using civil methods.

In truth, the current chill between them provided a needed opportunity for reflection. He had to find some distance from her, reconnect with his true persona, that of a gentleman and a duke. From the moment he'd found her crouching beneath the desk at Danbury House, something in him had changed. He'd become softer and weaker, more easily manipulated. He loved his wife but he could not allow her to run roughshod over him and his social circle. There must be a way to love her and yet preserve his own stringent standards, both for her and himself.

Lightmore paused in the middle of a step, asking the pianist to repeat a section. The dancing master conducted their lessons in the south parlor rather than the grand ballroom, so Lightmore's accompanist could be heard. The grand ballroom did tend to swallow the sound of anything less than a full orchestra. Lightmore had pretty manners and a pretty face. A little too pretty, especially when he smiled at Harmony. His female pianist might qualify as a chaperone, but Court still made a point of being there every time.

Not that he didn't trust his wife. He just didn't believe her impulsive nature would ever be curbed, and he wasn't sure Lightmore wouldn't try to take advantage and turn her head. He observed them as the lesson came to an end, but there were no overfamiliar or inappropriate exchanges.

She crossed to greet him once Lightmore took his leave, looking slightly pink-faced in her sage and blue floral silk. Was she blushing from exertion or from the assessing look on his face?

He'd promised her an outing to a local historical site in an attempt to warm the chill between them. He hoped it worked, since he intended to reassert his rights in her bed tonight. Her allotted time for sulking was over. There was still no heir, and this cooling could not go on forever.

"A very pretty lesson, my dear," he said, taking her hand and brushing a kiss across the backs of her knuckles. "I cannot wait to dance with you in the grandest ballrooms of London."

She made a soft, equivocal sound. As a polite gentleman, he ought to ask her next if she was too drained from exercise to accompany him on their outing, but he wasn't going to give her a choice. Instead he tucked her hand over his arm and walked her toward the foyer and then out to the coach. "I asked Mrs. Melton to arrange some refreshments for our trip to St. Alphage's."

"Thank you. How kind you are."

A polite response that nonetheless left him chilled. He tried again to engage her. "I think you will enjoy the site. There are church ruins and a park, and natural areas. It is rich in Roman history."

"I've been looking forward to it since you mentioned it yesterday. It's so kind of you to take me. It reminds me in some way of...well..." She ducked her face away from him. "It reminds me of our journey to the Roman wall."

He seized on her reminiscence and her amiable mood. "I hope it will be like that other trip, in a sense that we might feel a new closeness with one another."

Goodness, he would be spouting poetry next. But Harmony rewarded him with a faint smile, the closest she'd come to true smile in quite some time. He bit his lip against further babblings and handed her up into the coach. He sat next to her on the velvet cushions and they set off on their adventure. It had been a stroke of genius, planning this outing for her. For them. Fresh air, friendly conversation, and a chance to show her he still cared about her very much, even if he must discipline her strictly when her behavior went so terribly out of bounds.

They rode awhile in companionable silence, and Court thought that she really had been quieter of late, not that she'd ever been a chatterbox. The dowager approved of her new, more muted personality, and seemed to have softened toward her in the days since the incident. Perhaps it was because Harmony went out of her way to offer aid to the older woman in her convalescence. The Tremaynes and Runnenbarths reacted favorably to Harmony's apologies, and Gwen even came to call on his wife one day last week. Gwen could only be a good influence, although Court was still haunted by Harmony's words that night. *I want to be like her. I know you would be happy then. You wish I was her!*

He truly didn't wish it. He stared down at her hands clasped in her lap, at the skirt of her silk dress, the muted embellishments and trim that suited her station perfectly. With her blond curls and the stylish garments now available to her, no one could fault her appearance. She was more beautiful than Gwen, more beautiful than any of the ladies in her circle, both inside and out.

After a few minutes, he shifted and reached for her gloved hand. "I asked Mrs. Melton to have Cook pack some of those cherry preserves you enjoy."

"Thank you. How thoughtful of you."

She pulled her hand away to fuss at the folds of her dress. He wondered if she would ever wear the silver dress again. Of course she wouldn't. He would order her another one, differently styled. He would make a gift of it to her on their anniversary or some such thing. She really looked stunning in the color, especially with her light blue eyes.

Blast, she was quiet. What was she thinking about? He drew her into a desultory conversation about the weather, about books she'd recently read. When she stopped reading, then he would worry. She haunted his library more than ever, her nose always buried in some book. He talked to her about the St. Alphage ruins, about the old Roman roads and the history of London. She nodded and made interested noises but he realized after some time that she probably knew everything he told her, had probably already read it in the same books he'd read.

By the time they arrived, his good mood had eroded into something a bit more cross. He stuffed down his irritation and gave Harmony a tour of the dry winter park, the stone ruins and reputed Roman burial ground. Meanwhile, modern town life went on around them. There was no grand, great blue sky to gawk at, no expanse of vast moors, but there were old trees and some greenery and wildflowers. They came to one giant stone on their stroll and Court expected her to scramble atop it. When she stood beside it instead, laying her hand upon it, he felt disappointment. Why?

"This is a grand old rock," she said. "I like it."

"I wish I could put it away in my pocket for you then." She gave him a crooked smile. He wished he could keep *that* in his pocket. "Alas, I cannot," he said, indicating her rock. "Perhaps a smaller keepsake. A pebble? A winter rose like the one in our garden?"

She blinked and looked down at the ground, then back at him. "I need no keepsake, but thank you for bringing me here. It is a fascinating diversion."

They spread a blanket and had tea in a circle of shrubs, protected from the bite of the breeze. She perched primly in her dress and ate very little of the fresh bread and ham, though a bit more of the cherry preserves spread on thin biscuits. The conversation was polite but markedly strained. Or rather, he strained not to reach out to touch her, to seduce her back into his good graces. He wished he could lay her back on the thick blanket, roll her up in a bundle and make love to her beneath the afternoon sun.

Instead they packed the food away, took one last look around the historical site and walked a bit farther down the road, viewing more recent landmarks and some ramshackle houses in need of repair. They were not the only things in need of repair.

"Harmony," he said as they walked. "We must speak of matters between us."

She took another step and turned to face him. Her expression was calm, inscrutable. "What matters?"

What matters indeed. She would not make this easy. Her eyes were not Harmony's eyes, bright and inquisitive. They were closed off and emotionless.

"I fear we are not as comfortable with one another as we once were," he said.

She looked away from him, considering. "Do you think so? I have felt more comfortable these last few days. I feel as though things have…calmed down."

"Perhaps they have." What the deuce did she mean by that, "calmed down?" It would be too embarrassing to ask. He felt temper flare, helplessness. He reached to touch her cheek and the velvet curve of her jaw. "I miss you, my love."

She made a dainty feminine gesture that seemed false in the extreme. "How can you miss me when I am right here?"

Her falseness stoked his temper to ire. "Do not play the chirping ninny with me, for we both know you are no such thing." He softened his tone as her gaze dropped to his feet. "Harmony. My love. My wife. I will not ask for your forgiveness. If you are waiting for me to prostrate myself at your feet and say I was wrong for giving you a well-deserved punishment, you shall be waiting a long while."

"I want no apology. I demand nothing from you." Her tone was not rude, but exceedingly cool. "I expect nothing, and accept whatever I am given. If you are not happy with some aspect of my behavior, then tell me what you wish me to do."

Smile at me. Love me. Forgive me, damn it.

"I hope you will not object if I come to you tonight," he said instead in his most autocratic voice. "I have given you time apart. That time is at an end."

"As you wish. You might have come before," she added in the same cool manner, as if he were the one being difficult.

He studied her, noting the color in her cheeks. "I warn you, I will not allow you to lie beneath me and be distant."

"I can hardly imagine that being possible."

"Can't you?"

Were they to spar like children? He took her in his arms, in a forceful grip that shook the ennui, at least momentarily, from the depths of her gaze. "You promised once to stand my friend," he said. "At the inn at Newcastle."

Her lips tightened into a grim line. "It was not a promise, just naive talk from a silly girl. And that was before...before you ever...hurt me."

"It was directly after a spanking as I remember, and I was not gentle that first time." She looked down at his chest, her jaw working against tears. It was as if she would withhold all emotion from him, the very emotion he treasured, the emotion he couldn't express himself. "Cry, damn you," he said. "I ordered dozens of handkerchiefs when we wed, expecting to need them."

He'd teased, made a joke, but she hadn't even reacted. Her face was a blank mask.

"Where are you?" he asked in despair. Perhaps he shook her; perhaps she only trembled. "Where have you gone?"

"Nowhere!"

"Where is my Harmony? The woman I walked with beside the Roman wall?"

She swallowed hard, going tense but not pulling away from him. "I am right here. I am trying to change for you. If you do not recognize me, perhaps that is why."

"This cold demeanor is not the change I wanted."

Tears shimmered in her eyes. He pulled her into an embrace, prepared to produce his handkerchief after all, but she mastered herself before the glittering tears fell. He could feel the tension in her body as he held her. "Look at me," he said.

When she turned her eyes to his he saw his Harmony there, emotional and conflicted, fighting to get out. What did he want? The wildly unpredictable woman, or the hollow shell of her that made the polished and suitable wife? He took her face in his hands, the beloved face that hid so much anxiety and pain, and touched his lips to hers beside the weed-cluttered road.

"I want you to be happy," he said when he pulled away. "My punishments, my efforts to improve you, it is all in an effort to make both of us happy. To bring balance and structure to our lives."

"I find balance and structure very calming," she replied in a dead-sounding voice.

175

Court wanted to throttle her, but he kissed her again instead. At least in her kisses he had some sense that she still cared for him. Her fingers brushed up into his hair, her palm hot on the back of his neck.

"You torment me, Harmony," he breathed against her lips. "You ought to be spanked for it."

She didn't deny his words. She didn't deny any of it.

"Come to me tonight," she said when they broke apart. "Perhaps you will find I am not so changed."

* * * * *

Harmony sat at the escritoire in the dowager's room. Court's mother lay in her bed as if in state, her expression suggesting great forbearance with Harmony's faults. Well, that never changed. Harmony had learned, in assisting with the old woman's correspondence, that her given name was Ermengarde—not that she would ever dare call the woman anything but ma'am or Your Grace.

"Read it back to me, if you please."

Harmony focused on the letter before her. "*My physician says my wrist will be whole in five more weeks at the latest. We will not come to Hertfordshire, though the weather continues dry and mild.*"

"Did you spell 'physician' correctly?"

"Yes, ma'am."

"It is barbaric, the way you write with your left hand."

"I'm sorry."

"Then why do you not improve? It is not enough to merely repeat that you are sorry all the time."

You are always sorry. It won't be enough anymore.

The dowager's words recalled painful memories, thoughts of punishment and remorse, and the tension in her marriage. During today's jaunt to the St. Alphage ruins, Court had tried to re-connect to her, but to be *her* was to be a bad, inappropriate person. To be the calm lady he wanted—like Lady Wembley—she must be something outside herself. If she wasn't... Oh, she couldn't bear to be taken to that awful study again.

Of course, he did not seem to understand this. He thought she could magically remain herself and still be refined and well-mannered. He was making impossible demands, expecting her to fulfill them. Did he believe he could kiss her and give her a little shake and bring everything wrong in their relationship back to rights?

176

But she liked the kisses. Frustrated as she was, she still desired her husband. He could capture her so easily with his touch and intent gaze. She had tried to steel herself against him. She'd tried to hide herself away to give both of them peace, but now the cursed man didn't want that. He was as impossible to please as his mother.

Harmony scanned the other letters on the dowager's desk. Her gaze caught on one of the envelopes, on spidery handwriting she knew well. She would recognize her papa's peculiar left-handed writing anywhere, not least because it was similar to hers and because she received her own letters of him on a regular basis, calm, fatherly letters that made her heart ache for their modest but comfortable home. She was about to reach for it when the dowager's sharp voice stopped her.

"Do not poke among my things. What else does the letter say?"

Harmony swallowed back a retort about the fact that the dowager should very well know what it said since she had moments before dictated it. *"The duke and duchess are well, although she is mopish as always."* Harmony stopped, biting her lip.

"Go on."

"I do wonder if she is breeding," Harmony said. She felt herself go red as the dowager watched her expectantly.

"Well? Are you?"

She stole a look at the dowager from beneath her lids, hoping her agitation didn't show, but the woman regarded her with far too much acuity. She shook her head. "No, ma'am. Not yet."

"Does he still visit you?"

She would not, absolutely *not* answer that question.

"Answer my question, girl," said the dowager in a sharp voice. "What is going on between the two of you? You're like a flower without petals these days, and it doesn't suit you. You can't keep him from your bed. No wife does."

Harmony felt tragically, traumatically humiliated. "He wouldn't come," she said to the floor. She didn't say that he was supposed to come tonight, that she was beside herself to think about it.

"Stop chewing your lip," said the dowager. "Surely you understand your duties. You must make an heir. Several, it is to be hoped."

"I will try."

"Does he hurt you?"

The old woman's abrupt question resounded in the quiet room. Harmony picked at the edge of the letter.

177

"I don't know what type of hurt you mean, ma'am."

She rapped on her tea tray. "Answer the question."

"He doesn't break my wrist," Harmony said. "Nor any of my bones, so he is not as bad a person as me. He is still angry with me for what I did to you. For embarrassing him. He tolerates my company but I don't believe..." *I don't believe he loves me.* She swallowed back the words, expecting another sharp reprimand, but when the dowager spoke her voice was sad.

"It is an awful thing to only be tolerated, is it not?"

There was quiet, tragic pain in the old woman's words. Harmony stared down at her blurring fingers. "Please, ma'am, I had better go."

"No. Cry if you must, but we will talk together about your disaster of a marriage. You think I do not understand you, but I tell you I cried many tears in my day. I remember what you are feeling, how heavy it sets in your heart to be disapproved of. To be despised. My husband—"

The dowager's voice cut off and for a moment Harmony feared she would begin to cry too. She didn't know what she would do if that came to pass, but the old woman marshaled her control and lifted her chin. "In truth, my husband despised me. He told me so daily. He showed me hourly with his cutting glances and sneers. You believe that Courtland is cruel to you, but you don't know what cruelty is."

Harmony shook her head, staring at the dowager's trembling mouth. "No. I don't— I don't think he's cruel," Harmony said. "Only..."

"Only what? Rigid, unfeeling, inflexible? He was raised to be that way." The lady pushed out her lower lip. "Thank God I had a son. Otherwise I believe my husband would have divorced me. Or saved the trouble and arranged me a quick and tidy death."

Harmony gasped. "Oh, no. Surely it wasn't as bad as all that."

"It was." Her words burst out in a croak of agony that propelled Harmony to her feet. She stood beside the dowager's bed and touched her hand.

"I am so sorry, ma'am."

The woman swallowed hard. Harmony almost wished she'd release her tears. "So you see," the dowager choked out, "you are not the first one to suffer in marriage."

"No, of course not."

For a brief moment the dowager took her hand and squeezed it. Coming from her, it felt as intimate and shocking as a hug. Just as quickly, she released her hand and jutted out her chin again.

"You do not realize your good fortune, Harmony. My son does not hate you. You are better off than half the women of the *ton*."

Harmony studied the dowager, feeling as old and tired as the wrinkled woman before her. "Yes, I know he does not hate me. But he married me because he had to. Because you raised him to believe in duty."

"Foolish girl. Duty is all we have, though you scoff at it."

Harmony shook her head. "Duty is not all we have, ma'am. People can love. I love your son even though it hurts me. Even though I'm very afraid he will come to—to—" She stopped and traced a rose on the dowager's bed quilt. "That he will come to despise me in the way your husband did. I'm so afraid of that." She wiped away a tear and stared into the dowager's steely gaze. "I'm sure you think I'm an utter ninny. I know you have set your heart against me, with good cause."

"I have not set my heart against you. But I am a practical woman and you are not. I think you have to let go of this 'love' foolishness. It is not the way of our world."

Harmony touched the dowager's hand again, and took a very great risk in stating the obvious. "You loved your husband though, didn't you?"

The old woman took in a sharp breath, as if Harmony had slapped her. A gate came crashing down between them, and any bond Harmony had come to feel with her in the last few moments evaporated in the hardness of her glare. "You may take your leave."

Harmony stepped back at the ice in her voice. She had heard Court use the exact same tone when he was furiously angry. "I'm sorry. Please—"

"Get out. Leave me," she said. "Mrs. Lyndon is a less provoking companion. I will have her come and help with my other letters after my nap."

"Yes, ma'am."

"I shall let you know if I require your company tomorrow. I doubt I will."

"Yes, ma'am."

Harmony curtsied and backed away from her, repelled by the severity in her gaze. Not severity. Misery. The fearful woman was plagued with a broken heart. How sad, for all that heartbreak to be trapped beneath her cold and cutting manners. How sad that she was a widow now, with no hope of reconciliation with her husband, no hope of ever being loved as she ought to have been.

As Harmony left, she caught a last glimpse of her papa's letter on the desk. Why on earth was the dowager corresponding with her papa? Why would he write to the dowager, and why wouldn't he have told Harmony he was?

But the least likely people corresponded over the most benign things. She herself had begun an avid correspondence with Mr. Michael Thomas Burgermeister, an author and scholar of ancient history. He too had visited the old Roman wall at Newcastle, and numerous other grand sites in England, Scotland, and Wales. His letters painted vivid pictures of the various locales, and detailed a level of historical knowledge that astonished her. She enjoyed his letters immensely, enjoyed everything about them except that she had to keep them a secret from her husband.

She wasn't sure she *had* to, but somehow, from the start, she did. Now that they'd exchanged so very many letters she came to realize it was perhaps improper. Not that the man wrote anything impolite. He was a gentleman of advanced years, and starchy as anything. He was working on a new book, a companion to his last work *The Culture of Ancient Greece During the Bronze Age*, and he had asked her, as the Duchess of Courtland, to be a patron of his studies. Or rather, to help finance a research expedition to several ancient Greek sites. At some point she would have to ask Court about it, for the sum of money Mr. Burgermeister asked for, while reasonable, was not one she could disburse without someone noticing.

But she didn't ask yet, for she didn't want her husband to make her end the correspondence, and there was already too much tension between them of late. She didn't know what to expect tonight. She thought, with a kind of sick feeling, that she could win her husband's approval in one area anyway. She could please his physical natures and—oh, she prayed—become pregnant with his heir.

Chapter Seventeen: No Easy Answers

A winter storm arrived during dinner, pelting the windows with fat drops of rain and gusting winds, making a tense meal even more uncomfortable. Harmony could only bring herself to look at her husband twice, and both times the candlelight lent his face a severe air that made her chest go tight. The dowager sat across from her, glaring like a gargoyle.

Perhaps it was the dark storm that made Harmony feel melancholy, or the dowager's hidden pain, or her husband's grave looks, but she thought if she stayed at dinner one second more she might never stop crying, or she might run screaming from the house and ruin everything forever. Perhaps that was her fear—that her next mistake, inevitably looming, would be the last straw, the disaster from which there would be no return. Then she would have forevermore a cold marriage, a humiliating existence upon the fringes of life, being merely tolerated by those who moved around her.

She excused herself from the table, hiding the anxiety that choked her. She retreated to her room to wait for her husband, allowing herself to be fussed over by Mrs. Redcliff, who put her into pretty, sheer things His Grace had ordered from Paris. Harmony felt like an imposter in the delicate garments. If only she could give him an heir...

Above all, she must continue to pass muster in his bed, even if it gave her a fraught, uneasy feeling to lie with a man who'd become such a stranger to her. She must be warm and welcoming. Enticing. *I will not allow you to lie beneath me and be distant.*

Mrs. Redcliff left her in her grand bedroom chamber, the dim space going bright now and again with a flash of lightning. Thunder rumbled the flower vases and the very panes of glass in the windows. She walked to the largest window and looked out at the garden lashed with raindrops, her mind wandering until she heard his knock. He opened the door and entered, imposing as ever in his dressing gown. She remembered the first time she'd seen him this way, in private, a virile male arriving to lie with her. She'd felt the same type of panic she felt now.

His eyes fixed on her, dark in the low light. She jumped at a sudden crack of thunder as he crossed the room.

"Come away from the window," he chided. "The storm."

She let him lead her over by the bed. He smelled faintly of after-dinner wine and fresh soap. His hair was mussed as if he'd recently raked his hands through it. A strong pulse beat in the hollow of his neck where the dressing gown crossed into a "v." Why she noticed these things, she didn't know. His knuckles felt warm as he drew them down the length of her cheek. Then he cupped her chin and rested his head beside hers, leaving a whisper of a kiss against her ear.

Just like that, her body turned traitor to the warnings in her mind and warmed with an excitement that wasn't to be controlled. When he touched her with that needful look in his gaze, she melted into nothing for him. Nothing and everything. Whatever he wanted.

"Court..." she whispered. She didn't know what to say then. *How you frighten me. Can you fix things between us? I hope so.*

He, too, looked as if he was unsure of what to say, and so he kissed her, sweet loving kisses that progressed to an embrace as intense as the evening's storm. Through the tumultuous joining of their mouths, she clung to the lapels of his gown until he shed it, and then she clung to the hard planes of his chest, to the familiar shape of him. So much power.

He was all powerful now, his thick male member rising before him. He pushed back her robe, letting it fall to the floor, and regarded her in her sheer nightgown, his gaze hot with hunger. Her nipples tightened beneath the gauzy fabric. His arm came around her, bracing her, while the other traced those wanton peaks. Shooting, tingling desire arced through her body, making her tremble, making her knees go weak. She believed she would have fallen if he hadn't held her like a trapped, wild creature in his arms.

His jutting length pressed against the front of her, a pulsing reminder of what he would do to her. His magic. His mastery. The place between her thighs where she received him grew wet and ready without conscious thought. She breathed a small sound of lust, of surrender, a sound he answered with a baring of his teeth. He pulled her to the bed and sat on the edge of it, and began to draw her down over his lap. She stiffened, the erotic spell broken. Now she felt scared.

"No," he said. "Don't." He was telling her not to rebel, not to resist him. He looked kind but intent on his purpose. From their very first night as husband and wife he had been clear what he'd require of her. Still, it took all her willpower to bend her frame over his lap and give herself up to his desires. With a soft sound of approval, he pushed up the hem of her gown and bared her bottom. Cool air was replaced by the heat of his stroking, caressing palm. His other hand smoothed over her shoulders and rested there, calming her.

She moaned, and she realized it was from anticipation, not fear. This was not like the trip to his father's dark study. This was not punishment, but a nurturing interaction they shared. Her hips pressed against the hard foundation of his thighs, seeking she knew not what. Relief. Sexual pleasure. His palm slid down, his fingers exploring her until he found the sensitive button he sought.

"Oh," Harmony cried. Before his skilled touches could tip her over into that shattering place where the world stood still, he stopped his manipulations and landed a hard spank on her bottom. She jumped at the stinging contact—and arched back for more of it. He spanked her again, and again, leisurely smacks that spoke more of enjoyment than discipline. In between, he would again shift his palm down to torment her in that throbbing spot. She lost all sense of propriety and ladylike behavior and groaned like an animal. He didn't stop until she felt heated and tingling all over, and eager to receive him between her thighs.

They both jumped at a sharp clap of thunder. She turned up to him, needing to be in his arms. His expression was so fond, his eyes soft, and his lips...

Before she knew what was happening she was pulled up in his lap and kissed with ardent fervor. She could feel his masculine length against her belly as he lifted her gown over her head, tossing it away. They were naked together, hot and wanting. He turned with her, dumped her off his lap and down on the bed, coming over her with his long legs parting hers.

"I want you," he whispered. "God save me, I want you so badly."

He mounted her with one great thrust and filled her until she shuddered. She was so wrought up from his touches, his spanking, that this sudden deep possession ignited her. She grasped his arms, spreading her legs wider and begging for him to continue on, harder and faster. With a growl he pulled out of her. Before she could complain, he turned her onto her hands and knees and drove into her again, this time from behind. He pounded into her, and while she was not at all sure this was a polite and natural way of lovemaking, she didn't care. She felt hot shame and excitement as he reached down and parted the lips of her sex.

His pace slowed and became an almost sinuous perversion while his fingertips moved in accord with the erratic movements of her hips. He exhausted her with pleasure, with the intrusion of his phallus stretching her and leaving her again and again. When she arrived at her long-sought peak, she cried out from the sheer force of it. Rain pounded against the windows, an echo of the tumult shaking her limbs. She contracted around him as he bucked against her, his hands clamped on her shoulders, pushing her down even as her body seemed to hover in waves of pleasure. When she calmed and came back to her senses, he was there, right there, cradling her close against the broad warmth of his chest.

"Beautiful Harmony," he said against her cheek. "How you please me."

She ducked her head into the shelter of his neck. "Court..." She paused, gathering her courage. *Please accept me. Please love me as much as I love you.* She believed she loved him. At the very least, she needed him, even if everything seemed confused in the light of day.

"What is it you wished to say, my dear?"

"Do you love me?" she blurted out in anxious misery.

He stroked her cheek, once, twice, a fleeting touch that made her lift her head and meet his gaze. "God help me, Harmony. There are times I love you more than I can bear."

Just like that, he didn't seem a stranger anymore.

* * * * *

Court lingered, reluctant to leave her. He held her close until her chest rose and fell in deep sleep, until the storm outside blew over and silence reigned, and still he stayed and watched her. Wretched puzzle, this marriage. How could they be so connected in this way, and so frightfully disconnected in every way else?

He looked around her room in the candlelight. Everything appeared in order as it had always been. There were no clues, no easy answers to the problems between them. He eased from the bed, drew on his dressing gown and went to stand at the window, staring out at the wet grounds of the garden. Spring in England. It would come no matter what, bringing the cursed Courtland ball and the social season. If he couldn't fix their marriage, he wasn't sure they'd survive.

He crossed from the bedroom into his wife's adjoining sitting room, and prowled around and touched her things as if they might give him some idea how to mend their rift. He looked over her book collection, which was growing at an alarming rate. She needed more shelves to hold them all. Very well. He would have more added.

At the very least he could do that. Give her things. Dresses, jewels, bookshelves and books, horses and fancy bonnets and a grand old house around her. Material things. Despite his intentions to the contrary, he could envision his marriage becoming like so many of his friends'. An economic transaction, a lifeless and loveless arrangement only serving to secure the all-important family line. Harmony had not conceived yet, though. Why?

He paused at her desk, seeing a shuffle of papers in a pile. Notes, perhaps, on her most recent historical interests? He sat down to see what she was studying, what had captured her attention after her flurry of interest in Mongol civilizations. He did not find notes in her scrawled hand, however, but a letter.

Dear Michael,

What a pleasure to receive your most recent note. I look forward to them with a fervor you cannot believe. I am glad to hear you are safely returned and with so much of interest to share.

I have given thought to your request for a meeting but I'm not sure it is possible.

The letter ended there, still in progress, a note she had written to another man perhaps moments before he arrived at her bedroom to lie with her. He remembered her pensive, faraway look as she stood at the window. "Not sure it is possible" indeed. With shaking fingers he opened

185

her desk drawers, finding other letters in the top left one. Stacks of letters, all from this "Michael." Mr. Michael Thomas Burgermeister. Why did that name sound familiar?

How busy she had been, to have such packets of letters. *I look forward to them with a fervor you cannot believe.* When had she begun this acquaintance with her prolific Mr. Burgermeister? Perhaps before she and Court had even wed. He took the entire stack of letters and crossed back into his wife's bedroom.

"Wake up, Harmony," he said, nudging her shoulder. How innocent and sweet she could look in sleep, the little deceiver. All this time she'd been withdrawing from him, he'd blamed himself for being an inadequate husband, for being too strict and unbending to suit her, while she'd been writing letters to some mister who lived in Brook Street—the street where she used to live. "Harmony, awaken at once," he said as she stretched beneath the sheets. In *his* bed, beneath *his* sheets.

She blinked and raised her head. "What is it? What's the matter?"

He threw the pile of letters on the bed before her. She sat up, gathering them before they could slide to the floor. "What on earth?"

Court made a sound that betrayed far too much of his pain. "You won't pretend you don't know what these are."

She looked up at him, her brows gathered in those little thinking lines he used to find so sweet. "I know what they are. I don't know why you have dumped them on me at this hour of the night."

"Pardon me for not waiting until morning to confront you about your paramour."

She burst into laughter. "Mr. Burgermeister? My paramour?"

By God, he did not enjoy being laughed at. "You called him Michael in your letters," he said, pointing at the messy stack. "The one you were writing mentioned a meeting."

"You read my letters? What were you doing? Snooping about my desk?"

"Yes," he snapped, annoyed that she would attack him when she was the one who had behaved—yet again—so poorly. "Yes, I was trying to discover what it is that has so set you against me. Now I understand that another man has secured a place in your affections."

"My affections? Mr. Burgermeister is a scholar, a historian, not some paramour of mine! And if you wish to know what has set me against you, you are exhibiting a prime example of it right now. Will you always expect the worst of me?"

"A scholar?" Court scowled down at the pile of letters. "He has an exorbitant amount of time to write, for one engrossed in studies." A confusion of facts in his mind snapped together. "Michael Thomas Burgermeister. That damn book Lightmore brought you."

"I'd been meaning to explain—"

"Has he been ferrying notes for you two? Is Lightmore involved in this?"

"Involved in what?" Harmony sat up straighter, grasping the sheets to her chest. "We've been corresponding by post, and that is the extent of it. I've hidden nothing. Well, not intentionally." Her lips pressed into a sullen line. "I didn't realize I was supposed to apply to you for permission to write to those of my acquaintance."

"A *man* of your acquaintance," he pointed out. "You cannot imagine it was appropriate to carry on this sort of relationship without my approval." He gestured to the packets on the bed. "There are fifty or more letters here."

"Surely, not so many," she said, looking down at the pile. "I don't believe I've ever written fifty letters to anybody."

"Well, you haven't many friends, so why would you?"

He made a warning sound. "Do not test my patience, Harmony. You should be begging my forgiveness."

"For writing to a friend? Did you read them? We only spoke of Greece, of ancient history. Mr. Burgermeister is planning an expedition and he hoped I might become a patron of his. You've plenty of money. I was going to ask you about it."

"Ask me to finance this man's travels?"

"His historical expedition. It's a worthy endeavor. He is planning to go to Athens and Delphi, and Peloponnesia to study ancient villages and ruins. It is too costly without the aid of charitable patrons. We spoke of nothing inappropriate."

"If that's so, why the secrecy? You hid these letters from me."

"They were not hidden," she said. "The latest note was on my desk. Before you accuse and shame me, why don't you read them?" She picked up a handful and flung them at him. "Read them all if you wish, if I'm not to have any privacy or trust."

"Trust?" He waved a hand at the mess on the floor. "So many letters to a gentleman not even of my acquaintance. Don't you understand why this discomposes me? Who knows of these letters, of this correspondence between you? Lightmore? He will tell everybody—"

"Is that all you ever care about? What everyone will think? Meanwhile I cannot converse with another person on a topic I'm interested in?"

"This isn't conversing on a topic. This is a prodigious collection of letters, in which you address him familiarly as Michael!"

"In later notes I did, because we became so…familiar." She seemed to realize, at last, the impropriety that upset him. The blush deepened across her cheeks. "But we spoke of nothing but history. Niceties and news now and again, perhaps, as friends will do. But nothing torrid or in poor taste. We've done nothing to be ashamed of!"

"Haven't you? How different our morals are. And I daresay you will feel ashamed indeed when Mr. Lightmore and his foppish group spread rumors of your *affaire de lettres* with this thrice damned 'historical scholar.' The truth doesn't matter, only the gossip. You of all people should realize that."

"Oh, I realize about gossip, and I don't care. I am sick of it!" She threw another handful of letters at him. "Burn them, then. Do what you will. I will never speak to him again if it pleases Your Grace, and he shall never go to Greece or anywhere. I hate this. I hate these letters. I hate society and gossips, and your accusations. I hate this horrible house and I hate that I ever met you. I hate being your wife. I hate you! Now get out and let me sleep if you will not let me be happy. At least give me peace."

He could not say precisely what made him snap. Hurt feelings? Jealousy? How small of him. Perhaps he was only incensed by the boldness of her tirade. "I don't think I'll give you peace, Harmony. Not if you will persist in behaving like a disordered child." He crossed to her and pulled her from the bed, grabbing her nightgown from the nearby chair. "If you cannot be reasoned with, if you cannot behave as a thoughtful and respectable wife, I will not treat you as one."

She fought him as he worked to pull her garment into place. He felt ridiculous grappling with his wife but if he released her now, she would not respect his authority. He tightened his hand on her arm and gave her a sharp shake.

"Enough. Your behavior alarms me."

"Then don't pull at me." She gazed up at him with tears in her eyes. "Why are you always so angry with me?"

"I'm not angry," he lied. "Just resigned. Come."

She clung to the bedpost. "Where are we going?"

"To the place where misbehaving wives learn lessons. Your screaming and tantruming has pushed me beyond my limit." He kicked at the letters covering the floor. "Beyond my limit of patience and far beyond my limit of understanding."

"No," she wailed. "Please, no."

"Yes," he said, peeling her fingers from the bedpost. "And this time, hopefully, I will teach you a lesson you won't forget."

* * * * *

Harmony thought if she fought him hard enough, someone would intervene on her behalf. She cried out for the dowager when he dragged her past her rooms. She cried out to the footmen and servants they passed, but each and every one of them pretended not to hear her. At last, tired of her struggles, he lifted her and carried her in the bands of his arms. "The more you fight me," he said through gritted teeth, "the greater your penalty."

By the time he crashed through the study doors and released her, he seemed in a fury indeed. If she could have gone back then and done things differently, she would have. He was going to punish her, probably more harshly than he would have, because she'd so infuriated him. Now she'd also embarrassed him in front of the dowager and his servants. She'd behaved horribly.

As usual.

She couldn't help it. That must be clear to him now. Nothing he could do to her here would change the fact that she was impossible. "Just leave me alone," she said, turning on him and backing away. "You can't fix me. I don't want you to *fix me*." Her voice rose to a scream.

"I *can* fix you, and I am going to fix you," he returned in a stern and cool voice. "By whatever method it takes. Come with me."

He took her by the arm and dragged her over to the rack of rattan canes. "If you are so fond of being punished, choose one."

"I am not fond of being punished, and I will not choose one," she cried.

"Very well."

He promptly chose the stoutest one when she might have chosen a less threatening option. *Stupid, stupid girl.* As he walked her back over toward the desk, she broke away from him and ran. The cane clattered to the floor behind her as she bolted for the door, but he caught her long before she reached it, hauling her back against his front. He put a hand at her neck, not to choke her but to immobilize her. His voice was low and intent at her ear.

"Listen to me, dearest. You will submit to this punishment, willing or not. If you will not submit under your own power, I shall enlist the help of two strong footmen to hold you until I'm done. Which would you prefer?"

She shook her head against his palm. "You wouldn't."

With a violent sound of anger, he dragged her toward the door. "Once I call them," he warned, "I will not give you the chance to reconsider."

Harmony could not bear the ignominy of witnesses. It was bad enough to be punished again like this, but to be held down by servants? She dragged her heels, shaking her head. "No, please. I will... I will submit. Please don't call for anyone."

He hauled her back toward the desk. Harmony fought him, only because she was tired of being dragged around. "Release me, then. Stop it! I will walk."

"You had your chance to obey me with dignity earlier. Now you'll be treated like the headstrong termagant you are."

Moments later, she found herself bent over the horrible desk, gripping the hard edge of it. Her skirts were swept up, Court's hand braced at her back.

"I hate you," she screamed.

"I'm sure you do."

Whack! The pain was so much worse than she'd remembered, so hot and cruel.

"No," she wailed, arching off the desk. She must escape this. She must...

"Shall I fetch the footmen?" he asked.

He would. His voice communicated complete and utter inflexibility. He was angry and cold. "No, but...please..." she whimpered. "Please, I can't bear this."

"You will hold the edge of the desk. Each time you let go I will add five additional strokes to your punishment."

"But..." She could barely speak through her sobs. "How... How many will there be?"

"As many as you need."

What did that mean? His arm lifted again and Harmony braced for the pain. *Whack!* She held onto the desk for dear life. How was she to survive this? Each stroke was followed by an awful pause during which her bottom continued to throb in agony. Then another would come, and another. She wished she could go numb but the pain got worse, not better.

"Stop it!" she finally screamed, kicking back at him.

"If you do not keep your legs down and in position, you will be caned on the backs of your calves and the bottoms of your feet."

She went limp again and sobbed into the dusty desktop. Another stroke, and another, as she cried out in helpless agony. "You are killing me."

"I am disciplining you," he said, tapping the cane against the heated pain of her cheeks. "I'm trying to, at any rate."

"I'll write to my father. He will come for me."

"It's my right as your husband to discipline you. The fact that you aren't yet understanding the connection between your actions and this punishment compels me to continue."

"I understand." She jerked at a particularly vicious stripe. "I understand, but this is too much."

"On the contrary, I sense it is not enough."

Three more strokes, four. Oh, when would he stop? *Think, Harmony, how to make him stop?* "I'm sorry," she said over and over. "I'm sorry."

"I don't believe you. I think you simply wish this painful punishment at an end." *Whack!* "By tomorrow you will be back to your usual behavior, doing as you please with no thought to propriety or discipline."

In her hysteria, in her panic to escape, some glimmer of understanding penetrated her brain. The only way to make him stop would be to accept his discipline, whether it was fair or not. Perhaps the letters weren't enough to warrant this type of whipping, but the way she'd screamed at him was.

She truly cried then, cathartic, heartbroken tears for mistakes made and for the bleak future of her life. She couldn't change who she was, couldn't change her impulsive nature. Therefore, this pain and suffering would become all too familiar in weeks and years to come. She sobbed until she choked from it, but she held herself still beneath the fire of her husband's discipline, enduring the pain of each blow. She felt the hand on her back lose some of its tension. After one more measured stroke to her burning posterior, the cane ceased to fall.

Harmony waited, frozen, dreading more but resigned to it. She'd learned her lesson. The lesson was that each time she earned it, she would experience another session like this. Her husband's discipline would rule her life, and she had better get used to it.

"Stand up."

She wrenched herself upright, letting her skirts fall down of their own accord. She was afraid to rub her aching bottom or adjust herself or do anything without his permission for fear of angering him again. His steady gaze prompted the abject apology she knew she was supposed to deliver.

"I am sorry for my disrespectful and outrageous behavior. I will not... I will not..."

"I will not challenge your authority again," he suggested curtly when she got stuck. "I will not write to gentlemen without your knowledge. Repeat it."

"I will not challenge your authority again. I will not write to gentlemen without your knowledge," she parroted, not quite able to keep the bitterness from her voice.

He stood for long moments staring at her. "I hope you meant the things you just said. I hope they were not empty promises because I will hold you to them. You will be punished if you engage in these behaviors again."

She bit hard on her tongue. "Yes, sir."

"Why do I punish you, Harmony?"

"To instill discipline in me, Your Grace."

His face hardened at the terse honorific, but he let it pass without comment. He lashed her with cold words instead. "If this marriage cannot be based on trust and respect, *wife*, it will be based on discipline."

He said nothing whatsoever about love.

Chapter Eighteen:
Rescue

Harmony fought nightmares, sobbing into her pillow. Nightmares of Court's angry words and reproachful stare. Nightmares of his father's study, of being bent over the desk again and caned on her bottom while being lectured in the most cool and biting way.

Standing still for the strikes of the cane was not even the worst thing. Having her bottom—and her soul—bared for punishment, the humiliation of his hand forcing her down when she tried to struggle away. No, those were not the most heartbreaking things. The most heartbreaking thing was his contempt for her, and her reciprocal contempt for him. She hated what had become of their marriage. She hated that study. She hated that desk. She hated her husband for not trusting her and loving her.

She slept late the next day and kept to her bed, reading and occasionally repositioning herself so she couldn't feel the soreness of her bottom. There weren't many marks but there were enough to make her feel a continual shame.

Mrs. Redcliff knocked on the door and entered, dropping a curtsy. "Your Grace, will you dress for dinner?"

Harmony shook her head after a moment. She could not make it through dinner, not tonight. She could not sit across the table from him and respond to his small talk. She could not tolerate an hour of his mother's arch looks and Mrs. Lyndon's vicious prattle. "Kindly tell His Grace that I'm not feeling well enough for dinner."

The lady's maid flicked a glance over at the side table. "You haven't touched your tea tray. Is there anything I can bring that would be more appetizing?"

Harmony looked back at her book. "I am not hungry."

The kindly woman flushed and busied herself straightening things that didn't really need to be straightened. A few minutes later she returned to Harmony in entreaty. "If you do not eat, you will not fit in your lovely dresses."

Harmony shrugged. "He will buy me more."

"Shall I help you into your nightclothes then?"

Harmony forced a smile to bring her some ease. "I am still in my nightclothes from yesterday, since I am so lazy."

Mrs. Redcliff's hands shook as she trimmed the candles at the bedside. "Your Grace, if you don't wish to undress in front of me for fear I will see... For fear... I have already seen the marks, Your Grace. Forgive me, but—"

Harmony held out a hand, silencing the maid's words. "Don't fret, Redcliff. He believed I deserved it. He is my husband and..." She made a face. "I suppose it is within his rights to punish me if he feels it's warranted."

The woman set her mouth in a hard, firm line, letting her expression tell Harmony exactly how she felt about that.

"Perhaps you should send word downstairs that I will not be at dinner," Harmony suggested, to give the hovering woman something constructive to do. She bustled off muttering, and Harmony sighed in exhaustion. It was bad enough to deal with her own frayed emotions without Mrs. Redcliff storming about.

Harmony wished she had her mother.

She even wished she had her father or her brother. Anyone to accept her and love her unconditionally, just as she was. Awkward, impulsive Harmony Barrett. The merest thought of her childhood home across town in Brook Street nearly brought her to tears.

Mrs. Redcliff returned with a tray of milk and sandwiches, and Harmony ate a little to placate her. She was just finishing when a sharp knock sounded. Without waiting for an invitation, her husband entered and stopped inside the door, dressed for dinner in his usual starched finery. She sat up a little straighter, waiting to see what he would say, waiting to see whether his present mood was as prickly as hers.

He looked at Mrs. Redcliff. "Leave us."

Yes, prickly. The maid's spine snapped to stiffness as she faced him, and for a moment Harmony feared she would redress him. To her vast relief, she drew up her skirts instead and took her leave. As she exited through the dressing room, she shot Harmony a fortifying look.

Brave Mrs. Redcliff. If her husband were to dismiss her for such insolence, there would be nothing Harmony could do to stay his hand. That was the main lesson he had driven home the night before—that he had all the power in this marriage, and she had none of it. What she intended by her words and actions had no meaning to him. Everything she did or did not do would be reflected through the lens of his will, and the lens of the greater society.

Oh, she had warned the man, warned him clearly so many months ago. She had told him what a trial she would make of their marriage. Now he surely understood what she'd meant, but it was too late for both of them. She had begged him not to marry her but he had insisted. Now it had come to this. She was his prisoner. His burden. A wife he could not fix and could not love.

He turned from the dressing room door, regarding her with the full force of his gaze. "How long are you planning to hide here and sulk?"

Harmony closed her hands on the edge of the sheets. She would not let him goad her into more misbehavior. "I am not sulking," she said without rancor. "I do not feel well."

"It is time for dinner."

She didn't move from her place in the bed, not even when he crossed the room at a brisk pace to pick up the book on her nightstand and look at the cover. *Great Disasters in the Age of Modern Politics*. He sighed and put it back down.

"You have a new interest in politics?"

"I have a new interest in the inability of people to get along," she said.

His gaze snapped to hers, then traveled down to the bodice of her nightgown. "Did you even dress today? Did you rise once from your bed?"

She yanked the sheets up to her neck, feeling bared by his stare. "I told you, I am not well."

He crossed to her, making a show of feeling her brow. "You are not well, or your pride has been injured?" He put his fingers beneath her chin and raised her face to meet his. "Did you learn nothing last night? This immature, self-centered behavior greatly disturbs me. I will not tolerate it."

"Will you take me to the study again?" She flung the question at him with false bravado, pushing his hand away.

"Perhaps," he said. "If I think you need it. In this battle of wills, you shall come out the loser. That, at least, I hope you understand."

I hate you. She had screamed it at him last night, and his hard, cold authority only exacerbated the feeling. *I hate you. I hate you. Where is the Court I love?*

"You can take me to the study a thousand times," she said, "and I will still be me."

"And I will still be me," he replied. "You behaved badly and I punished you."

"You were unjust. I did nothing wrong."

"I read the letters, Harmony. Every one of them. They were not lurid but they were inappropriate. You are a married woman and he is a man."

"He is an *old* man fixed on history and travel. How silly you are."

Court drew himself up tight, as if he were restraining some very unpleasant words. He let out his breath and spoke in a steady voice. "If you cannot recognize the fault in your actions, I fear you may be beyond redemption." His eyes left her, looked past her with a new indifference that devastated her. "Stay here in your rooms if you like." He made a dismissive gesture and started toward the door.

"I want to go home." She didn't yell the words, or sob them—although she felt like sobbing. She spoke them with the same quiet and cool tone he used. When his back stiffened and he turned to her, she said again, "I want to go home. Right now."

"Right now? Impulsive as ever. You are truly beyond the pale."

"I want to go home," she repeated stubbornly.

"To Hampshire? I don't think so."

"To Brook Street. Father is still in town. He will take me in." She had no idea if that was true, but she said it anyway. "I will go there this very night."

196

His gaze was glacial. "Will you? I hope you are prepared to walk."

She shivered under his regard, remembering another time and place when she felt helpless, furious and thwarted. When she had indeed been desperate enough to walk. She could tell from the look on his face that he remembered too. "This time," he said, "rest assured I will not rescue you from your folly."

She sat straighter in the bed, blinking back tears. "It is not so far to Brook Street as it was to Newcastle."

His expression frightened her. "Do not attempt it," he bit out. The door slammed behind him, the starkly echoing bang hurting her heart much more than her ears.

* * * * *

Court arrived to dinner a short while later with his wife's words still echoing in his head. *How silly you are. How silly.*

Silly indeed, to have such bruised pride over the words of a sulking wife. If she had called him *brutal* or *unfeeling*, or *horrid* or *mean* or *cruel*, he could have coped with it, but *silly* cut him too close to the bone. Since the day he met her, he had had a sinking feeling of becoming ever more ridiculous. To be called a silly man by Harmony, the silliest, most unreasonable creature in the world, was very nearly an unbearable blow.

Even more unbearable—she wanted to go home.

She would not go home. He'd sent a man to alert the gatehouse that she was not to call up carriage nor horse for her own use without his permission. It was petty, yes, and the servants undoubtedly thought him a tyrant. He was becoming a tyrant, because of her. Not just a tyrant, but a jealous, abusive husband.

Oh, God.

He had abused his wife.

He could try to excuse his behavior the night before by saying it was his right, by saying she deserved it for being disrespectful to him and corresponding with another gentleman behind his back. None of those excuses rang true to him though, not in his heart. He had lashed out at Harmony because his feelings were hurt and because he feared losing her. Now he wondered if he'd lost her for good.

He moaned inwardly, or perhaps he moaned aloud, since his mother and Mrs. Lyndon looked up at him with curious glances. The footmen took forever to serve, or maybe time was taking forever now that

Harmony wanted to leave him. Of all things, he had not expected her to give up.

As soon as the last uniformed coattail swished out of the room, his mother turned on him.

"Where is the duchess this evening?"

Court picked up his spoon and hunched over the bisque. "She is unwell."

"Unwell or unhappy?" his mother persisted.

He frowned into his soup. "Both, perhaps. Does it really matter?"

Silence spun out across the table. The soup, though rich and flavorful, tasted like ashes in his mouth. His mother glared at him from beneath bunched eyebrows.

"I did not think you a foolish man, Courtland."

He paused as Mrs. Lyndon's spoon clattered onto her plate.

Court blinked and began to eat again with renewed focus. It was bad enough for Harmony to think him silly, but his mother too?

"Do you think you will fix her by breaking her?" she prodded when it became clear he would not engage her in this conversation.

"It is none of your business."

"I have had letters of her father," the dowager said. "I don't know what to tell him anymore."

It was Court's turn to fumble his spoon. He put it beside his plate and stared at his mother. "You have been in correspondence with Lord Morrow?"

"Ladies will engage in letter writing," she said with a subtle note of reproach. "It is one of the few pastimes allowed to us."

"One of the few," Mrs. Lyndon parroted, with her eternal head bobbing.

Blast. Of course the old women would know everything that had gone on the last pair of days, from his wife's misbegotten letters to Court's ignoble and jealous reaction.

"Will you take her side?" he asked. "That is certainly a change."

"There can be no sides in this," said his mother. "If we are to have our heir—"

"Courtland will have its heir," he snapped. "Courtland will continue on, if only from your heavy-handed insistence that nothing else matters."

The old woman's eyes went wide as Mrs. Lyndon feigned a swoon. "Whatever do you mean by that exclamation?" asked the dowager.

"I mean that—" The footmen entered with the main course of roast quail and vegetables, plunging all of them into tense silence. As soon as they left, Court dug into the small, tasty corpse, feeling destructive in the extreme. For long minutes there was only the sound of utensils clicking on bone.

"Lord Morrow believes his daughter unhappy in marriage," his mother finally said, eyeing the carnage on his dinner plate. "I have endeavored to convince him otherwise, but now I must say—"

"What? That we are unhappy? Were you and father ever happy together? Was I a happy and joyful child?" He stabbed a fork in the air. "It is the Courtland legacy. Refined misery. Why should things change now?"

"Well," Mrs. Lyndon gasped.

"Because," his mother said, speaking over her friend. "I did not have a choice in your father. You had a choice. I thought, when you chose her, that you had made the correct choice. That you would find rare happiness in marriage. Now I am not so sure."

Court stared at the herb-seasoned *haricots verts* beside his quail, befuddled by his mother's words. "You did not wish me to marry Harmony. You wept and sobbed. Don't you remember? You took to your bed."

"It was a shock."

"What changed, that you will support her now?"

His mother poked at the bones on her plate. "You changed, my son. For a short time, anyway. She made you happy...but not anymore?"

She was fishing for information, practically pleading for it. What had gone wrong? If he could explain it to his mother and the gawking Mrs. Lyndon, he would not be so miserable himself. He rubbed his forehead and squelched the urge to run like a coward from the room.

"I—I cannot say what has gone wrong," he said. "She wants to leave."

His mother stiffened. "You cannot let her leave."

He shook his head, burning with shame. Guilt. "I thought we could have a good marriage. I wished for her happiness." *Make a wish...* Why couldn't he have made one damn wish for her? One wish for them?

Why did she want to *leave?*

"I wished for more children," his mother said in the silence. "Not because you were not a perfect son, but because it was the way of the world. A man wants many sons for peace of mind. I often thought, as you suffered—"

"I did not suffer, mother."

"As you *suffered*," she insisted, "that if only I had been able to bear more children, you would have had a lighter burden. I prayed on my knees to conceive, thinking of your large, solemn gaze and all the weight of responsibility on your small back."

"Mother," Court said, rubbing his eyes. "I beg you. Please."

"I also tried to be perfect for your father. It never mattered. He had no use for me and went about with hundreds of other women. Oh, I knew," she added as Court turned to her in shock. "What could I do about it but grow old and bitter and nurse a vast emptiness in my heart? But you, my son. You and Harmony had love. I recognized it, though I was never fortunate enough to experience it. I was angry. Jealous. I wanted you to fail as your father and I failed, but that was the emptiness in my heart speaking."

"Oh, Mother," Court said. He had no idea what this confession cost her, nor what to say in response.

"The two of you had love," she went on, "and you are destroying it. I tried to destroy it with my own treatment of your wife." She shook her head, her face drawn with regret. "I thought you could fix her and she would still love you. Now I'm not so sure. But I am sure of one thing. It is more important to love and be loved."

"More important than what?"

"Everything else."

Mrs. Lyndon heaved a quiet sob, swiping at tears, but his mother's eyes were clear with the staunch spirit that defined her. "Courtland, I'm sorry for the ways I failed you. I wish things might have been different, but they weren't. Your marriage to Harmony, like my misfortune in bearing children, is something which cannot be changed. But you can make the most of things as they are, as your father and I made the most of your qualities and talents. You have been a resplendent son," said his mother with quiet affection. "I daresay if you give Harmony a chance to prove herself, she will make you a resplendent wife."

"But...I've been trying... I've been giving her chances," he said in a choked voice.

"You've been trying to force things, out of fear, or worry," his mother said. "We did the same to you and I think you suffered greatly for it. The sins of the father should not be repeated by the son."

"What do I do?" he asked over the sound of Mrs. Lyndon's sniffling. "I want her to be happy, but she won't be happy...none of us will be happy if she's not accepted by the *ton*."

"She is a very perceptive girl." His mother nodded and put down her silverware. "I think with a little more time, and a little less pressure, she may discover her place in our world." Her lips tightened into a small smile. "I have come to know your wife rather well over the course of my recuperation. I have some vague hope for her eventual success."

It was a resounding commendation coming from his mother. Court excused himself to the sounds of Mrs. Lyndon's emotional exhalations. He went in search of his wife, to apologize, to beg her forgiveness, only to be brought up short by a stammering maid. He pushed past her into Harmony's rooms. Her bed was empty, made up and smoothed over to perfection as if she hadn't been frowning at him from there a short time ago.

"What do you mean, she is not here?"

Mrs. Redcliff wrung her hands and curtsied for the tenth time. "As I said, Your Grace, she wished to go home. She will doubtless return when she has visited with her family."

"Doubtless," he said. "But how will she reach them without horse or carriage?"

The maidservant paled. "How else would she go?"

Good God, not this business again. "How long ago did she leave?" He knew the grooms would not counteract his orders, even for a prettily begging duchess. "What did she wear? Did she take money?"

"She took nothing, Your Grace," said the maid, curtsying again, and then again. "She dressed as if to go calling and..." She curtsied again. "It was half an hour ago, perhaps. She took only her reticule and bonnet."

"Redcliff, if you curtsy again I will break your knees." His heart pounded and his blood thundered in his ears. His wife, on foot at night in London! Heading for Brook Street, for God's sake. "Tell me what color dress and cloak your mistress wore when she left."

"Deep purple with lavender lace and insets. And a striped bonnet, with her silk aubergine cloak."

"Come with me."

She curtsied once again and tried to pass it off as a temporary loss of balance. He ignored her and clipped down the stairs, taking up his hat and gloves in the entryway. His wife was going to be the death of him— if he didn't kill her first. He turned back to the lady's maid.

"Pack Her Grace's things and let the head housekeeper know we will be leaving tonight for Hertfordshire." He turned to the butler as the man helped him into his cloak. "I want every man in the household on foot looking for Her Grace. Not just in the direction of Brook Street, but every direction from St. James. She cannot have gone far."

"Yes, Your Grace," the man said with a bow.

"Your— Your Grace?" The maid's voice trembled. "Will I be accompanying Her Grace to the ducal seat?"

Court didn't have time for the maid's fretting, not now. "You will remain here. If you are needed, you will be called for."

"But Your Grace—" she called after him as he swept from the main house.

He waved a hand. "Your mistress will be returned to you in good order."

The butler shut the door on the maid's deep and abject curtsy. These women would all be the death of him. He knew that for a fact above everything else.

* * * * *

Harmony trudged along shadowy lamp-lit streets, pulling her cloak closer around her. If she did not have a talent for getting lost, if she were not so horribly impulsive, she would not be in such a muddle. She knew the streets around Brook Street innately, but these were not those streets. These streets were empty of life, cold and glittering with monumental edifices as grand as the Duke of Courtland's.

She did not belong here. One thing for certain, she would not go back even if she didn't know her way forward. Brook Street was west so she would walk west and eventually reach it, and while her father would be angry at her for leaving her husband, hopefully he would not turn her away. If he did, then what?

She couldn't think about that now. She must walk faster. It was full dark and the risk of her behavior wasn't unknown to her. She was precisely the immature and reckless person her husband reviled, and well she knew it. Why did she never think through things before she did them?

She heard voices and felt panic. She should not be walking alone. Polite women did not do it, not in town and especially not at night. Two men walked toward her deep in conversation, and she did the only thing

202

she could think to do. She hid against the shadow of a building and stood very still.

The men continued by, unaware of her presence. They were not cutthroats or criminals, only gentlemen like Court, smartly turned out in their greatcoats and tall hats, their canes tapping the ground as they walked. She wondered if they were married, if they loved their wives. She made a small sound of misery and one of them turned. His eyes sought the source of the sound and she shrank back in the darkness. What if they addressed her? Should she run away? Walk in her own direction and ignore them?

She held her breath until he turned around and continued to walk with his companion. By God, she could not do this, make her way through London at this hour in a direction she didn't know. But she must. She had defied Court—again. If she slunk back to St. James he would take her to his father's study—again.

She must get home, she must find her way to safety. If she came to a frightening area of town she would change direction and avoid it. As soon as she saw a respectable person, she would inquire of Brook Street. Or hail a ride. Yes, that was the answer. She would hail a hansom cab when she came upon one and direct it to Brook Street. Foolishly, she had quit Court's house without any money, but her father could pay the driver on her arrival.

Once the gentlemen were well away, she set off to walk again, straining to perceive the sounds and lights of more populous streets. After some time, she began to suspect she was going the wrong way altogether. She turned in frustration. Had she been walking an hour? Two hours? Half the night? She felt suffocated by the still darkness, and then she heard the sound of hoof beats.

"Harmony!"

Her name sounded half-curse, half-prayer on her husband's lips. He reined in a few paces from her and she wondered to herself, *Should I face him or run?*

"If you run I will chase you," he said, answering her unspoken question. "What in sorry hell are you about?"

"I am going home. I am going to Brook Street."

His lips tightened and his eyes flashed angrily. "You cannot walk all that way."

"I most certainly can!"

"You can't," he said, swinging off his horse and stalking to her, "because you are headed in the wrong direction. The complete opposite direction, if you must know."

"I wish you would not mock me!" The emotion that had built up for hours erupted in an outburst of tears.

"And I wish you would not defy me." He reached within his coat and produced a square of monogrammed silk, pressing it to her cheeks. "I told you you were not to go home. I told you not to dare attempt it. Why did you leave? Why?"

She stared at him through a blurry haze of tears. "You don't want me anyway. You said so."

"I did not."

"You said I was beyond redemption."

He flung out his hands. "You've done nothing to prove me wrong."

She turned her back on him and started walking. Why had he even come for her? She wiped her eyes and squared her shoulders. "I'm going home, right now, tonight. I don't care what you think about it."

He made an agitated sound and grabbed her. "Curse you, Harmony. You are going the wrong damn way!" He turned her around and stabbed a finger in the opposite direction. "It's that way to Brook Street. If you're going to run away from home, at least do it correctly."

"I'm not running away from home. I'm running *to* home. My home where I can be myself, and do whatever I want."

He shook his head and tightened his hand on her elbow. "Nobody can do whatever they want. You can't run away from your duties, your responsibilities. My entire household is searching for you." He dragged her toward his horse. "Your home is with me now."

"I don't want to go home with you," she sobbed. She pushed at him, although he easily subdued her. "Anyway, you said you wouldn't rescue me this time."

"I am not rescuing you," he said, tossing her onto his stallion and mounting behind her. "I am rescuing us both."

Chapter Nineteen: Revelations

They left London for Hertfordshire within the hour, with four grooms and one hastily-assembled baggage cart trailing behind. Court rode on the seat opposite her, smelling of horse as she smelled of night. They did not converse and he did not touch her, only sprawled out his legs and watched her from beneath his lashes. Harmony wrapped up in her cloak and stared out the window as they left the town behind.

He was taking her to his country home, to Courtland Manor, perhaps to imprison her in its prodigious rock walls. Well, she wasn't sure if it had prodigious rock walls but she'd always pictured it that way. And it was unlikely he would imprison her. Surely gentlemen didn't do that in this day and age.

In truth, she had no idea what he was going to do to her. She just knew it would be bad.

At some point she drowsed and they arrived in full black night to the welcome of a skeleton staff. The house—the palace—seemed a ghastly edifice, with vast walls and towers standing out against the moonlit sky. Inside, the corridors seemed to close upon her as she was turned over to a silent and stone-faced housekeeper.

The woman took her to a large dressing room where Harmony bathed and wrapped up in a nightgown and dressing gown taken from her trunks. The housekeeper and two younger girls unpacked her other items, placing them in armoires and on shelves.

"Please," she said to them. "It is so late. You must leave that until the morning."

"Your things will wrinkle, Your Grace," said the housekeeper with a quick curtsy. "If it pleases you, your sleeping chambers are just through that door."

Harmony did not feel like sleep but she passed through the wide, carved door and closed it behind her. The room was warm with a fire, and someone had set a tray of cakes and tea on a table near the fireplace. She stared at the tray, at the delicate china and gleaming silver, and dropped her head in her hands. What now? How badly was he going to punish her this time? Why was he making her wait until morning, so she had to dread it all night?

"You may eat first or come to bed," said a voice behind her. "It is your choice."

She turned to find her husband lying beneath her bedcovers, propped on one arm watching her. He didn't appear to be wearing clothes.

"Oh," she said. She looked away and sat by the tray feeling the weight of his stare on her. She felt nervous, too breathless to eat or drink. She forced down some sips of tea anyway. Why was he here? Would he punish her now, or...? She stole a glance back at him. No, he was not here to punish her. Why did he want to lie with her tonight, after everything?

The heir, of course. This would continue, this charade, until she gave him what he needed—an heir to carry on his name.

She took one last sip of tea and rose, going to the bed as if to battle. He still watched her, an unfathomable look on his face. She discarded her robe and stopped with her hands on the ribbons of her nightgown. "Do you wish it on or off?" she asked curtly.

"I prefer off, but the choice is yours. And you don't have to lie with me. That is also your choice."

She looked around in confusion. "Where else would I lie?"

He made a huff of a sound and held out a hand. "Come here. Leave it on for now." Once she climbed into the bed, he drew her into his arms. She held herself stiffly, unsure of his mood. "Don't worry," he said. "I understand you haven't the fondest regard for me at the moment. If you cannot endure my caresses, we will merely sleep together."

"You will not...?" Her voice trailed off in a question.

"Force you? I can't imagine any circumstance in which I'd do such a thing."

"What about the heir?"

Court snorted and rolled away from her. "This confounded heir. He's a third person in our marriage. Or rather a fifth, after my mother and the specter of my late father. How crowded our bed has become."

Harmony stared down at the embroidered sheets. "Well..."

He turned toward her again. "I imagine you rode uncomfortably in the carriage. Turn around if you please, so I can see how the marks look today."

She felt sharp, hot shame as he moved her onto her stomach and drew up the skirt of her nightgown. His fingers brushed the tender stripes, raised by his own hand. "I am sorry," he said quietly.

She didn't move. Couldn't move. His apology meant the world to her but what did it really change? Silent tears dropped onto her pillow, creating a spreading ivory stain. His hand slid higher to touch her hips, her waist, her back and shoulders beneath the whisper-soft gown. She wished she understood her feelings. She wished she understood how he could be so threatening and yet so tender to her.

"Poor Harmony," he said against her ear. "What a beast I've been."

She shook her head. "Not a beast, exactly. I should not have screamed at you, or written so many letters to Mr. Burgermeister. I deserved to be punished."

"But I disciplined you in anger. I broke a promise to you."

She slid her hand across the pillow and sighed. "In some way it comforts me to know that I'm not the only one in this marriage who makes impulsive mistakes."

He made a small, choked sound like a laugh, but it wasn't quite a laugh. "You are certainly not the only one. I am deeply ashamed."

She turned to him, meeting his tortured gaze. "I did warn you. I told you I'd be the very devil to live with. You married me anyway."

"I had to marry you. How couldn't I, after you spoke to me so passionately of Joan of Arc? After I saw you almost cuff Sheffield in the Darlingtons' garden? How couldn't I, once I saw you walking that damn road to Newcastle with your back stiff as a poker? I wonder if I didn't want you from the time I found you under Darlington's desk. I'm sorry, but I'm going to stay married to you forever, devil or not."

Harmony stared at her husband. Her lover. She did believe that he loved her. His gaze spoke of longing, fear, regret. His fingers traced over her tear-dampened face. "You told me once to make a wish. I think I did, Harmony. Now we have to make it come true."

"We need an eyelash," she whispered through the tightness in her throat.

"No, we need each other." He brushed away her tears and kissed her, then nudged his face into the curve of her neck with a groan. "Curse you for all the turmoil you've brought me. Your name, my darling…it's such a lie."

Harmony half-chuckled and half-sobbed. "My playmates always made fun of my name. I wanted so much to be Arabella, or Caroline or Jane. I asked my father once why he called me Harmony and he said it was because I brought harmony to his heart. That after Stephen, he had hoped for a little daughter, and there I was." She took a shuddery, miserable breath. "And I think I was never the daughter he wanted. And you…" She hid her face against his hair, fresh sobs pouring out of her. "I shall never be the wife you want either. I'm terribly afraid I won't be, no matter how hard I try."

Court could only hear one thing over the clamor of his wife's tears, and that was his own heart breaking in half. "Good Lord," he said. "This has gone on far enough." He shushed her and drew her right against the shelter of his body. "You are overwrought, I fear, and it's my fault. But all shall be well now."

"How?" she cried against his shoulder. "You should have let me go home. You should have made me go long before now."

He grasped her, this wild, puzzling woman that had become so necessary to his happiness. He smoothed his hands over her bottom, over the fading welts he'd put there in jealous outrage, welts that had taught them both a lesson. "You cannot go," he told her. "I don't want to let you go!"

His palm slid between her thighs, over her secret wet curls, teasing and playing there until her sobs weakened into moans. He pressed her down to the bed, the soft gathers of her gown bunching between them. In a tangle of limbs and fabric, he stripped off the ruffled confection so he could lie with her as he wished, skin to skin with nothing between them. He suckled at her breasts and traced their generous shape with his tongue, and was rewarded with greedy thrusts of her hips.

He couldn't rule such passion, he realized now. He could only stoke and nurture it, taking his own pleasure as reward. When he slipped inside her tight warmth, everything broken in the world seemed right again. "My beautiful love," he whispered. "My Harmony." They moved together with an intensity matched only by the risk of this reconnection. If he lost her now, he thought the pain of it would kill him.

Long after they tired of lovemaking and fell into an exhausted huddle on the bed, he stayed awake whispering promises to her—promises he meant to keep.

* * * * *

Harmony awakened alone, exhausted and emotionally wrung out from the night before. Where was Court?

Sunlight poured through the high windows of the bedroom, illuminating heavy and ancient furniture and wall hangings, and the expanse of her curtained bed. Seven generations of Courtlands had lived in this imposing castle. Her husband was the eighth duke, and she must bear the ninth, or bring the long and honorable line to a close.

Was that why he'd brought her here? To show her what was at stake, what necessitated her cooperation and courage? This land, with its properties and tenants, was a great part of his purpose, and she realized now it must be her purpose too.

A servant knocked at the door and helped her dress. Harmony worried for poor Mrs. Redcliff back at St. James Square. Her maid had been frantic about their overnight flight to Hertfordshire, perhaps fearing the duke planned retribution. Last night hadn't been about retribution at all. The memories of their passion had her blushing to her toes.

A footman led her to a breakfast room, a parlor with a great table and chairs and more sunshine in the windows. Her husband stood staring out one of them, and she recalled the time she'd opened the door to Lady Darlington's parlor to find him silhouetted in a similar window, a tall, proper man of great nobility. He'd been His Grace then, as untouchable to her as the stars, telling her gently and apologetically that she must marry him. He looked very much like that man today.

"Sit and have some breakfast," he said, coming to her. His hand touched hers, a reminder of his tenderness last night. "There are eggs and ham, and cakes."

He knew she loved cakes and pressed them on her unforgivably. There were buns and coffee too, and tea and a salad of fruit and sweetmeats.

"Your home is beautiful," she said once she'd seated herself with a laden plate. "Truly, it amazes me."

"It is your home now too." He sat across from her, gazing fixedly into a half-filled cup of tea. "I should have brought you here before now. I stay in town too much. When we have children..." His voice trailed off.

"This would make a fine place for children," Harmony said. Her neck and cheeks heated in a flush as she thought about the night before, the way he'd held her and caressed her, and whispered of better times to come for them. *Please*, she thought, pondering magic and wishes. *Please let me give him an entire castle full of children...and at least two sons.*

Breakfast was delicious and Courtland Manor not as forbidding in the daytime. He explained that there were two wings, each with sixty to eighty rooms, all of them serviced by scores of maids and footmen. There were outbuildings too: stables, servants' quarters, a carriage house as large as entire streets back in town. She asked questions only to hear the measured pride in his answers. He told her the year the windows were installed, the origin of the intricately carved molding, the number of candles in each jeweled chandelier. When Harmony could not eat another bite, her husband asked if she would like to walk with him.

"I could use a walk," she said. "After so much breakfast."

"Feeling bloated, are you?"

She gave him a sheepish look. "Must you remind me of that?"

"If you hadn't told Lord Monmouth you were bloated, we might never have met." He took her arm and led her toward the double front doors. "That was the night I lured you alone to the Darlingtons' ballroom and spoke with you of Romans and an ancient northern wall."

It had been the first time in her life that any gentleman besides her father had encouraged her to speak of her interests. As they moved into the sun of the front lawn her eyes grew wet and hazy from the glare. "I liked that painting in the ballroom very much. I think I will always remember it."

He gave her a long and enigmatic look. "You enjoy history," he said. "Let us talk of history. Courtland Manor's and my own."

He took her first to the gardens and surrounding woods. Court seemed in his element here, seeking out long-unused paths and stomping about in his dust-covered boots. He showed her where he played as a boy

210

with his beloved dog Mercury. He described everything about his childhood pet, from his glossy amber eyes to his coarse red fur. His tales were so vivid she almost expected old Mercury to come bounding from the surrounding trees. He showed her where he hid as a child and played forest games with one of the servants' boys, at least until they were found out and forbidden to speak to one another again.

From there they went to the stables where she learned of his boyhood mounts and extensive riding instruction. He'd only been allowed the gentlest sort of horses as a child, lest he meet with disaster. One old nag was still there, cosseted and sheltered in her old age. His miniature-sized tack was there, his initials engraved on the fine leather. They went into the house then, shed hats and cloaks and ventured into musty, dark rooms where he told more tales of his childhood. So many of them were sad. Stark lessons learned, harsh discipline meted out for one thing or another. She'd understood he had an unusually rigorous childhood. It was something else altogether to hear about his everyday experiences within these walls.

He told her of servants dismissed for being too kind to him, relating the exact places where they were sacked as he looked on in horror. He showed her the places he'd hidden when his parents fought, great screaming fights that terrified him, fights about his father's extramarital affairs and many, many fights about him, Courtland's sole heir. "And here," he said, leading her to the middle of the great room just inside the door, "here is the first and last place I ever cried in public. I was six years old. My dog died...Mercury, you remember."

Harmony nodded with a hot, tight feeling in her throat.

He stared at the parquet floor as if he could see his own self in the gleaming tiles. "I was looking for my mother, to tell her, and my father found me crying and knocked me to the ground. 'A gentleman never cries in public. Especially a future duke.' And so it was." He looked up at her and touched her cheek. "And I have never cried since, not like you, who cries so gustily and sweetly whenever it moves you to do so."

Tears filled her eyes. "I shall cry now, unless this tour is at an end. I can't bear much more of this."

He reached in his pocket for a handkerchief. "I love that you cry. I pray you will never stop." He made a face, rocking back on his heels as she dabbed at her tears. "Well, I don't mean that in a literal sense, of course."

211

She giggled through sobs. "I didn't think you did." She fluttered his wet hanky in frustration. "There has got to be some middle ground, hasn't there? Something between never crying at all and always making a scene. And you, and this childhood... There has to be some center ground where one can be disciplined and mannerly, and yet enjoy the fullness of life's pleasures. There must be a balance between joy and duty. There *must* be."

Her husband brushed away her tears and looked intently into her eyes. "When we return to town we shall dismiss your tutors and instructors and find this middle ground so we can both be at peace. We shall endeavor to make our marriage as harmonious as your name."

"Do you believe that's possible?"

"We'll find a way." He sobered, stroking a ringlet of her hair drawn askew by her bonnet. "For one thing," he said, lowering his voice, "I don't intend to spank you anymore."

Harmony couldn't say why, but the idea troubled her. "Why have you decided that?"

"I don't want you to get the idea that you are not good enough as you are. That you need improving. Because you don't."

She made a face. "Sometimes I do."

"You don't."

"What if I am terribly stubborn and start calling you Benedict even though you hate it? Or Benny?" she persisted. "What if I started calling you Benny from this moment forward?"

His lips twitched in a shadow of a smile. "It is not worth a spanking."

"What if I put pepper in the dowager's unmentionables? That is surely worth a spanking."

"You would not."

"I might, to get what I wanted. I am terribly headstrong and reckless when it suits my needs."

"Harmony."

"What if I stuff bits of odiferous leaves and grass into Mrs. Lyndon's hats where she cannot see them? She'll be sniffing about everywhere, trying to discover who smells so bad, and the whole time, it shall be her. What if I publish my own book about Mongol hordes and pass it about at the Courtland ball with my name emblazoned on the cover?"

Court cupped her chin, stifling laughter at her wild examples. "Why must you plague me? You have, you know, from the very first. I am not a man who can be comfortable with women hiding under desks, or conversing of hordes, or sponsoring historical expeditions. How on earth have you ended up in my life?"

"Fate."

"Chance," he countered.

"Magic," they both laughed at once. She threw her arms around him, pressing her face against his chest and breathing in his reassuring, familiar scent. "But if I am good enough as I am, so are you. I don't want you to change to suit me. If I earn a spanking I wish you would give it to me. Otherwise I shouldn't know what to do with myself. I'll be an utter mess."

"And what of the sulking afterward?" he asked, leaning in so she was on level with his raised eyebrows and teasing gaze. "How shall I deal with that? And your petulant moods?"

She melted against him, feeling the evidence of his burgeoning desire thick and hard against her middle. "I think you will find a way to bring me out of them."

He held her tightly, brushing his lips across hers. The kiss deepened, a celebration of closeness and acceptance, of divisive problems solved, at least for the moment. She sighed against his mouth as he embraced her without the least of gentlemanly manners. "Oh, Court," she whispered.

"Courtland!" Her father's loud voice carried across the soaring room.

Court released her with a jolt, and Harmony turned to find her papa stalking toward them, the tutting dowager at his heels.

"They are perfectly fine, Harry, you see?" said the dowager. "I told you they only needed a little time away."

Harmony's eyes went wide. "Did your mother just call my father 'Harry?'" she whispered to her husband.

"I believe so," he muttered back. "What the devil's going on?" He addressed her father, holding out a hand to greet him. "Welcome to Courtland Manor, Lord Morrow."

"I'll speak to my daughter before I accept your 'welcome,'" her father snapped.

"Papa!" Harmony shot Court an apologetic look.

"Come with me, dear," the old man said. "We'll have some words in private. I got a letter yesterday eve that deeply unsettled me."

"It was not from me," the dowager protested to her scowling son as Harmony's father pulled her from the room into a smaller, adjoining parlor.

"Well, you have made an entrance," Harmony said to him once the door closed. "But I am happy to see you anyway." Was it only yesterday she'd so desperately wanted to seek shelter in his arms? She hugged him, thinking how much everything had changed in the meantime. Then she drew away and frowned. "Now, tell me. What on earth has got you in such a temper?"

"What has he done to you, poppet? I got this letter yesterday at the house. No signature or direction, but I'm sure it came from St. James Square. Here."

He held out the note. Harmony recognized Mrs. Redcliff's hand in the hastily scrawled missive. She hadn't the heart to read it, thinking of what her protective lady's maid might write to her father after the uproar of the past couple days. "Papa," she began. "Well, we have had some recent difficulties...but..."

Her father threw himself down on a yellow chintz sofa, beckoning Harmony to sit at his side. "I tell you true, I figured the duke for a fine man. I trusted he'd make you happy, but even before you married I'd heard things about him that didn't sit well with me."

Harmony recalled the barrage of caricatures in the papers. They'd been embarrassing enough, but the thought of her father seeing them...

"What does he do to you?" he asked. "Does he beat you? Make rough with you? If he does, I'll take you away from him this very moment. Duke or no, I'll not allow a daughter of mine to be abused."

"It's not at all like that." She was blushing to her ears from this mortifying conversation. "He doesn't beat me. He doesn't do anything outside the law. It is...oh, how to explain? He likes a...a disciplined sort of lifestyle. I've agreed that this is good for me too. It keeps me focused and thoughtful. After all, I'm a duchess now." She'd exhausted the extent of her capabilities to explain the matter. "Please trust me. All is well. If it wasn't, I'd send Redcliff or one of the other servants to tell you right away."

He didn't look convinced. "You know, I never laid a finger on your mother. I never hit her—or you—even though it was within my rights to do it."

"I know. You were a gentle father."

"I loved your mother just as she was. There are other ways to enforce discipline, such as kindness and loving guidance. These are skills every husband should have."

"He does have those skills." Harmony twisted her hands in her lap, then looked back up at him. "Papa, I knew when I wed him what our marriage would be like. I agreed to it. In some way, I wish for order and propriety too. It comforts me to know that he will gather me in when I go too far. And I always go too far, you must admit. I was allowed to run...perhaps...a bit too wild in my formative years."

Her father bit at his lip. She didn't mean to chastise his parenting skills. His voice was gruff when he spoke. "I wronged you, poppet. I abandoned you after your mother passed. You see, it was so difficult when you got older, because...well...you recalled her so much to me. You have her same beauty, her same energy and charm." His eyes misted over, and Harmony's throat tightened with emotion. Her father composed himself and took her hand. "I miss your mother so, even to this day. I'm sorry I wasn't a better father to you these last years. If I can do anything to contribute to your happiness, I will. Stephen too. That scapegrace has been tamed something awful by his Meredith. You wouldn't recognize him. There's a baby on the way, he's just written."

Harmony clasped her hands. "Truly? How wonderful. I'm to be an auntie. But, father." She lowered her voice. "What is afoot with you and the dowager? How did you arrive here together?"

Her father puffed up with a pride she hadn't seen in evidence in a while. "Why, I'll tell you how. We rode here together. A gem of a woman, the dowager Courtland, when I can steal a moment without that Mrs. Lyndon by her side."

Harmony had to laugh at that picture. Her father and the dowager, evading Mrs. Lyndon like two young people dogged by a chaperone. "You are not... Surely you are not courting the dowager?"

Her father waved a hand. "I am too old to court anybody, and she's too high above me anyway. We talk and write letters. Perhaps one day I'll marry her or perhaps I won't. Depends what she wants, if you know what I'm saying. She's the type to rule the roost. These Courtlands," he said, with another wave of his hand. "What are we to do?"

"I don't know, papa. I really don't know." Harmony's head was reeling. The dowager and her father?

"Harry?" The dowager's voice shrilled from the doorway. She poked her head into the room with a beleaguered expression. "My son

215

would like to have a word with you in the library. Something about discussing the honor of your intentions."

"What?" Her father rose from his chair.

"He believes we should not have ridden all this way without a chaperone!"

"That young upstart." Her father crossed the room and offered the dowager his arm with a lazy bow. "I'll tell you this, Ermie. I shall set him straight if he thinks to trap me into marrying the likes of you."

The Dowager Courtland giggled—*giggled!*—as her father turned and winked at her. Then the two of them put their heads together and sailed out the door.

"Oh my goodness," Harmony said, burying her face in her hands. "Oh my goodness, it is too much."

Chapter Twenty:
The Ball

Two Months Later

They decided—together—on a weekly system of accounting for her transgressions. Not that he didn't occasionally spank her in a rush of exuberance, or lay on some heat before he made love to her. Harmony loved those spankings tossed over his knee in the bedroom. But for purposes of discipline, both of them found a weekly session suited them very well.

These sessions did not occur in her bedroom, or his, or in the study, but in his very stark and male dressing room, where things like belts and straps naturally abounded, and where he discreetly stored other tools such as riding crops, paddles, and various sizes of birch rods. The canes were left in the study. "A possibility," her husband warned, "for the very worst misbehavior."

Harmony tried not to think about that, but she did wait with a queer and excited feeling for Sunday evenings to arrive. She would sit at dinner with Court, barely noticing any other family members or guests, thinking only of what she had done that week in the way of naughty acts. She would stare at her husband's hands and his stern and handsome face and wonder how he would choose to punish her. Sometimes he would catch her eye and she would shiver in guilty anticipation.

"You enjoy this far too much," he teased one Sunday. After that, he had introduced the use of ginger figs into their punishment sessions. He'd procure lengths of the root from the kitchen gardens and carve them into slender phallic shapes with a flange at one end. He would carefully feather the edges of the ginger while she watched with wide eyes, and then...

Being spanked or whipped with ginger burning in her bottom was so very different than being spanked without it. When she admitted to Court that it made her feel much more punished, he made it a regular feature of her weekly disciplinary regimen.

This Sunday he had moved their session to an earlier time since the Courtland ball was to take place that night. Harmony headed toward her husband's rooms just before the appointed hour in a pretty flocked dress and stockings, with her hair drawn up in a fetching style. At these weekly sessions, she took care to present herself in her very best light, and to accept gracefully his efforts to discipline her. In truth, these sessions kept her dearly connected to him. Even if they hurt like the devil most of the time...

The closer she came to his chambers, the harder her heart beat with excitement and alarm. She was already fit to fall apart over the ball and her role as hostess. Perhaps this time with Court would help her calm down and refocus her wits. It seemed the sessions always ended with her feeling clear-headed and relieved of stress.

That's because he makes love to you so thoroughly afterward... Would he do so today, with the ball to prepare for? She hoped so, but it would be his choice, not hers. The last thing she could do after a spanking was make demands on her husband. But if he wanted her, even now in broad daylight, she would gladly submit to his whims.

Her fantasies along these lines became so ribald that by the time she arrived at his door and knocked upon it, she was blushing hot. He admitted her with an all-too-knowing smirk. "Improper thoughts?" he asked. "What a naughty wife you are. If not for these sessions, I believe you would be completely lost to the civilized world."

She dropped an apologetic curtsy. "I am guilty as charged."

"We had better begin then." He removed his coat and draped it across the back of a chair, then his waistcoat, carelessly flicking open the buttons. He turned up the frilled cuffs of his shirt, exposing the muscled grace of his forearms. Harmony's heart accelerated and her mouth went completely dry.

"You will remove your gown, please."

"Yes, sir."

She struggled out of it with her husband's help until she stood only in a short chemise and stockings. His gaze raked over her with carnal heat, and then he crossed to a bureau and lifted the lid of a silver-domed plate. The ginger. He took up his carving knife and stood facing her, preparing the gnarled root just prior to her punishment so it would be in its most fresh and potent state.

"Shall we talk about this week?"

She watched his fingers work. "Yes, sir."

"We have been very busy with preparations for the ball, so some of your harried and disrespectful behavior toward my mother might be excused. For instance, when you made fun of the turban she specially commissioned for this evening's revelries."

She felt a snort of laughter rising in her throat.

"Harmony," he chided.

The laughter burst out, bold and disrespectful. "It's only that there were so...many...birds...upon it."

He pursed his lips, focusing staunchly on the ginger. "You are not helping your cause."

She clamped her mouth shut, knowing he, too, was trying not to laugh.

"Then there was the matter of my mother's favorite bonbons mysteriously disappearing."

"I only ate three of them," she protested. "My papa ate the rest."

"Ah, but I cannot punish your father, only you. I trust they were delicious enough to be worth a sound switching."

Harmony's galloping heart turned over. He hadn't yet punished her with a switch! Her eyes went to the table where he normally laid out the implement of his choosing and there she saw it, slender and newly peeled by the looks of it. "Oh," she said softly.

"Oh," he repeated, mimicking her. "I believe you will find it very instructive. Quiet in application too, with the house so crowded today. I cannot be lenient only because of the circumstances."

"No, sir." She curtsied again, bowing her head with true remorse for all the mischievous and mannerless things she'd done over the course of the week.

"Lastly," he said, beginning to shape the ginger's flange, "there is the little matter of your dress for the ball."

"What matter?" Harmony asked innocently.

He flicked a bit of peel onto the tray. "I believe it to be scandalously alluring. You cannot think I would have nothing to say on the matter."

"The dowager approved it, sir." His eyes fixed on her, and she wished she had used a more submissive tone.

"The dowager lives to torment me," he said. "And sometimes I believe you do too. I shall spend the entire evening trying to discipline my gaze from the display of your glorious bosom."

"I meant to please you."

"Oh, you please me." He stepped closer, his fingertips teasing at her waist. The scent of ginger wafted between them. "You shall also please every other man there and cause me to burn with jealous ire."

"Jealous ire?" she repeated weakly. "That sounds like a very impassioned thing."

His fingers spread on her back, his features tightening into a strict mask. "Turn around, wife. It is time to pay the price for your shenanigans."

She turned as he bade her and he gathered the back of her chemise, handing her the ruffled edges to hold out of the way.

"Bend forward slightly."

Harmony bit the inside of her cheek as he parted her and seated the shaft of ginger into her bottom. She straightened and fidgeted, agitated by the invasive feeling of it. She always, always clenched around it when it first slid in her. It was a helpless reflex invariably answered by an aching burn. She made a moan of complaint which her husband ignored.

He walked her to a chest of drawers near the wall, conveniently waist high, the top kept free of any clutter or decoration. "Over," he said when she stiffened. "Bend over and present your bottom for the punishment you've earned."

She obeyed, clutching the hem of her chemise in now-sweating palms. This was the moment that addled her the most, the moment when she stood positioned and waiting while he crossed to the bureau to fetch whatever he planned to spank her with. She stared down at the top of the chest, her bottom already feeling punished as the ginger released its sting within her sensitive nether passage. She heard his measured steps returning to her.

"I feel you have earned twenty strokes of the switch due to your behavior this week."

Harmony gulped. She knew he'd deliver them carefully, due to her pregnancy, but she also knew he wouldn't shirk on the heat. The first stroke came in a swish across the juncture of her bottom and thighs. *Oh, God help me.* The switch, while thin and not particularly heavy in impact, delivered a shocking amount of sting as it flicked across her skin. She cried out and clenched her buttocks, gasping at the answering burn of the ginger.

"I am waiting for your count," said her husband after a moment. "Or shall I begin afresh?"

"One," Harmony said. She didn't want even one stroke to be repeated, which is why she tried to be accurate at her counts. Of course, the whole purpose of making her count was so she must stay alert throughout her spankings, and not drift away from the sensation and pain. That would make things far too easy for her.

"Two," she cried at the next whistling stroke. "Three!"

Four, five, and six fell in a heated lattice of lines. She decided as she counted through the following volley of lashes that she despised the switch, and all trees everywhere for providing the torturous things. "Ow! Twelve!"

"Eleven," said Court acerbically. "You are getting ahead of yourself."

"Oh, sir!" She pounded her palms against the top of the chest. She used to beg him to stop, but eventually learned that got her nowhere. "Twelve," she said on the next stroke. "Thirteen. Fourteen! Ow!"

"If you clench, my dear..."

"I know," she wailed. How could she not realize by now that clenching her bottom only added to her misery? "Fifteen. Oh, it hurts," she said, shifting from foot to foot. "I do not like switches."

Court made a soft sound of amusement. "I will be certain to remember that."

Oh, curse him and his predilection for spanking. Curse her for going along with it and marrying the man and submitting herself to his hand. "We are nearly finished," he said. "Perhaps you will bear it better if you think at the same time of how you will improve."

"Perhaps I would bear it better if you removed the ginger," she said, shifting again. "This fig seems unusually potent."

"It is newly harvested. You will be pleased to learn I have instructed the gardener to increase the ginger yield this coming year by at least fourfold." He paused in the act of drawing his arm back. "I did not tell him why."

Harmony's face burned as he pushed her down a bit more over the unforgiving wood surface. The strokes began again, in such quick succession she could barely count the numbers. She hopped in agony on her toes, then reached behind to cover her bottom.

Court tsked and seized her hand. "Where does that belong?"

"In front of me," she cried as he placed it on the chest again.

"You know the penalty for reaching behind you. Five extra strokes. That will bring us to twenty-five, dear, and we were so close to finished. Pray, control yourself so we needn't make it thirty."

"Oh, no." The very thought of it had her grasping the edge with renewed focus. Each stroke in itself was not unbearable, but her backside and upper thighs throbbed with a vicious-feeling heat, and the ginger seemed to burn hotter, not milder, as the spanking went on.

"Eighteen. Nineteen." Oh, the burn of it—and he was not even hitting her full force. "Twenty. Oh, please, sir! I have learned my lesson. Please, no more. I can't bear it." Penitent tears dripped down over her nose, into her mouth, wetting the wooden top of the chest—not for the first time.

"Harmony, there are five strokes remaining and you shall take every one. How you manage is up to you, but I suggest relaxing and accepting this as your due consequence. You may cry and you may flinch, but you must take it."

She shuddered and squeezed the hem of her gown in her hands. "Yes, sir."

The last five strokes fell with strict, controlled regularity, and Harmony accepted each blow as it came. Resignation did help. When she relaxed, the ginger didn't goad her as much, and he had explained many times that her buttocks bruised less when they weren't clenched tight. Somehow she never managed to relax until the near end of these sessions, but when she did there was something transcendent about the pain. "Twenty-five," she finally gasped out.

"Very good."

With those words, her husband crossed to the bureau to put down the implement, and then back to her, brushing his palms across the heated skin of her bottom. Even though it hurt, she lived for this moment when he would measure out the damage he'd done to her and give her a couple of sharp, finishing slaps. It gave her some sense of accomplishment—and relief.

"Stand up, my dear." She stood and turned, and let him wipe away the sheen of her tears with one of his ever-present handkerchiefs. "Do you feel better now?" he asked. "Cleansed of your petty sins?"

She nodded and leaned toward him, letting her chemise fall down over her smarting bottom. He kissed her forehead, her eyes, her cheeks, her mouth, an ending ritual of nurturing that always made her squeeze out a few more tears. "Well then," he said, releasing her. "Go into my bedroom and await me there."

"Yes, sir."

She only visited his bedroom at this time—after spankings. The way he made love to her here was quite unlike the way he made love to her in her room where they slept together every night. His room was a place of mystery and authority, and his bed...his bed was only used for one thing.

She heard him enter and turned to face him. He was fully naked now, an aroused and vigorous male, his body enticing even after months of intimacy and marriage. Now, in the light of late day, the windows cast warm shadows across the sculptured beauty of his muscles—and the more compelling features of his physique. He was prodigiously erect. Her center tightened and even the biting retort of the ginger couldn't dampen her body's reaction to his virility.

"Remove your chemise," he said, "but leave the stockings." Some savage wildness sparkled behind the benevolent regard of his eyes. He came toward her as she shimmied out of the filmy garment, letting it drop to the floor. He turned her away from him, delivering another smart slap to her bottom before he pressed his front against her back. The ache in her bottom—doubled by his hard spank—now faded away, replaced by the sensation of his hands cupping her breasts. He manipulated them with care, knowing they'd become more tender with her condition. So far, they were the only area of her body where her pregnancy showed.

"Bend over the bed." His voice was hard yet affectionate. Bending over for this was so much easier than bending over the chest of drawers. He pressed behind her, fitting his long legs to her shaking ones, and fastened his hands to her hips.

This was never like their marital bed, but she liked it anyway. Guiltily, she liked it perhaps a bit more. The slow invasion of his thick length nudged her forward and she braced on the bed for balance. The ginger's burn intensified in a thrilling way as he seated himself inside her

223

and began to take her with firm, measured strokes. Her hips arched to him, her entire body feeling opened and given to him without resistance.

While his thrusts were crude in nature, his hands were infinitely gentle. He caressed her, tracing every part of her with a touch that bespoke ownership as much as love. When he neared his release, and his strokes grew quick with intensity, he helped her find her peak too, deftly massaging the pearl between the secret lips of her sex, the pearl he knew how to manipulate with magical skill.

"Oh…oh, it's not possible," she sighed. "It cannot feel this good."

It was possible, though. Her husband urged her to nerve-rending completion and embraced her through the fit of his own release.

"Again, beloved?" he sighed after they'd rested.

"Oh, yes, please." She slid her hands about his neck. "Yes, please. Again."

* * * * *

Court stood still and let his valet fuss over the folds of his neckcloth while his mind wandered miles away. Or rooms away, where he'd left his wife to prepare for the ball with the help of Mrs. Redcliff. Their magic afternoon of discipline and lovemaking lingered in his mind like the scent of flowers on a breeze. When his lace-edged cravat was finally arranged and pinned to his valet's liking, Court set off to fetch his Duchess of Chaos and escort her downstairs to a ball that had become the talk of the *ton*.

God help them all.

Not that he cared what happened, good or bad. He had made peace with his wife's oddities and accepted that he would be ridiculous in his love for her. In fact, he was eager to see what kind of bedlam she'd cause with the guests, especially her dance partners. His wife was the curiosity of the budding season and everyone wanted to observe her in person. Calling cards had accumulated at a shocking pace as the gentry returned to town from their country homes. Court believed they would all come to love her, but whether they accepted or rejected her this evening, he did not care.

He knocked and entered his wife's dressing room. Redcliff blushed as she curtsied and greeted him with a mild "Your Grace."

Harmony did not stand on such formalities. "Oh," she exclaimed, clapping her hands. "You are too dashing." She flew to his side with a gratifying squeal. He was in his most formal wear of tightly fitted breeches, coat, sash and glittering medals. He allowed her to coo and flutter over his decorations while he stole a look down the bodice of her gown.

"As for your finery," he said, nudging her away so he could drink in the full effect, "your gown is far too beguiling. I must insist you take it off."

She giggled at his lurid stare as Redcliff clucked and quit the room with mutters of "husbandly rogues." Court watched her go with a smile. He would charm the old biddy yet and win her over. But apparently not tonight.

He turned back to his wife, making her turn and pose for him. The dress was a silken sky blue chosen for the way it flattered her eyes. Pearls, lace, and bows framed the stylishly low neckline and the cut of the dress accentuated her petite stature and curves. The tips of shimmering blue slippers peeked from beneath the gown's embroidered hem. To complete the effect, Redcliff had woven matching blue ribbons into his wife's hair, along with artfully placed miniature white flowers. Beneath her halo of soft curls her face shone with delight. "Is it not a magnificent ensemble, Benny? What do you think of it now that you see it on?"

He shook his head as he drew her into his arms. "It is much worse than I imagined. Really *de trop*. The other ladies will wilt into vapors with jealousy, and the gentlemen run riot with lust. You will ruin the ball and I'll hear no end of it from my mother."

She waved her fan at him, her giggles rising to shrieks as he buried his face in the pillows of her breasts. "Stop it, you barbarian," she cried, rapping him on the head. "That is undignified."

"Your dress is undignified," he moaned against her cleavage, but he released her. He made a great show of rearranging his cravat, but it was the engorged cock in his form-fitting breeches that really needed adjustment. "I shall have to punish you for torturing me with this dress."

She plucked her matching gloves from a table. "You may punish me for it next week. I cannot withstand any more today." He stared at her as she smoothed the pretty things up her arms, adjusting the fingers with care. He made some audible lusty noise even though he meant not to. She looked up at him. "Or any more of that either," she said in a husky undertone. "Please, love, have mercy."

225

He took her proffered hand. "Yes, I will have mercy, only because we are unforgivably late. Mother will want your head."

She blew out a breath, her pretty blonde curls dancing against her cheeks. "More punishments! If I manage to please her tonight, perhaps you will establish a period of clemency in reward for my efforts."

He believed she only teased him, but he took her in his arms with all seriousness and held her close. "Do not worry about pleasing me or her," he said feelingly. "That silly competition with my mother is a thing of the past. You never believed I cared about it, did you?"

She glared into his eyes. "Yes, I believed you did, or why would I have tried so hard to put up with that provoking Lady Archleigh and that blasted deportment tutor? What was her name?"

"Lady Renfrew-Burress," provided Court, blithely recording Harmony's heated trespasses to use against her later...for both their pleasures, of course. "Your conversation still tends to the rough side. Perhaps I should re-engage the ladies' services."

She poked him and palmed her fan. "Do not torment me. This ball shall be trying enough, although this gown is truly beautiful. I feel like a princess."

"Or a duchess?"

"Especially a duchess," she said, grinning at him. "Thank you for giving it to me."

"It is my pleasure to give beautiful things to my beautiful wife. Now..." He reached beside him to the table where he'd laid a weathered mahogany box. He opened it to reveal a velvet-lined interior and the richest and most famous of the Courtland jewels. "The matrimonial set," he said, tilting the box so the polished sapphires sparkled in the light. "As reprehensible as it is, they were never given to any Courtland duchess until she showed a talent to breed." Harmony made a face at that. "Yes, it was positively medieval. Nonetheless, we will cleave to tradition since you are so conveniently in the family way."

Her mouth made a round, admiring "o" as he drew the pieces from their velvet pillows. "My goodness," she breathed. "Are they horridly valuable and expensive?"

"You are very gauche to ask it, my darling. But yes. Endeavor not to lose them in one of your quintessential scrapes."

He fastened the heavy rope of sapphires about her neck and fixed a pair of matching teardrops on her ears. A glittering sapphire bracelet completed the set, slipped over her glove to nestle perfectly about her wrist. Knowing Harmony, he'd had the clasps specially reinforced just in case. He regarded his adorned wife, feeling a primal surge of ownership, of provision for this otherworldly creature of beauty.

"They are captivating with the blue of your eyes, dear. And the dress." His voice choked off, with emotion and pride and who knew what else. Ridiculous things that he now accepted as his bride price. He kissed her forehead, then cupped her chin to brush tender embraces across her lips. "The entire *ton* can see you wear them tonight and make of it what they will. I love you and claim you, rapscallion or no."

She touched his cheek and he thought he would lose his manners altogether if they did not leave the room. "Come," he said gruffly. "Our guests await."

The ballroom was awash in a sea of gaily attired ladies and proper gentlemen, even though the night was young and the dancing not yet started. His mother the dowager stood near the east entrance, beaming in her specially commissioned gown. The confection of deep green and tea-brown lace was complimented by matching gloves, another set of Courtland jewels—emeralds—and, oh, a truly unfortunate hat. The "barnswallow" turban, as his saucy-mouthed wife had christened it, but his mother loved it and felt pretty in it, so it made her look beautiful. Lord Morrow much admired it, whether from true regard or self-preservation, it was difficult to say. He was as much a rapscallion as his daughter, Court was coming to learn. Perhaps more.

Even though his mother had chosen to retain her title rather than take Morrow's, the love between her and Harmony's father was evident. Court would never have imagined it, their quiet wedding in a glade at Courtland Manor. Thus were Court and Harmony made into step-siblings, an unfortunate outcome they both chose to ignore.

"Lord and Lady Wembley are here," Harmony pointed out. "How kind of them to attend."

"You mean, after you caused them to be doused in soup and dog fur?" His jest was met with silence. He looked down to find his wife regarding Gwen with such an air of vulnerability, it was all he could do not to gather her in his arms.

"If you are wondering whether I still have feelings for her," he murmured, "I do. But only as a dear old friend. Come, we will make our addresses."

They crossed to welcome the couple, who greeted them effusively.

227

"I can barely believe it," said Gwen. "Another Courtland ball already. Hasn't the year flown by?"

Court looked sideways at his wife. "It has been a particularly eventful year for us. For you too," he said, congratulating them on the upcoming anniversary of their marriage. They talked briefly of local Hertfordshire matters and other niceties, and then Gwen touched Harmony on the arm.

"Your Grace, how beautiful the Courtland jewels look on you." Her eyes shone in earnest admiration. "Truly, they are a perfect fit." Then Gwen looked to him, and some silent understanding passed between them, an acceptance of their past and an avowal of continuing friendship.

"I think so too," said Court, as Harmony blushed and stammered out thanks. A short time later they took leave of the Wembleys, exchanging promises to pay calls.

"Oh, Courtland," Harmony said. She used his formal name in public, even though she'd trained him to answer to Benny now. "Look who's just arrived."

"I know. I was looking for a place to hide."

Harmony forced him over to greet her brother Stephen and his wife, the Lady Meredith. After smiling embraces, Meredith and Harmony put their heads together and Court could guess of what they spoke. Meredith's eyes went wide. "Oh, that's marvelous news. Now our child shall have a cousin close in age."

"A cousin?" Stephen overheard this and exclaimed without couth, "You are having a baby too?"

Harmony shushed her brother. "Must you blurt it out like that, here in the middle of a crowded ballroom?"

"I suppose not," he said good-naturedly. "But congratulations." And to Court, "Good work, old chap."

Court managed, despite his pained sensibilities, to manage an answering smile. "I suppose everyone will know shortly," he said to Harmony as the Barretts moved away. "Oh, my dear. There is someone you must meet this very minute." He led her over to an older gentleman who had just arrived.

"Your Grace," said the man with a bow. "I am so grateful for the invitation. And this must be"—he swept into a deeper bow, nearly to the floor—"your wife Her Grace, the Duchess of Courtland."

Court turned to Harmony and nodded at the guest. "Madam, it pleases me to introduce you to Mr. Michael Thomas Burgermeister."

"Oh!" Harmony's initial flush of embarrassment soon receded into comfortable conversation. After all, the studious scholar and his well-read patroness had much to discuss. From Hertfordshire, two month ago, Court had decided to support the gentleman's expedition, only for the pleasure his published research might bring to his wife.

"My dear," he said when the old man began to sag under her volley of questions, "perhaps you should allow Mr. Burgermeister to mingle with some of the other guests."

"Oh, of course," she said, blushing beneath her curls.

Court squeezed her hand once the gentleman left. "You must share a dance with Mr. Burgermeister later. He is one of the few men in town who will not take offense at your talk of Mongol hordes."

Harmony laughed behind her fan. "Thank you for inviting him, my love. And for being...understanding. Patient. Wonderful."

"Reasonable?" he suggested lightly. "I thought you should meet him face to face before he sets off on these adventures you have financed."

"You financed them, not I."

"Because I had a debt to pay." He touched her waist, deeply aware that she carried their future nestled within her. "Perhaps we can accompany him on some other expedition, next time when you are not...in the family way."

She put a hand over his. "Everyone will know our secret if you stand and gaze at me so, with your hand over my waist."

"Everyone will know because you told your brother and his wife," he teased. "And my mother already knows. See how she beams at you the entire length of the ballroom."

"She beams more often at my father. Look at how she hangs on his arm and sets everyone whispering."

He chuckled at the scandalized look on his wife's face. "Let them be the object of gossip for a while," he said. "I have tired of it. We have become a very conventional couple, don't you think? I daresay we will retire to Hertfordshire all too soon to raise the Courtland heirs on a steady diet of rapscallionism and history texts."

Harmony laughed out loud. "There is no such thing as 'rapscallionism.'"

"Isn't there?" he said, eyeing her. "I disagree."

She looked away from him, her mouth turning down at the corners. Oh, no. The little thinking lines. "What if I have a girl?" she asked.

Court leaned closer to her. "I wish on every eyelash for it to be so. The world needs more ladies in your mold. Wild, stimulating ladies to draw the stuffy peers of the realm out of their misery. And if it is a girl, we shall have no choice but to keep trying for a brother." He gave her an edifying look. "It will not be so bad."

She gazed into his eyes, with that liquid, emotional expression she sometimes had, and he readied his handkerchief in his pocket. But she managed to govern herself, smiling instead with the bright intensity that lit up all his days.

"I love you so dearly," she whispered, only for his ears. "I know it is not fashionable, but I do love you so."

Court brushed a secret kiss against her cheek. "Let us not be fashionable, then," he whispered back. "Because, God help me, the depth of my love for you is not to be believed."

Epilogue

Five years later

Newcastle in late summer was the most beautiful place on earth.

Court lounged on a blanket across from his wife near the old Roman wall, enjoying the bright day. Now and again Harmony leaned back to peer at the sky.

"Lie down," he finally said to save her neck. "No one will have anything to say about it. We are quite alone."

She scanned the immediate environs. They were not actually alone. Three shouting little boys grappled and tumbled on a nearby carpet of grass while two nursemaids warned them to be careful of their clothes. Court chuckled as the Marquess of Raymore, his first born, scattered handfuls of grass over his younger brothers' heads and then led them both on a merry chase beside the ancient, crumbling wall.

"Wherever do they find the energy?" Harmony mused, following their darting movements. "I am exhausted."

He ruffled fingers through her hair. "You are not expecting again? We've been taking precautions."

"I don't believe so." She took his hand and pressed a kiss to the center of it. "I am merely tired of travel. It will be pleasant to go home again."

"I agree." He leaned back on an elbow, watching his rambunctious sons with equal parts pride and amusement. "Next time I take it in

231

consideration to visit Greece with three young boys in hand, followed by a side trip to the north of England, you will kindly dissuade me."

"Or?" she asked.

"Or you shall pay the price," he warned, nudging her over and landing a furtive smack on her backside.

Harmony grinned, not at all intimidated, and pointed at the clear sky. "It looks the same," she said. "Don't you think? It looks almost exactly the same as it did the first time we were here. Do you remember?"

"How could I forget? You were full of wonder that day."

"Wonder?"

"*I wonder this. I wonder that.* You wondered about everything. It was charming."

His wife pulled a face. "I am certain you were anything but charmed, considering you'd just found yourself saddled with me for all eternity."

He tugged one of her curls. "Things did not turn out so bad."

The nursemaids finally settled the children and brought them over to share a picnic lunch. Henry, the oldest, was dark like him, while Arthur and young James favored his wife, down to their heads of raucous blond hair. "Use your manners," she chided when they poked at one another. "You must grow up to be refined gentlemen like your papa. See how politely he eats."

Comically, all three boys began to ape him. They straightened their backs and used flawless manners, not for fear of reprisal, but for love of their mama. It occurred to Court they also probably did it because they admired him and truly wished to be like him one day. It was an affecting thought. He looked at his wife, who had been, from the start, such a serene and proficient mother. He would never have imagined it. He would never have imagined any of this magic in his life.

After the children had eaten their fill, they went for a walk along the wall, shepherded by their nurses who seemed determined to give the duke and duchess a moment of peace. Harmony rested her head on his shoulder. They held hands, enjoying the fresh breezes of the summer day.

"Do you know," he said quietly, "I believe I feel the earth moving under us."

She peeked up at him, flushing pink. "Did I truly say such things to you?"

"You did. You also compelled me, quite against my nature, to lie down and stare up at the sky alongside you."

He lay back upon the blanket, pulling her with him. They sprawled shoulder to shoulder, their fingers linked.

"I wonder," he said after a moment, "if someone ever lay here and fell in love with an impulsive young woman who was not at all the thing?"

"Hmm." Harmony's voice held a tender note. "A duke perhaps, falling in love with a mere 'miss' who was very poorly behaved?"

"Yes, something outrageous like that. I wonder if such a thing has ever happened, quite near this spot. Perhaps in this very place where we lie."

She grinned at him, rising up on one elbow. "I'm certain it's happened at least once in the vast history of the earth. Quite certain, in fact."

"Well." He tapped her chin. "You are the historian. I shall take your word for it."

He kissed his wife, long and deep, here in this place he'd first come to know her, here where the earth rocked them both to a fragile understanding, then a blessed marriage and three strong sons.

Fate?

Chance?

No. Magic. It had to be.

A Final Note

If you enjoyed *Disciplining the Duchess*, you may want to do more reading in the area of spanking and domestic discipline. They're fun kinks—even more fun when you add the period costumes! You may also want to check out my other historical spanking novel, *Lily Mine*.

In closing, I have to thank my editor Audrey as well as my beta-readers extraodinaire: Linzy Antoinette, J. Luna Scuro, Renee Regent, Doris S., Melisa T. (who devoured it in one night!) and Melissa R. You always make my books better and I treasure your advice.

Disciplining the Duchess

**An excerpt from *Waking Kiss*, an upcoming
BDSM contemporary romance novel
by Annabel Joseph**

Chapter One:
Act Three

Since I was a little girl, I've wanted to be invisible. Not in a cool, magical kind of way, but in that way of *please don't look at me too hard*. Ballet has always been a compulsion for me, not a pleasure. It was something I got serious about because I had to, despite the trauma of being poked and prodded from the most tender years of my childhood, judged and lambasted because my turnout was weak or my *port de bras* one degree off center. That stuff will drive you nuts, but it's always been worth it to me, like jumping upstream is worth it to a salmon. It was a survival thing.

That's why I really didn't want to dance center stage with The Great Rubio in our company's heralded production of *Sleeping Beauty*. I'm not being coy. I'm not pretending I didn't want to when secretly I would have killed for the chance. No. I really didn't want to do it and it never should have happened in the first place. There was a clause in his contract with the London City Ballet to prevent such a farce. *Mr. Rubio will dance with prima level ballerinas only. In the event a prima dancer is not available, Mr. Rubio shall not be compelled to perform and a substitution shall be made.*

But in this case, Princess Aurora pulled a muscle stretching backstage before her Act Three entrance and I was the only other available dancer with her shade of jet black hair. A stagehand yanked me from the palace set by the long skirt of my ball gown.

"What are you doing?" I asked, pulling my costume from his grubby fingers.

"Do you know it?" His words didn't make sense until I saw Mariel, the injured Sleeping Beauty, sobbing a few yards away as a swarm of helpers stripped off her crystal-embroidered tutu.

"Do you know it?" He shook me, tugging at the straps of my "Fourteenth Wedding Guest" costume. Of course I knew it. Every corps girl knew the part of the Sleeping Beauty from the opening *pas de chats* to the closing *arabesque*. Every one of us had watched Mariel dance it in practice over and over while imagining ourselves in The Great Rubio's arms. Fernando Rubio was a God to us—capital letter. He was a celebrity recognized by people who weren't even into ballet, a superstar we'd all been warned not to look at or talk to backstage.

"Yes, I know it," I said automatically, before I processed what that meant.

Four pairs of hands stripped off my ball gown costume and strong-armed me into Mariel's tutu. Oh, okay. Oh. *No*. I couldn't dance with Rubio, not center stage in front of a packed theater. I averted my eyes from him not because I was contractually obligated to, but because I wasn't worthy to look on him. I certainly wasn't worthy to dance with him.

"I can't," I said in a panic. "I won't be able to do it. My shoes are too soft."

They were twisting knots in the stretchy clear shoulder straps of the costume since Mariel was taller than me. I tried again. "Uh, guys, I can't do this. My shoes..."

See, the boxes, or tips, of toe shoes are constructed of layers of fabric, material, and glue hardened into a molded point. If they're not broken in, those boxes sound obnoxious on stage, like the clopping of a horse. If they're very broken in, like mine, they're nice and quiet but it's impossible to do demanding pointe work—and Princess Aurora required demanding pointe work. "My shoes are too soft." I think I said it two more times but everyone ignored me. "Why aren't you listening to me?"

A vein throbbed in the stage manager's temple. "You've got to dance, shoes or not."

"Then I need to go grab a better pair."

"You're on in eight minutes." He looked around for someone to send but they wouldn't know which pair I needed. Hell, I didn't know which pair I needed. I didn't have a single pair of shoes that would make me good enough to dance with Fernando Rubio. *Oh my God.* "I'll be back," I said, darting away.

He trailed me for a second but then he stopped and hissed, "Seven minutes, or else!"

Shit. Shit. *Shit.* I banged through the door into the backstage corridor toward the dressing rooms. I took the corner so fast I almost slid into the opposite wall. I couldn't fall down in this two-thousand-dollar tutu, and I definitely couldn't dance in these flimsy shoes. I reached the corps dressing rooms and yanked the doorknob to the women's door. No. Oh God, no. *Locked.*

"No, no, no, no," I pleaded with the universe. "Oh, no. No, no, no." Every time I said no, I yanked down on the doorknob, like maybe this time it might miraculously open. I turned in a panic. Someone backstage had to have a key. How long would it take to find them? Oh God, I was fucked. I was going to have to dance the third act of *Sleeping Beauty* with my idol in the world's shittiest pointe shoes.

I barreled down the corridor and collided full speed into what felt like a brick wall but was actually a very solid man.

"Hey," he said, catching me. "Where's the fire?"

"Key," I said, shaking my hands at him. "Key, key, key, key. *Key!*"

"I'm sensing you need a key," he said, his lips quirking into a half smile. I gave myself a second—no, half a second—to appreciate how handsome he was. Designer suit, long honey brown hair curling around his shoulders, gorgeous amber eyes and a strong shape to his face. He had a golden-tan complexion like Rubio but based on his accent, he was American like me. I gave myself another half second to mourn the fact that this guy probably didn't have a key.

"I need to get into the dressing room," I practically sobbed. "It's locked."

"Show me. I'll open it for you."

"I need a key."

"Show me," he said again. I took him to the women's dressing room and started rattling the doorknob. "I only have about...I don't know...five minutes to get back to the wings."

He looked over my costume. "Okay. Stand back."

For one wild moment I thought he was going to shoulder through the door. He looked strong enough to do it, but what he actually did was bop the doorknob with a quick, smooth movement of his palm. I heard a popping sound. He turned it and held the door open for me.

"Oh my God," I babbled. "Thank you. *Thank you.* How did you do that?"

"It doesn't always work. It depends on the make of the doorknob. With this kind of door—"

"No," I said, cutting him off. "I don't have time."

"What can I do to help?"

"I need shoes. New shoes." I ran over to my carrel, crouched down and pulled out my basket of pointe shoes. I started knocking the toes on

237

the floor trying to find a pair that was adequately broken in. Oh God. "I'm so screwed," I said. "So screwed. These are all too hard!"

He took one in his hand and started kneading it. "Want me to help you soften them?"

I grabbed the shoe back. It looked too vulnerable in his huge hands. "No! Oh, God. There's no time." I sat in my chair and leaned forward, batting away a faceful of stiff, sequined tutu. "Oh, please. Help me," I said, trying to reach past the layers of tulle to the ribbons on my ankles. "Help me take these off."

I was barking orders to a perfect stranger but he complied, untying the pink ribbons and unwinding them from my ankles while I picked out the pair of shoes that was least noisy. I dug my toe pads out of the discarded pair, wrapped them around my toes and jammed them into the new pair. He held my tutu down and out of the way while I bent to adjust the elastics and tie the ribbons.

"Hey," he said over the rasping of my frantic breaths. "It's going to be okay."

"It's not going to be okay," I snapped. "I'm about to dance *Sleeping Beauty* with The Great Rubio. And listen to this." I clopped the toes of my shoes on the floor and then kicked my old, soft ones across the room.

"*The Great Rubio?*" he repeated, chuckling. I was almost to the door when I realized how rude I'd been to him.

"I only had seven minutes," I said. "I'm sorry. I—" I stammered, not finding the words.

He gave a little wave. "Fly free, little ballerina. Go."

I ran out the door, thinking I should have at least thanked him. It was too late now. The stage manager was a deep shade of scarlet when I skidded up to him. "About time," he said. "You're on in thirty seconds."

Grunts attacked my scalp with hairpins as they affixed Princess Aurora's aluminum and rhinestone crown to my head. At least my black hair would hide the blood. *Ouch.* There had to be blood.

"Shake your head," the lead costumer barked. The crown didn't budge. Some woman pushed past him. These were Mariel's people. Me and the other corps dancers didn't have dedicated staff to do our costumes and makeup. The woman grabbed my face in one hand and used the other to apply a haphazard slash of the dark red lipstick Sleeping Beauty wore. Out of the corner of my eye I noticed the man from the dressing room observing this backstage chaos. His unkempt hair contrasted with his sedate expression, his cultivated bearing. He had a great body but he wasn't a dancer. I wondered why he was hanging out backstage.

"Do your lips. Do your lips!" the makeup lady hissed, smacking her own together until I mimicked her, smearing oily crimson in what I hoped was an adequate outline.

Someone tugged at my back, fluffing the tutu. The waist and bodice fit like a second skin. Apparently Mariel and I were the same size in the middle if not in height, and in fact we looked very much alike, with pale complexions, black hair and blue eyes. Only difference was that she was a principal who'd danced this role for weeks now, and I was a faceless member of the corps. Also, my shoes weren't broken in and I was about to possibly have a heart attack.

I looked around for my lockbreaking savior but he'd disappeared again. "Just get through it, Ashleigh," said a low voice at my side. The company director. His name was Yves Thibault but I would never dare call him by his first name. The Great Rubio could do such a thing, but not me, never. Mr. Thibault was a great director because he understood his dancers. For instance, he understood that I danced best in a group, at the back of the stage out of the spotlight. I appealed silently for him to intervene and save me, perhaps by canceling the rest of the ballet or delaying it until another principal ballerina could be fetched.

It wasn't happening.

Rubio stretched on the other side of the stage, oblivious to the drama, deep in performance mode. He wasn't called The Great Rubio for nothing. Such focus, such artistic brilliance—and the body of a Brazilian Adonis. He'd jeté'd from the slums of Rio de Janiero to the top of the ballet world on pure, glorious talent. Me, I'd scratched my way into the City Ballet corps and that was probably as far as I'd manage to go.

I scurried to my mark, or maybe one of the stagehands pushed me. I heard the cue to enter and looked up at the same moment into Rubio's dark, wide-set eyes. My inspiration, my idol—this was both a dream and a nightmare. We moved toward each other, arms outstretched. My smile said *oh God, help me*, while his was more *WTF?* He fixed his expression first, turning to the audience with a blazing smile. I did the same. We posed, the happy couple, Sleeping Beauty and her prince.

The orchestral cue straightened my spine like the demanding tap of a teacher. I could do this. I'd been dancing for twenty of my twenty-four years. I could do it—I just wasn't ready to. Rubio swept me forward to center stage and we struck another pose. His whole body tensed, vibrating beside me. I could sense his fury like a palpable thing and it shook my already-faltering confidence. *Don't mess up. Don't dare*, my brain screamed. *Don't do one thing wrong or your idol will hate you forever.*

The dance began with a sustained *développé* facing away from the audience. I had to extend my leg to the front and then lean backward in a very slow, graceful, controlled movement. One wobble, the slightest falter, and I'd fall on my ass in front of four thousand eyes. My balance depended solely on his skill as a partner. My hands were so sweaty I was afraid my fingers would slip, but his grasp tightened like a vise. He centered me, supported me. In those slow, panicked seconds he sent me a message with his stance, his grip, his balance.

I got you. This is yours to fuck up.

Oh God, I was going to fuck it up.

Follow Annabel's blog (annabeljoseph.com) and Twitter (@annabeljoseph) to learn more about the summer 2013 release of *Waking Kiss*.

About the Author

Annabel Joseph is a multi-published BDSM romance author. She writes mainly contemporary romance, although she has been known to dabble in the medieval and Regency eras. She is known for writing emotionally intense BDSM storylines, and strives to create characters that seem real—even flawed—so readers are better able to relate to them. Annabel also writes vanilla (non-BDSM) erotic romance under the pen name Molly Joseph.

Annabel Joseph loves to hear from her readers at annabeljosephnovels@gmail.com.

CPSIA information can be obtained at www.ICGtesting.com
Printed in the USA
LVOW07s1533100815

449554LV00022B/1613/P